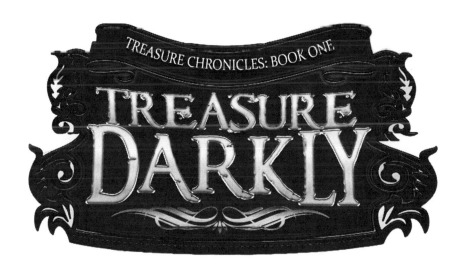

TREASURE CHRONICLES: BOOK ONE

TREASURE DARKLY

JORDAN ELIZABETH

CURIOSITY
QUILLS PRESS

A Division of **Whampa, LLC**
P.O. Box 2160
Reston, VA 20195
Tel/Fax: 800-998-2509
http://curiosityquills.com

Cover Art by **Amalia Chitulescu**
http://ameliethe.deviantart.com

ISBN 978-1-62007-694-1 (ebook)
ISBN 978-1-62007-695-8 (paperback)
ISBN 978-1-62007-696-5 (hardcover)

For my mother, Cynthia, who introduced me to the Wild West, with all of its horses, heroes, bandits, big skirts, and ranches.

TABLE OF CONTENTS

CHAPTER ONE

His mother's voice carried through the cracks in the wooden wall to let him know it was safe. She sounded hoarse. Tired. The final syllables of each line hovered as if she waited for a response.

"The day the sun dies,

"Radiance lost to the reaches of space.

"Water boiling,

"Bubbles of blood...."

Clark eased the dressing room door open enough to slip through. Good thing he'd oiled the metal hinges. He kept his shoes slung over his shoulder to creep across the cold, plank floor, his bare feet silent.

She'd hung her client's clothes on the pegs near the bathtub. In the attached bedroom, the client snored and Clark's mother kept singing to let him know he had time to act.

"Midnight blood staining shredded white,

"No power to surpass,

"No power left to shine...."

A faded curtain of green brocade separated the two rooms. Morning sunlight filtered through the threadbare patches to provide the only light. He might be hidden from view, but he had to move fast and keep quiet.

Holding his breath, Clark eased his hand into the pocket of the client's blue jacket. A copper penny, probably to tip Clark's mother, and a leather pouch of silver coins for the actual payment at the desk. Clark counted ten coins, more than enough considering his mother, one of the Tarnished Silvers, only cost two. He removed one coin and dropped it into his own pocket. The client might miss more than that.

Clark fished through the man's black boots and brown leather spats, but didn't come across any hidden valuables. From the crossed pistols emblem on the cap, the client had to be a general from the army. The clothes were strong quality, made with sturdy fabric and machine stitching. He had to have something else of worth.

Clark checked the silk vest. The front pocket contained a brass watch on a chain attached to a brass button: too noticeable to steal. He slid his hand underneath and grinned when his fingers brushed a hidden opening with a bulge. He lifted out a glass vial and swished the thick, green liquid. It crawled up the sides and dripped off the cork.

Absinthe. Clark caught himself before he whistled. His mother wouldn't allow him to touch the stuff in the bar downstairs, but he'd always wondered what it tasted like. When the customers knocked back the shots, they started laughing and hallucinating. People they knew, but who'd died, would visit them in their minds. One man had thought his dead father sat on the stool beside him.

If Clark drank it, he might see his dead relatives, too.

"Nasty stuff," his mother would say, but she drank it over a sugar cube if a client bought it for her.

Clark yanked out the cork. It popped and the liquid fizzled. Bubbles crept to the surface before the substance stilled, and he sniffed the rim of the vial. Absinthe smelled like anise hyssop, a plant in the garden, but this had more of a metallic odor. Maybe it was fresher than the stuff shipped to the bar.

He tipped it to his lips for a sip. The liquid burned his tongue and scalded the roof of his mouth. Fire flared along his nostrils. Clark choked, but the drink had spilled down his throat before he could swallow, as if it were heavily weighted somehow.

His mother broke away from her song as the client snorted.

"Wuz zat?" a man grumbled.

Clark froze. Brass glass, he should've left the potion in the vest. The burning faded, but left a metallic aftertaste, like when his mouth filled with blood after a fistfight.

"Just the folks downstairs." His mother's mattress, stuffed with dried cornhusks, rustled. "It's still early if you want to catch more shut eye time."

Two thumps sounded on the floor. Feet? The man grunted. "Can't be wastin' all day with the likes of you."

Clark stiffened. His mother wasn't worthless. If she hadn't had him fifteen years ago out of wedlock, she might've found a husband or a decent job besides being a Tarnished Silver, or doxy, her boss's name for her profession when she didn't bring back enough customers.

"You was real sweet." The man's voice softened. At least generals had manners. "I might come back to see ya real soon. Leave ya a big tip, ya hear?"

Clark tried to jam the cork back into the bottle, but it wouldn't fit, as if it had expanded. By black steam, he couldn't put the vial back if it was open. He couldn't stay to force the cork, either. He ran on his tiptoes to the door and eased it open again.

"You was real sweet, too," his mother said as Clark shut the door. He took the spare key from his pocket and relocked the door.

The second floor hallway of the Tangled Wire Saloon and Brothel lay empty. A few muffled voices drifted through the closed doors. He wandered toward the stairs, shoving on the cork. As he reached the first floor, it slid in with a pop.

Hmm, keep it or leave it? He could drop it under a table in the saloon so the client could think he'd lost it. If someone else took it, that would be their problem.

Clark glanced around the front room. The old man who owned the establishment stood behind the main desk, which stretched six feet long in the corner. Customers paid for drink and prostitutes there. No one sat at the tables, but Clark glimpsed one of the other Tarnished Silvers in the gambling room beyond. One of them might wonder what he was doing under a table.

"Goin' to work?" a girl called from the stairs: Mable, only twelve, identical to her mother, who used the room next door to his mother's. Mable wore her ginger ringlets pulled back in a ponytail with a wide, silk ribbon. Pearl earbobs hung from her earlobes and a silver chain with an owl charm dangled around her neck. Her pink dress draped too low in the front, exposing her prominent collarbone, and sagged around her waist.

"Sure thing. Can't be late." Clark tucked the bottle into his pants.

"Whatcha got?" She ran her painted fingernails over the railing as she descended.

"Nothin'." He shrugged. "Just somethin' for lunch." He usually ran back to the kitchen for a hunk of bread and milk, or a customer's leftovers, but she wouldn't know that. The old man used her for serving food and drink during the days.

"You wanna play with me tonight?" Mable asked. "I was thinkin' we could throw rocks at the stream. Maybe we can gig a couple frogs to cook up for supper."

"Sure thing." Clark leaned against the wall to tie on his shoes. Mable stood in front of him, rocking on her heels with her hands clasped behind her back. When he headed toward the door, she followed.

"Lots of soldiers in here yesterday," she said. "Why ya think the army's back?"

Clark pushed open the door and stepped onto the front porch. A calico cat curled on the top step, asleep in the sunshine. "Dunno. Maybe they wanna build the railroad this way."

She skipped at his side as he walked. "That'd be real nice. They might open up more stores. Ma said the city she used to live in had a theater, a real theater with actors and stuff."

He stopped himself from saying that all real theaters had actors.

Wind blew along Main Street, shoving dust into Clark's face. The buildings consisted of wood slapped together, some sturdy, some seeming to sway. The saloon and brothel were the biggest, with three floors and walls that didn't shake.

A mechanical horse clattered by on the dirt road and the soldier in its leather saddle lifted his cap to them by the short visor in greeting. Clark nodded and Mable curtsied. Most of the army ignored them, but a few took offense if a resident of Tangled Wire wasn't polite. More soldiers strolled along in their crisp blue jackets with brass buttons and automatic rifles in hand. Mable ogled them, her lips parted.

Clark pulled out the vial and bit off the cork. She might think soldiers were fascinating, but he had absinthe. Clark held the bottle to his lips and knocked back a swallow. It still burned, but he fought the sputtering cough. Alcohol was supposed to burn at first.

Mable slapped his arm. "Yer Ma don't let you have liquor."

"Neither does yours." Clark knocked back another gulp. Half remained in the vial.

"So, did you swipe it?" Her crooked, yellow teeth gave her a childish gleam when she grinned.

"All mine. I'm a man now." The next swallow didn't burn at all. It kept the metallic taste, though, and his mind buzzed. Could he be drunk already? They wouldn't let him work if he was inebriated. He couldn't have had that much already. Clark swigged the last bit and tossed the empty bottle to Mable. "All yours, sugar."

"You finished it," she yelped.

He waved two fingers overhead. "Getting to work now. I'll be home tonight."

The mine lay at the edge of Tangled Wire, nestled in the narrow valley amongst the jagged hills. Two soldiers guarded the gates at all hours, but today there were five. Other workers spoke to them before filing inside to retrieve their gear.

"Captain Greenwood should be here soon," one guard said to another. "Thought he'd have arrived by now."

"What do you think his big experiment is?" Another guard chuckled.

"Who knows, but he said he only had enough supplies for one. Whatever that one is. Maybe an explosion." The guards laughed. It must have been grand to be that jolly at work.

"Clark Treasure," he told the guard checking the workers.

The soldier lifted his thick brows and grunted. "Treasure, eh? No relation to Captain Treasure?"

"Course not." Another soldier laughed. "You think he'd be related to that tycoon while working at a place like this?"

The first soldier scanned his list and checked it with a stylus. "Get inside, boy. You'll be in chute five today."

"Good morning right back."

"Oaf." The soldier swung at him, but Clark ducked past the arm and into the grounds.

He retrieved his helmet, gas mask, leather gloves, and pickaxe from the supply shack before heading into chute five. Once the machines ground away most of the rock, robots worked until it became too fine. Humans needed to see and gage where next to hit.

He fit the helmet over his oily yellow hair and slid the goggles down to cover his eyes. The air chilled and dampened as he headed into the mine, stepping over the uneven rocks strewn across the floor. He turned to the right at the first division, which led to chute five. Four other workers had begun for the day; their pickaxes rang against the rocks.

Within two hours, sweat beaded on Clark's skin despite the draft in the tunnel. He paused to pull a red bandana from his pocket and wiped his neck. It came away black with dust. At least the gas mask kept the debris from his lungs. Before he'd been old enough to work, men had died from the fumes. Hertum, a white rock that crumbled into dust, was harvested for the government. If a person breathed the dust for too long, it would make their throat bleed.

Clark shuddered, stuffing the bandana back into his pants. The thirteen other men around him worked their tools in a steady rhythm. The thump-thump-thump helped Clark concentrate on the rocks, kept his mind from wandering.

Something crashed toward the entrance, followed by another, louder, and chute five trembled. The men lowered their tools, stiffening.

Clark sucked a breath through his gas mask. "No, there hasn't been one in two years...."

"Cave in," someone hollered.

Clark jumped against the wall and crouched with his hands clasped behind his head. The army had taught them to hide like that in the case of a cave in, but if a rock fell on a person, they still died. Tears burned his eyes. No, he was too old for crying. Mable never wept anymore, not even when the men called her names.

After what seemed an eternity, the mine stopped shuddering and the roaring ceased. The men stood from their walls and edged toward the entrance. From that direction, men screamed.

Go slow, if anything changes, crouch. Clark nodded as he repeated the mantra in his mind. His body shook and his heart pounded so hard his veins ached. He grabbed at the wall with his gloved hands to stay steady.

The entrance to chute three had caved into a mess of rocks and dust. Workers tugged on some of the larger pieces to move them aside.

Clark yanked off his mask and let it hang by its canvas strap around his neck. "Anyone trapped in there?"

One of the older men shoved a rock aside. It rolled against the wall with a thump. "All of Team Three."

While other workers staggered out, shaken from the shock, to await next orders, Clark fell into line with those who wanted to help. He gripped the rocks and heaved, although the muscles ached along his back and shoulders. His arms tingled and his palms burned beneath the worn out leather gloves.

If he were trapped, he would want his coworkers to help him. As long as they got them out soon, they would survive…

Clark coughed. Blooming gears, he should put his mask back on. Stepping away from the crowd, he lifted the mask, but a new cough wracked his body. It tasted metallic, like the drink. He coughed again, so hard his lungs throbbed. He doubled over. The hertum mineral mined from the rocks shouldn't have harmed him so fast. Impossible.

Blood sprayed from his mouth with the next cough. Hands pushed him. Someone rubbed the back of his neck.

"You'll be fine." The male voice didn't sound familiar.

Clark staggered to his knees and coughed. More blood, hot as burning coals, shot from his lungs. It strangled him like a thick mass. He couldn't die. His mother needed his pay so they could leave the brothel. They could buy a farmhouse. He could learn how to farm.

He couldn't die on his mother.

Clark pounded on his chest until the panic lessened and he could breathe again. His lungs wheezed, but they worked. He dropped his helmet, goggles, and mask onto the stone next to him. He'd gone without his mask before without almost dying. Had it been the panic from the cave in? He leaned back and closed his eyes while he panted. He'd have to get outside, no more helping.

Something soft but firm twitched beneath his hand. Clark glanced down and bile rose in his raw throat. An arm protruded from the rocks, a leather glove on the hand and the black jacket sleeve shredded. Clark had rested on it. Sputtering, he twisted away. That poor worker… gone. It could be any of them, any day of the week.

Despite the pain in his lungs, Clark pulled off his glove and pushed the sleeve up to read the victim's brass identification bracelet. He might've known the fellow, so he could tell the family himself, rather than have the army deliver a letter they would have to pay the priest to read for them.

Clark's fingertip touched the man's dry, hairy skin. Warmth shot through the contact.

Suddenly, he stood in a desert with endless sand and an orange sun above. A man in black dust with mining gear faced him, the outline too blurry for Clark to know who he was.

The man lifted his hands. "Bring me back. Don't let me die."

"I...." Clark sputtered, and the man grabbed him. Tingles shot along Clark's nerves from the contact to his scalp. Heat baked into him from the surrounding air.

Clark screamed as he pulled away. The image of the desert shattered back into the mine. Could he be hallucinating? No, that had happened; somehow he'd been transferred to the desert.

The fingers on the arm uncoiled and stretched, as though reaching. The arm shifted, as if the man were still alive. A moan elicited from within the rock pile.

"Help him," Clark rasped. A headache pounded against his temple, blurring his eyesight like in the vision. Where had that headache come from so fast?

The man had wanted Clark to bring him back to life. Had he, somehow, when the perished mine worker touched him in that desert state?

"Git outta here, boy. It's too dangerous." A man grabbed his shoulder. Clark stumbled into his chest and reached up to brace himself; his hand brushed the man's neck. At the touch of skin against skin, the headache vanished and the man gulped. Blood spurted from his lips and he collapsed, his eyes wide.

Dead? How? The world had to have an explanation for it. He wasn't going crazy. Something unnatural had happened, something far more than a collapsed mine chute. Wait, that did sound crazy?

"Get up," Clark whispered as images whirled past him. Other workers rushed over to see what had happened to the man.

He had to escape the mine. The dust had done something to his sanity. Clark ran, shoving people aside. Sunlight slammed his senses. Soldiers shouted orders that jumbled into gibberish.

"That's him." The soldier from the gate that morning grabbed him by the collar of his jacket. "Clark Treasure."

He tried to ask why they were mad, but his lips sagged. Saliva dripped down his chin. His heart thudded and the metallic taste filled his mouth again.

"Clark Treasure," a soldier behind him said, "you are arrested in the name of our good Queen for stealing a vial."

Someone waved the bottle from the general's pocket in front of Clark. His eyes wouldn't focus on it despite how many times he blinked.

Mable had told someone he'd had it. She'd given him away. How many coins had the army promised her?

"Looks like he did drink it up." The general client spoke from the right. "Must've interacted with all that bloody hertum. Look at 'im, he's bleeding already."

"What's it gonna do to him?" the guard from the morning asked.

"Lots of stuff." The general laughed. "When he touches the dead, he'll be able to bring them back, and exchange that life for another. Perfect soldier, huh? We only have one vial ready and I was going to give it to a lucky fellow. Guess it will be this boy."

"Whatcha gonna do with him?" The guard snickered.

"Have to be a test subject," the general said. "Sure thought it was that Judy who stole my bottle. Pity I killed her. She sure knew how to make my pecker sing."

Judy.

Clark's mother.

Clark bolted off the ground and ran. He could hide in the hole under the shed behind the brothel. Mable never found him under there. He might be cursed with raising the dead—he'd already done that to the poor mine worker—but it didn't mean he'd let them take him for tests.

CHAPTER TWO

Two Years Later

Amethyst tossed the six dice into the velvet-lined gully in the center of the table. They struck each other with tiny taps as they rolled. Each side of the die contained carved images of cogs to symbolize their worth. She held up her crossed fingers and flashed a smile at the crowd. "I hope for sixes!"

Some of the young men and women cheered; others held their breath, leaning over the table beside her.

The dice stilled.

"Five sixes and one two," the Game Master announced.

"I won!" Amethyst bounced into a twirl, waving her hands overhead. Joseph caught her with a hug to swing her off her feet. She bent her knees, leaning into him; he smelled of sandalwood and musk, exotic. The gold buttons on the front of his jacket pressed into her cheek.

"Amethyst Treasure, a picture?" A photographer pushed through the crowd. He cradled his camera against his chest with its metal legs stabbing the onlookers. Green-lens goggles covered his eyes beneath a brown top hat.

"Certainly," Joseph answered for her. He set her down and her heeled slippers clicked the marble floor. She leaned against his chest and he rested his arm over her shoulders as the photographer steadied his camera on its tripod.

"What does it feel like to have just won four hundred dollars at Sixes?" The photographer fiddled with the camera's dials and levers to get the settings correct. Chains on his leather armbands jingled.

Amethyst smiled, her classic look: the wide eyes to keep wrinkles at bay, lips parted to show the perfect teeth she paid to have straightened and whitened, the chin tipped to make her neck appear longer. She could've said that she'd lost almost five hundred earlier in the evening, so she'd almost broken even, but the photographer must've missed those rounds. She might've commented on how Sixes was the only game women were allowed to play at the club.

"That's what we Treasures do. We win." She tossed a yellow ringlet over Joseph's arm to give the picture flair. Her father's latest gift, a sapphire as large as her thumbnail, hung around her neck above the top of her silver corset.

Gift? She refrained from flaring her nostrils in disgust. The necklace had been more of a bribe.

"One moment." The photographer ducked beneath his robe and lifted the flash pump.

The flash blinded her. As she blinked to clear the stars in her vision, Joseph kissed her cheek. His breath smelled of absinthe.

Tomorrow's headline in the city's top selling newspaper: Treasure Heiress Wins Big at Star Club.

"You've come every summer to my beach house." Joseph's lips felt like velvet against her rouged cheek. "This year will be extra special."

Her heart thudded and she stepped back. The gas lamps cast shadows over his sharp features. Would this be the year Joseph proposed? At sixteen, she was old enough, and he would be twenty-five come winter. Did she want to give up flirting already?

A girl with a peacock feather protruding from her chignon bumped her arm. "Amethyst Treasure! I'm so excited to meet you. Can I get your autograph?" The girl pulled a miniature, leather-bound diary from her silk reticule and stabbed it toward Amethyst. "I have a stylus, too."

Amethyst stepped back into Joseph and smiled at the younger girl. "I don't do autographs." It always felt sweeter when they begged.

The girl's eyes widened and Amethyst swore she saw tears in them. "Please? It would mean so much." Her painted lips trembled.

Amethyst sighed and shot Joseph a patronizing look. "If you insist, but only this once."

"Thank you!" The girl grinned as she thrust the book toward her. She yanked an electronic stylus from her bag. "My name's Drusilla."

Amethyst opened to a page in the middle rather than searching for the next clean one, and signed her name with a dark swirl. She added **To** and glanced up. "Debbie, you said your name was?"

"No, *Drusilla*."

"Of course." People reacted so well when she teased them about their names. **To Drewciluh.** She hoped that was the correct spelling as she handed back the book. "Our secret." She winked.

"Right, of course." Drusilla clutched it to her chest before scampering into the crowd.

She would tell the first person who would listen.

Shrugging, Amethyst turned back to Joseph "I'm sorry about this summer. You know I love spending time with you." She trailed her fingertip up his jacket and tapped his chin. "My father has such crazy ideas."

If Joseph really wanted to propose, he would find a way. Maybe he would prepare a ball in her honor. Chandeliers and gas lamps. Dancing until dawn. In front of everyone, he would kneel before her and lift a diamond ring on a satin pillow.

"I'll be back for winter," she added. He needed to understand she didn't leave him by choice. Maybe this absence would help him realize he needed her in his life. Forever. The Treasures would unite with the Velardis, two of the most prominent families in the kingdom. Apart from royalty, of course.

Amethyst laughed. Most people considered her father equal *with* royalty. He was the fourth richest man.

"It seems so far away." Joseph tucked a yellow curl behind her ear, so she batted her painted eyelashes. Two could play at flirting. This must've been why her parents left her in the city when they moved out west—so she could find an appropriate husband.

"You'll have to visit me." To keep him aching for more, she twirled away and grabbed a champagne flute off a passing waitress's tray. The bubbles tickled her nose and made her tongue tingle. A buzz started in the reaches of her brain. Perhaps it should be her last alcoholic beverage. She could always ask for a goblet of ice water.

The band struck up a song in the next ballroom. The drumbeat vibrated through the wooden walls, painted white with gold-embossed wainscoting. A violin and flute added to the upbeat tempo, followed by a young man's strong voice.

"I'll sing for you,

"If you sing for me.

"I would dance with you,

"If only you would dance with me."

Amethyst drained her glass and set it on the nearest card table. "I love this song!"

In the adjoining room, people clapped and stomped their feet in time to the beat. She grabbed Joseph's hand to tug him toward the doorway. A waiter in a black suit with an emerald green bowtie stood with a tray of red wine in crystal goblets. Joseph accepted two and handed her one.

"Here's to your farewell night." He kissed her cheek.

"Here's to a grand time." She clinked her goblet against his before gulping a mouthful. The buzz grew harsher. The gas lamps and candlelit chandelier cast bright glows across the public, but the shadows lingered, hiding the distinctness of faces.

Bugger it. Joseph would be certain she got home even if she passed out. She finished her drink and dipped her finger in a lingering droplet. Giggling, Amethyst smeared the wine across her lips. Most of the rouge had worn off. Now she would get back that pouty look.

"May I have another?" She staggered on her feet and laughed louder. The music picked up its beat, so she nodded her head and waved her hand along with the other cheering listeners.

She should live the party to the fullest. Who knew what excitement lingered in the wilderness out west?

CHAPTER THREE

The scream fired from Jeremiah Treasure's lungs so harshly it burned his throat. A hawk took to the sky with a cry just as ragged.

If only the noise could reach his father. Instead, it faded into the desert. His horse nickered from behind, but Jeremiah screamed again. His throat and lungs throbbed, his heart raced, and sweat coated his palms. He should feel better, but the irritation lingered.

Panting, he sank onto the dirt beside the pond—or, watering hole, as his father called it. The trees surrounding the area cast shadows across the brownish water. Jeremiah grabbed a rock and skimmed it over the surface, sending ripples to scatter the shadows. It sank with a gurgle.

Why did his brother get to be the one to go to war against the natives? Jeremiah was older by two years. He should get to kill those savages. He should be the hero that navigated the peace between the upper and lower classes.

He stood and kicked his knee-high leather boots through the dust. Jeremiah could still be his father's heir, even if he became a soldier. Of course, his father ignored that idea.

Scowling, Jeremiah pulled his brass watch from his jacket pocket. He still had fifteen minutes until noon, when his sister's train was due to arrive in town. His parents would want him back at the ranch house when she returned. He would have to smile, laugh, and pretend he'd missed her shallow ways. The wisest thing his father had done in the past ten years had been to leave Amethyst in the city. She didn't belong in the wilderness.

His horse whinnied and swung his head toward the field. Jeremiah stood, brushing his palms across his denim slacks. Perspiration dotted across his brow from the sun in the cloudless sky.

The low rumble of a steamcycle reached his eardrums and he frowned. No one should be on Treasure property except for the hired hands, and he hadn't assigned anyone to work these fields today.

Jeremiah stalked to his horse and laid his gloved hand against the neck, sensing strong muscles beneath the flesh. He pulled a hay stalk from the ground and chewed the end of it to calm his nerves.

The rumble grew louder and the knee-high hay swayed as the rider approached. Wire protruded from along the cycle's sleek metal body, with black handlebars and a leather seat. Much too city-like for ranching.

Jeremiah ground his teeth; the fool ruined the field. He could have him arrested for that, make him pay for the spoiled crop. What if the driver didn't stop? Jeremiah gripped the leather reins. He could mount within a second and chase after the intruder. Although a steamcycle could outrun a horse, the hay would slow down the wheels. Plus, the idiot wouldn't know the dips in the land.

The driver turned his cycle toward the watering hole and stopped alongside Jeremiah. Jeremiah stepped forward, while keeping hold of the reins in case the intruder darted off.

The young man on the steamcycle pulled off his hat and pushed his goggles onto his forehead. Yellow hair, long enough to brush his broad shoulders, stuck to his sweat-soaked forehead. His black, leather jacket had tears in the elbows and the front of his white shirt was missing buttons. Patches covered the knees of his denim pants, with the hems tucked into the tops of his ankle-high boots.

"You can't ride on this field," Jeremiah said when the youth switched off his steamcycle. Since he didn't look familiar, he might be a new hired hand for one of the neighboring ranches.

"I'm lookin' for the Treasure Ranch. Fella in town told me to come this way." The young man pulled a crimson bandana from his jacket pocket and wiped sweat off his upper lip. Pale stubble decorated his jawline.

Jeremiah frowned. "What you want with that?"

"Some old business. Name's Clark."

New to town, then, and looking for work. Someone who didn't know enough not to ride through hay fields didn't belong with the Treasures. "Going the wrong way."

Clark wrinkled his long nose. "You sure? Fella told me—"

"Positive," Jeremiah interrupted. "If you turn around, keep going until you reach the main road."

"Just came from there."

Impertinent goof. He couldn't be much older than eighteen, if even that old.

Jeremiah snorted. "You listen then. You keep heading right. Bound to reach the Treasure Ranch." The right way that wouldn't cause any trouble to the land. It would take him an extra hour, too, since the road wound along the stream and followed the fields.

Did he really want the idiot to show up?

Jeremiah chuckled, patting his horse's neck. They could all laugh as Jeremiah's father kicked the idiot back into town.

"I dunno...." Clark squinted. "How long will that take?"

"Not too long. It's really the only way." Jeremiah shrugged. He would have to look into putting up a fence along the main road to keep other trespassers out.

"Well"—Clark snapped his goggles back into place—"thanks for your help, mister. I'll be seeing you around."

"See you," Jeremiah echoed.

Clark revved the engine and the steamcycle rumbled forward. He turned it in a wide arc, crushing more of the hay stalks, and headed back the way he'd come. At least he knew enough to follow his tracks instead of making fresh ones.

As soon as he'd become a speck in the swaying hay, Jeremiah swung into his saddle. "Hi-yah, boy. Best get back before Father comes home with Amethyst. You're going to love her. From what I recall, she's scared crazy of horses."

The steamcoach pulled into the gravel circle in front of the Treasure mansion. Sunlight glinted off the brass decorations and glass windows. The mutt who hung around the stables ran to meet it, yipping at the metal wheels as they rolled over the gravel pathway.

Jeremiah leaned back in the white wicker chair and rested his ankles on the porch's railing. Dirt flaked off his knee-high boots onto the white paint. More filth caked around the buckles on his ankles. He would have to get one of the servants to clean them before his mother saw it.

His mother and Zachariah stood waiting for the steamcoach on the top steps, clutching hands as though the world were about to crack open. He'd never seen his mother so pale beneath her face paints before; as for Zachariah, did his brother really think their sister would be happy? Amethyst would return to the city within a week.

Jeremiah grinned. He had a bet going with the barn hands. They'd all assumed she would obey Master Treasure's wishes and remain on the ranch. Jeremiah chuckled. He knew far better how Amethyst acted.

The steamcoach halted and the driver hopped down from his front bench to open the side door. Master Treasure stepped down, dressed in his black suit with the brocade necktie. His top hat hid his thick, wavy hair. Jeremiah patted his own, glad he'd inherited that trait. Perhaps he should've put on a hat, too. Zachariah wore his army cap, with the brass symbol on the front. He polished it every morning and evening, as if he would perish if it dulled. No wonder Amethyst got along best with him.

Their father, his face covered by a smile, reached into the steamcoach. From the dim interior, a tiny hand emerged, clothed with a white silk glove. She wrapped her fingers around his and descended the stairs attached to the side of the blue coach.

Ah. Amethyst. How long did she think white would last in the territory of Hedlund? Even their mother had given up her pale colors in exchange for dark cottons.

His sister left the hood of her red velvet cape over her head, but yellow curls long enough to reach her waist cascaded down her chest. A robin's egg blue dress peeked out, with silver embroidery along the hem.

"Amethyst!" Their mother stepped down the front porch to the driveway with her arms outstretched. She stopped once she reached the gravel, as if expecting her daughter to come to her. "How I've missed you. It's wonderful to have you here."

Amethyst slid her hand from her father's grasp, but remained beside the steamcoach, smoothing her cape. "It's dreadfully hot here. What do you suppose the temperature is?" She tipped her head toward their father.

"One hundred degrees? One hundred eighty?"

Jeremiah snorted. Could she be serious? They would be cooked if the temperature reached one-hundred and eighty degrees Fahrenheit. She still had that annoying lilt in her voice, too, where she accentuated the start of each word and heightened the end of her sentences, as if everything counted as a question. Snob.

Their mother coughed, probably from the dust, and strolled to Amethyst. "Afternoons are always warmer here. You needn't wear such a heavy thing." She pushed back her daughter's hood. "There, darling. Much better."

Amethyst had lined her eyes in thick black kohl, and her lips were so red they seemed to gush blood. She'd left her curls down, with the front sections pulled back in a braid. Didn't she know hair needed to be tied back on a ranch? It was too dangerous to leave it down. One of those curls might be caught in farm machinery and rip off her scalp. Jeremiah had seen it happen to one of the serving women last year.

"I'm glad to be here." Amethyst's words sounded rehearsed and her smile barely moved her lips.

"It was a tiring train ride," their father said as the driver drove the steamcoach toward the barns.

"How many hours?" Zachariah sauntered to them and kissed Amethyst's cheek. She stiffened, but at least she didn't wipe it off.

"Three days." She glanced at their father. "Thank you for purchasing a private bunk for me. It made the journey much more relaxing."

"You must've gotten a lot of work done." Their mother unfastened the front of Amethyst's cape and swept it aside, the hem stirring dirt off the driveway. "Needlepoint and reading. Perhaps some tatting."

"Some." Amethyst blinked, as if she had no idea what tatting meant— Jeremiah assumed it was one of the needlecraft activities his mother did in the evenings.

Her dress hung straight; at least she'd known better than to wear a hoop. The sleeves laced to her elbows and the front pinned from waist to bosom, where a lace chemise poked over the low neckline. A silver charm hung from a choker of indigo velvet.

"Come inside." Their father cupped her elbow, tugging her toward the front door. "There's some lemonade prepared. We can sit in the back garden and talk."

"You can tell us about New Addison City," Zachariah added.

"Where things are wonderful." Now, her smile appeared genuine, wicked even.

Jeremiah scratched the stubble on his chin. If she hadn't wanted to come, she should've whined her way out of it.

She paused on the front porch to face him. "Good afternoon, brother." Cold. Unattached. Yet, with an emotion underneath it, as if she pleaded with him for something.

He studied her from beneath his lashes. Straight back, stiff shoulders, pursed lips. What could she want? Knowing Amethyst, it would be something trivial, like a compliment.

"You look pretty." He made his tone sound as detached as hers.

She walked across the porch to bend over him, her lips to his cheek. Her breath, scented with peppermint, tickled his ear. "Tell me how dangerous it is. Order me to go home."

Home—back to New Addison City. He stared at the field beyond the driveway where the horses grazed. So, that was her motive. "Sorry, sister. You're here now. You figure out how to leave before winter."

He loosened the leather ties on the front of his blouse to let the air tickle his chest and cool his skin. If he helped, he'd be cheating on his bet. Besides, she didn't need him.

A steamcycle rumbled toward the ranch. Their parents turned to the driveway, while Zachariah slid his arm through Amethyst's. "I'll show you the back garden. Mother's done a wonderful job with it—considering our dry climate."

The vehicle swerved along the driveway and halted in front of the porch. Jeremiah frowned. The boy from the hay field had shown up after all. He pulled off his hat and goggles before sliding off the leather seat of his steamcycle. Leaving his gear hanging from the handlebars, he strutted toward the Treasures.

"Howdy." The young man ran his fingers through his shaggy hair.

Amethyst sucked in a breath. Jeremiah glanced at her, chuckling when he saw how wide her eyes had gotten. Leave it to his sister to flirt with every guy she came upon.

"Can we help you?" Jeremiah's father asked.

"Are you Captain Garth Treasure?"

Master Treasure removed his hat and nodded. "That I am."

The young man wiped his palms on his denim pants and held out his right hand. "Then it's high time you met me. I'm Clark Treasure, your bastard son."

CHAPTER FOUR

Clark flexed his arms, his biceps pressing against the sleeves of his leather jacket, as he faced the Treasures. He'd rehearsed what he would say to them every night as he camped in a Bromi tent, and those hadn't been the words. The *real* words—"I'd like to sit down to discuss something important"—had more of a professional ring.

One of the Bromi men who'd sheltered him from the army had suggested approaching unarmed and naked.

"You will be yourself," the native had said. "He will have nothing to fear from a man who bares himself, open to attack, fully trusting his words."

Showing up naked might work for the Bromi tribes that lived off the cliffs, but other men might find it unsettling.

Master Treasure stared at Clark with flared nostrils, as though smelling him for confirmation of his claim. Could this man be his father? Yellow hair peeked from beneath the ten-inch high top hat, and beneath the rim shown blue eyes. Clark recognized his features there, as seen in his mother's cracked mirror. Master Treasure also had his six-foot height and broad shoulders, unmistakable beneath his black suit. Clark had never seen shoes that shone so brightly, nor a diamond-encrusted pocket watch like the one the man wore in his front jacket pocket. Those were definitely not Clark-worthy. He'd never owned something that clean or costly.

Clark swung his gaze to the woman, Mistress Treasure, who clung to her husband's arm. Her wide, gray eyes appeared to glisten with tears. A silver chain rested on her forehead and draped around her pale brown chignon. Her green dress hung straight to the porch, with a lace-trimmed bodice and tight sleeves that ended in V's over her middle fingers. The other wealthy women he'd seen wore corsets that kept their waists mere inches wide and skirts hung out with outrageous hoops. Even his mother, in all her frills and bows, looked as if she wore a costume. This woman, although elegant, appeared serviceable, reliable.

The young man at her side, with his brown hair and gray eyes, had his jaw hanging open. Clark stiffened, his hands tightening into fists. The man wore a soldier's cap, but not the full uniform. Instead, his suit matched Master Treasure's. One of the rich soldiers, then, who never served the country, but used the title for personal gain. Clark peeled back his upper lip in a sneer before catching himself. Enemies wouldn't help him explain his point. At least as a soldier in title only, he wouldn't be a threat to Clark's anonymity.

The other young man on the porch was the one he'd met in the field, wearing the same clothes, and stretched out in a chair. Like the other boy, they matched Master Treasure in height. It could go either way with this fellow. He might be an ally, since he seemed smart enough, or he might be an enemy, the temper apparent in his scowl.

Then, the yellow-haired girl. She covered her mouth with one hand. Was she about to vomit? That had to be improper.

Laughter bubbled up from within her. She rocked back on her heels and pressed her hands over her stomach.

"Amethyst," Mistress Treasure exclaimed. "Hush. Don't be rude."

"I thought this was going to be a terrible bore." Amethyst dragged her fingers over Mistress Treasure's arm. "I love it. How did you know to hire an actor to liven up my homecoming?"

Clark smiled. Could she be his sister? Her giggle reminded him of young Mable's from the saloon. He'd never had a sibling, and even though he'd known Master Treasure had legitimate offspring, he'd never considered them as being close relatives.

Master Treasure coughed. "Excuse me, lad. Who paid you to come here?"

Clark slid his hands into his pockets. He'd expected that question and had rehearsed the answer. "No one, sir. I came by myself."

Mistress Treasure clicked her tongue. "Nonsense. This must be a joke."

"No, ma'am." Clark patted his pocket. "I have proof. From my mother." They wouldn't turn him away without an argument.

"Perhaps we should go inside. There's some lemonade, isn't there?" Amethyst swung the front door open. "I, for one, am quite parched."

Master Treasure stepped down the porch to stand in front of Clark. Clark stared him in the eyes, unwilling to flinch. If he backed down, the man might never think of him as an equal. He wouldn't get another chance to prove his worth. Clark's heart thudded in his chest, but he breathed through his nose to calm his nerves. A son of Master Treasure's had to be worthy of the surname.

"Come into my study." Master Treasure spoke in a soft voice, little more than a whisper. He inclined his head before striding inside. That could be a good sign. If they wanted to dismiss him, they wouldn't go to the trouble of inviting him in.

Clark drew a deep breath before he followed, careful to keep his steps slow, deliberate. Jogging might make him appear desperate. The younger Treasures watched him pass, the soldier gaping and the field one scowling deeper. Amethyst kept laughing. Mistress Treasure trailed behind Cark, her skirt clutched in her hands to avoid tripping.

The foyer opened into a grand room with a marble floor and a crystal chandelier. Portraits hung on the beige walls and a wide staircase, carpeted in maroon velvet, occupied the right, while the left contained a door opening into the front parlor. A Bromi slave stood in the corner of the grand room, bowed at the waist, staring at his shoes.

Master Treasure led the way through the parlor into a room in the back. Clark watched his rear side to avoid ogling the interior. This joint belonged in a major city, not the middle of untamed Hedlund. Sure, it was a ranch, so they had money…but this? He'd never been anywhere so amazing.

Clark kept his hands jammed in his pockets so they couldn't say he'd swiped anything.

If they accepted him, he could have all of this. Excitement raised the hairs on his arms. He wouldn't have to work odd jobs that paid in pennies, worrying if he'd have a next meal. No more rags. He'd gone without food and shelter to save enough for this outfit to make himself appear presentable.

No more running. The army wouldn't dare to touch a Treasure.

Master Treasure held the door open for Clark and Mistress Treasure to pass through. Clark blinked at the office, where floor to ceiling bookshelves lined the parts of the walls not occupied with windows. Brocade curtains were drawn back; the view overlooked the veranda and a field.

Master Treasure reclined in the chair behind the desk and folded his hands across his lap. "Sit. Please."

Clark kept his gaze locked with… his father's. The thought sent a shiver across his skin. This happened; it wasn't a joke or sick dream. Forbidding his limbs to shake, Clark sat in one of the high-backed chairs facing the desk. Mistress Treasure perched in the one beside him.

"We will start at the beginning," Master Treasure said. "How old are you and where were you born?"

Clark kept his voice steady. "I'm eighteen years old, born in Tangled Wire. You have a mine there."

Master Treasure nodded, and he folded his hands over his stomach, constrained by a blue velvet jacket with brass buttons. "I have many mines throughout the state of Hedlund. Tell me about your mother."

"Judith Kurjaninow. Her father built steamcoaches until he and her mother died. Train accident. She was fifteen."

"Judith Kurjaninow," Mistress Treasure repeated. Her gaze lingered on her husband, as if gauging his reaction to the name. Clark eyed the desk instead of her. It would have to be tearing her apart to know her husband hadn't been faithful.

"She responded to an ad for a waitress in Tangled Wire," Clark continued. "It turned out to be a brothel. You were her first customer."

When she'd described it, she'd shivered.

'Garth Treasure didn't look at me like I was dirty,' she'd said. *'The place was horrible, but he made me know I couldn't help where life put me.'*

For that alone, Clark would always be grateful to the man who'd given him life.

"Over nineteen years ago," Master Treasure mused. "I would've just been opening the mine there. I stayed for a couple months and kept returning to make sure things ran smoothly."

Clark admired how straight Mistress Treasure remained. He'd expected her to succumb to hysterics when he told his tale.

"You got my mother pregnant," Clark stated. "You left her money and this letter." He peeled the letter from his pocket and smoothed the well-worn creases. As a child, he'd begged his mother to read it to him instead of telling bedtime stories. A photograph rested in the middle— Master Treasure as a younger man. Clark passed both over the desk.

Master Treasure read the letter in silence, then handed both the paper and photo to his wife. Clark had memorized the words. Master Treasure apologized for not being able to marry her, but would give her enough money to survive and take care of the child.

"You left before I was born," Clark added.

"Where is your mother now?" Mistress Treasure asked.

"A soldier killed her." The truth would help explain his avoidance of the military. They wouldn't question an army man killing a Tarnished Silver. Mining town whores didn't hold much esteem. The Treasures wouldn't need to know she'd been killed over a potion meant to raise the dead.

"So, then you came here seeking a home," Master Treasure whispered.

Seeking protection. "Yes."

"I'm sorry to hear about your mother." Mistress Treasure laid the items on the desk as she stared at her husband. "Is this true?"

Clark held his breath. If Master Treasure denied his claims, Clark had no other proof. They could have him arrested for fraud.

They may not give back his belongings.

Master Treasure sighed. "I never thought this would come up again."

"So...." Clark trailed off. Something had to happen now. They had to say something else.

"It's true." Master Treasure glanced at his wife before he stood. "Welcome home."

CHAPTER FIVE

Amethyst winked at the young man seated across from her at the dinner table. If any man alive was noble enough not to sire a bastard, it would be Garth Treasure, her father. This boy—Clarence or Claremont or whatever he claimed for a name—couldn't be her brother. Her father would've needed to bed his whore mother between Amethyst and Zachariah. As far as she knew, her parents hadn't fought. She hadn't been born then, but surely their life had been as perfect as it was now.

"I apologize for my transgression." Garth stood at the head of the table holding a crystal goblet of red wine.

Why hadn't the servants offered her any? Despite the entertainment with the bastard business, she would've loved a glass of the tart stuff. Amethyst wrinkled her nose at the cup of water beside her porcelain plate of…farm fare. She poked her fork into the mashed potatoes to make a river for the melted butter; if anyone in the city had offered her *mashed potatoes*, she would've laughed in their face. The wealthy ate potato cubes with garlic gloves, ricotta cheese, and parsley flakes, served in hand painted bowls. The china her mother had chosen for the meal had printed blue lines from a *factory*, as if they were commoners. Her father could afford any porcelain he wanted.

"Father, you really went to a *brothel?*" Zachariah sputtered. His face reddened above the buttoned collar of his silk shirt.

Amethyst tapped her painted fingernails against her lips to stifle a chuckle. Zachariah had never looked so pale before. Didn't he know what real men did? In the city, men had birthday parties at the more upscale pleasure houses. It didn't mean they were unfaithful to their intendeds or brides—it was just once a year or only one night.

It wasn't that Garth had taken a whore, but that he hadn't known enough to use a rising wrap, that burnished her nerves. Rubbers weren't that expensive.

"For shame, Father," she muttered under her breath.

The woman was a country whore; she might've had the pox. Garth Treasure could've taken his pick of upscale Tarnished Silvers who were safe.

Her father stared into his wine. "We're all adults. I apologize if this offends my women's delicate ears, but it must be said. Yes, I visited one of those establishments. I had recently opened a new mine in Tangled Wire and I was young, restless. A friend of mine," he lifted his gaze to meet his wife's eyes, "egged me on, so to speak. I stayed for a few months to make sure the mining operation progressed smoothly. Clark's mother approached me before I left to admit she was with child."

Clark. Right, his name. Amethyst winked at him to coax a smile, but the young man stared at Garth as though he were suffocating and her father held all the oxygen. Perhaps Garth did, only with gold, not air. Anyone would want to be related to Garth for a bit of that fortune.

"How do we know he isn't lying?" Jeremiah glared at Clark. Her older brother's face resembled a beet in coloring. Veins protruded from his thick neck and sunburned brow. Didn't Jeremiah know how unfashionable a tan was, let alone such dark burns? The city would ridicule him to no end.

"This letter." Garth tapped it where it rested near his plate. "I remember writing it to the young woman. It even has my picture. Besides," Garth rested his hand on Clark's shoulder, "he looks like me."

Amethyst choked on a giggle. Jeremiah must have loved Clark sitting at Garth's left instead of him, the heir. Sure, Clark could inherit some, but as a bastard, it could only be a small sum in the eyes of the law since Garth already had three legitimate children. Whatever Clark received would be from Garth's kindness.

"You can't really believe this." Jeremiah rose with his fists on his hips. "Mother, tell me you recognize how stupid this is."

"Jere, stop." Their mother stroked Garth's hand where he held his drink. "I know this is all a shock, and while we wish your father had mentioned this sooner, we can't ignore it now. The past is there, but we can make amends. I'm glad you're here, Clark. You belong with us. Family."

"He's not family," Jeremiah spat.

Clark winced. He didn't seem the type to make up an elaborate lie. Amethyst had seen that type—lots of flattery amongst the oiled words. Clark seemed genuine. He didn't throw in extra words to make himself seem more trustworthy. It shone through his calm, but nervous, demeanor. He kept licking his upper lip. She'd spotted that tic before when playing cards in the gaming establishments.

What fun it would be to hit a club. The music could play so loud the walls vibrated as if about to cave in. It could be one of the dark clubs, where the girls wore black wings over thigh-short dresses and the men sported masks with their suits. Did "fun" exist in Hedlund?

She peered out the floor-to-ceiling dining room windows, at the fields stretching over their land, and sighed. No night club, then. Bullocks.

Garth set his goblet down. "Clark is exactly that. Family. I want you to treat him the exact same way you do each other. Family belongs together. He may only be joining us now, but that doesn't mean he should be shunned."

"We would never shun you," Amethyst's mother said. How could she be all right with this? Amethyst cocked her head as she studied the woman she'd idolized as a child. Her mother's calm demeanor could quell any argument.

"Mother," Jeremiah roared. "Father was unfaithful to you!"

The woman blinked at her son. "I understand that. Amends have been made. Clark should not suffer for any of that."

Amethyst nodded. Despite the years, her mother still had that awe-inspiring ability to radiate authority.

If Amethyst's husband had been the one fooling around with a whore and got her pregnant, Amethyst would've kicked him away. She sipped her water and wrinkled her brow. It just couldn't quench this antsy mood of hers like alcohol would have. It didn't give her that buzz that made everything bright, cheerful.

"I want to thank you," Clark began when Jeremiah slammed his fist into the table. The chill from his blue-gray eyes could have frosted the windows. Ah, if only. That would have been another intriguing sight.

33

Jeremiah drew back his upper lip in a sneer. "What's he going to do here? Use up our money on education? Join the army? This is *my* ranch. You told me I'm inheriting it."

Garth cleared his throat. "This is *my* ranch. Clark will work here. He'll defer to you, but he'll still be considered my son. The rewrite of my will is not under discussion at this point."

"This will make a scandal," Zachariah said. He pulled on his linen napkin as though wanting to rip it apart.

Amethyst leaned back in her high-backed chair, grinning. Scandals were always fun. Some of the city papers called her the queen of them. Although, to be fair, she hadn't known that particular Mr. Smith had been married when he'd wanted to court her. The other instances…well…at least she'd never let them get under her skirts.

"We will endure a scandal." Garth lifted his goblet again. "Together."

Her mother lifted hers, so Amethyst joined in. Maybe they'd give her something a little stronger. Clark lowered his gaze to the embroidered tablecloth, but joined in. After a pause, Zachariah did, too. Snorting, Jeremiah stomped from the room. The front door slammed, the sound echoing from the hallway.

"He'll come around," Garth said. "I'll see to it."

"It will take some time," his wife added.

"I want to thank you with everything in me." Clark blushed. What a sweet comment.

Amethyst sipped her water again. Yes, he did think he really was her father's bastard. Maybe he was. How delightful. A scruffy brother who would know the best places in town to have fun.

Clark gasped at the bedroom Garth had given him. It had to be the same size as most saloon halls, with an attached bath and sitting room. The walls were painted a pale red, with a green carpet on the hardwood floor. Brocade curtains hung on the two windows facing his four-poster bed, complete with blankets and pillows. The other furniture consisted of a wardrobe, desk, and bedside table. The bath had a real porcelain tub and one of the new toilets that sported a brass chain used to flush. He'd only ever heard about running water in houses, but never expected to actually use any.

"Are you certain you don't have any luggage anywhere?" Mistress Treasure inquired from the doorway. She clasped her hands in front of her belly, smiling with her cherub lips, smooth and dark, not chapped and peeling like his mother's. She'd caked them with cosmetics to hide the imperfections.

"No, ma'am." Clark met her gaze. He owed her that. She could've thrown him to the streets from spite. "No luggage." Those on the run didn't own a lot.

"I won't ask you to call me Mother. I know that would be too personal a request. Georgette will work fine."

No one of worth had ever asked him to be so familiar. "Thank you, ma'am." How could she be so understanding?

She trilled a laugh as she hung the door key on a brass hook. "Georgette. Please."

"Georgette." He nodded. What a wonderful woman, too perfect to be true.

"Although we are rich, we still work. There is always something to do. I expect you to earn your stay." She trailed her fingernails over the doorframe. "You will have the same privileges as my children. If you desire to attend a university, so be it. If you want your own ranch, we can arrange that, too."

Clark bowed. "Your kindness is incredible." He would stay there, though, safe beneath the Treasure name. The army could reach him if he left.

"For now, I ask you to stay and accustom yourself to your new family." She swept into the room to press her hand over his heart. "Thank you for coming here, Clark. Thank you for finding us." She kissed his cheek before leaving, closing the door behind her.

He rubbed his face and whistled. Hope for a welcome had been a given, but he'd never expected such a warm opening.

Clark wandered into the bathroom. The claw footed tub called to him, but so did the bed. He should bathe before getting beneath the covers. It had been months since he'd gotten to wash more than his hands and face. Clark peeled off his jacket and shirt, but when he started on his slacks, he realized he would need something else to wear. Although he slept naked, he shouldn't his first night in the house. Anyone might come in. He didn't know the household routine yet.

The wardrobe stood empty and Clark swore beneath his breath. Of course they wouldn't leave clothes in a guest room. The sitting room might have a robe, though. Didn't rich folk lounge in robes?

He stepped into the room and froze. The Treasure girl lounged on the velveteen settee with a glass of chardonnay balanced against her lips, one arm flung over the back of the furniture. If he were back in Tangled Wire, the wine would be cheaper. They only had the good stuff when the army brought it along.

"Cheers." She raised her glass. "I've been dying for something like this since I left New Addison City."

"What...?" Clark coughed when his voice squeaked. "What're you doing?"

"Waiting for you." She rolled her blue eyes, stretching her slender legs across the settee, her ankles hooked together. She wore a white silk robe with yellow flowers embroidered across the wide sleeves. It hung open in the front to reveal a lacey camisole and pale blue corset. A gold chain hung around her porcelain neck.

He could almost taste her pulse if he leaned over.

Clark jerked back. He couldn't think like that. She was his *sister.* Half-sister, sure, but family. Real family.

"You have to leave." He pointed at the main door. "Now."

"Why?" She poured the chardonnay down her throat and gulped it.

"This isn't proper." The last girl who'd confronted him like that had been a Tarnished Silver. He'd known what she'd wanted and he'd paid her extra for it, in his mother's memory, no matter how twisted that sounded in his mind. "Brass glass."

Her eyes widened at the cuss. "I hope you don't mind if I drink this. It was in the liquor cabinet up here. I worried Father would miss the stuff downstairs." The Treasure girl set the glass on the floorboard. "So, are you really my brother?"

"Yes." He steeled his voice, and another part of him stiffened. Bloody wretch. Had the Treasures sent her up here to tempt him into admitting he wasn't one of the brood? Curses to her—he was blood related. The letter and picture, and his mother's claims, proved that. Garth had agreed.

"Huh." She hiccupped and giggled. How much had she drunk before he'd arrived upstairs? He glanced around the room, half the size of the main bedroom, until he found the liquor cabinet. A half-empty bottle rested on top. Quite a bit, then.

"Do you know if there's anywhere around here for a party?" She picked at her white, fingerless gloves. The lace seemed to stick to her fingernails. At first he thought they were painted black, but it was a dark crimson.

"How did you get in here?" Mistress Treasure had unlocked the door for him when he first entered.

She pointed at the glass doors in the back of the room. "The second floor balcony goes all the way around. You can visit anyone. Maybe"—she blinked her kohl-streaked eyes—"you should lock them."

"I will." He hoped the ice in his voice scared her.

She giggled. "You're so unfriendly." When she stood, she wobbled, but caught her balance on his arm. Her breath smelled of peppermint and alcohol, her blue eyes glazed.

It would be too easy to push her back onto the settee and nip her shoulder where the robe had slipped.

Clark nudged her toward the open glass doors. "This isn't proper." The wealthy clung to manners far more than the penniless. Manners didn't mean much in the scheme of survival.

"We're *family*." She swung her hips on her way to the balcony, pausing with her hand on the brass knob. "I like a good time. I like you. My parents will help anyone. It's surprising they have anything left. Zachariah will do whatever Father says."

"All right." The breeze brushed his chest and he remembered he'd taken off his shirt. She could see his bare skin, his scars.

She bit her lower lip, already dark from paint. "The real challenge will be Jeremiah. Be careful he doesn't kill you."

"He can't," Clark whispered. The tonic he'd drank those years past would make that near impossible.

CHAPTER SIX

C lark leaned his arm against the bedroom window to watch
the morning unfold on the ranch. If he craned his neck, he
could see part of the barnyard. A worker crossed the gravel
path with a sack slung over his shoulder and another worker
fed the chickens in the fenced-in area behind the barn. Jeremiah rode
across the field atop his horse.

Clark had risen with the sun, watching it streak purple and gold in
the sky. He'd dressed and waited for a servant to fetch him…only, no
one had come. If Jeremiah was up, then Clark would have to do
something besides sit on the bed and read from the bookshelf of
classics over the nightstand. The Treasures would have to find him
something to do while he sought refuge with them. He could work on
the ranch with the best of anyone. He'd done odd jobs like that since
he'd fled Tangled Wire.

Shuddering, Clark headed into the hallway. Some of those odd jobs
still haunted him, like the time he'd needed to play butcher. This ranch
would provide him the cover he needed to drift into the background:
another rich man's bastard, another ranch worker. Clark grinned as the
perfect disguise slid over him. The army would never guess.

The air smelled of cinnamon potpourri wafting from porcelain bowls
on velvet-draped shelves along the hallway. The doors remained closed,
each covered by damask curtains; most were pulled back and hooked into
brass holders near the door hinges. He expected to meet a servant—
weren't these places crawling with them?—but he didn't find anyone until
he ventured downstairs where Georgette Treasure arranged roses in a
crystal vase on the marble table near the front door. Beside the vase

rested a bowl of peppermints. She turned to him with a smile brighter than he would've expected. Could she really be pleased with his presence? Clark wiped his palm across his mouth to hide his wince.

She held out her hand. "Good morning. Jeremiah wanted to wake you, but I wasn't sure what time you rise."

He hesitated before taking her hand to kiss her knuckles. He'd been around enough wealthy folk to know they craved obedience. "Early. I wasn't sure what to do, so I stayed in bed."

"Come down whenever you want. There will always be something for breakfast." She tsked her tongue. "This way, please." The bustle on the back of her red dress bounced as she led him into the kitchen.

A servant kneaded dough on the table; flour puffed around him. From his dark skin, Clark realized he was Bromi, one of the natives the president had driven from Hedlund so he could build ranches. Clark averted his gaze to the cauldron bubbling over the hearth fire. If the man was Bromi, then he was a slave, not a servant.

"Anytime you're hungry, Nolan will fix you something. He's in charge of the kitchen." Georgette nodded to the slave.

Clark refrained from snorting. The Bromi named themselves after aspects of nature. He doubted this man had been given the name "Nolan" by his parents.

"I can cook for myself," Clark said. It might not be as delicious as the supper the day before, but it would sustain him: meat, potatoes, and hardtack. If he were lucky, a farmer might give him leftover crops that weren't sellable. His mouth watered remembering the old turnips he'd gotten a week before.

"Of course not. If you want to be a Treasure, then you'll act like one of us." She brushed her painted fingernails over his cheek. "Don't worry, dear. You'll get used to it. Although we don't cook our own meals, we're always eager to help. Anytime you want to try out the kitchen, Nolan will assist you."

What would it be like not to worry about being too tired to cook, not wondering if he would have something to eat the next day? Clark glanced at the Bromi, but the slave didn't look up from his bread dough.

"My husband is attending to paperwork this morning and Jeremiah works the ranch every day. Zachariah took Amethyst into town. Things have built up since she was here last."

Georgette stared at him with her unblinking gray eyes, so Clark figured he should say something cordial. "How long ago was that?"

"About three years, I would say. I thought you and I could get to know each other today, if that's suitable."

She didn't want to replace his mother. She wanted to welcome him entirely. Clark grinned despite his thumping pulse. "That'd be great." They'd be less inclined to come after him if stunning Georgette Treasure had him beneath her wing.

"We'll visit the seamstress and have proper attire sewn for you."

"Ma'am, I don't have any money." As a Treasure, would she be willing to pay? His father had begotten him, after all.

"Nonsense. I'll put it on my husband's tab."

Excellent.

"Then, I thought we could go to Tangled Wire."

Clark choked on his saliva. "W-what?" The army might still be there even though the mine had run dry. One of the soldiers might recognize him, and if not them, then one of the villagers. They'd been searching for him when he fled.

"My husband had an affair without my knowledge." Georgette didn't blink as she spoke, each word slow and spaced. "I want to see this Tangled Wire. I want to speak to people who knew him and your mother." Her lips softened. "And you."

His heart thudded. "It ain't a great place, ma'am."

"Isn't," she corrected, "and I know. That's why I want you to take me. I trust you."

"Ma'am...." Pressure built along his forehead and his eyes watered. Everything might be ruined if they returned. They'd lock him up. Use him to try out their stupid invention.

"I have adopted my husband's secret love child. As a family, we work to help each other, to care for one another. You will do this for me." Her lips pursed, Georgette turned away. "Nolan, see that he eats. Clark, as soon as you're through, we'll depart." She marched into the hallway with her heels clicking the hardwood floor.

"Brass glass." Clark sank into the chair at the table. If he wanted the Treasure protection, he'd have to brave the waters, and pray he would escape.

Nolan chuckled.

Clark fidgeted on the seat of the open steamcoach. The driver sat on the bench behind him and, across from him, Georgette smiled at the countryside. Clark had never seen anyone take so much pleasure from burnt grass nature. The way her eyes twinkled beneath her wide-brimmed bonnet, she seemed to love the open fields and sparse trees, the dry dirt that showed signs of drought. Soon they would reach Southern Hedlund, where the drought would be more apparent.

Clark tapped his heel against the floor and clicked his tongue. In two more hours, they would reach Tangled Wire. Without the mine, the town might've dried up like the dirt that blew around the steamcoach's wheels. Nothing but shacks might remain.

"What education have you had?" Georgette smoothed her gloved hands over her brown skirt. She'd changed into a corduroy outfit and leather coat. The wealthy dressed for the occasion. Clark glanced down at his clothes, the same from the day before, the only set he owned.

"Mama taught me to read so I'd know what the letter from…Mr. Treasure said." *My father* might be awkward to say. "The saloon owner showed me my numbers so I could help with the accounting. I got a few extra pennies if the books came out right."

"Would you like to attend more schooling?"

"No, ma'am. I know all I need." The hot wind blew over the back of his neck where his ponytail bared his skin.

She pursed her lips. "As a Treasure, you can never learn enough."

He picked at the cushion on the seat. Great, he'd offended her. "Begging your pardon, ma'am. I've never needed education."

"Jeremiah will show you the ranch books and my husband can teach you some of his files. Zachariah can tell you about the army. You might be interested in joining."

Clark stared at the passing desert so she wouldn't see his glare. Blast the army. "Yes, ma'am. Thank you."

"There are also boarding schools and universities, if you decide to take that path." She removed a canteen from beneath her seat and took a drink before passing it to him. He nodded his gratitude and sipped it. The water tasted lukewarm, but it helped his dry tongue. He pushed the cork back into the top and handed it back. Sometimes, he'd gone days without fresh water.

"All these years, you must've dreamed about meeting your father." Georgette tapped her fingers against the sides of the metal canteen. "How did you imagine it? I assume it was to be more graceful than what occurred."

Clark shrugged. He'd known what his father would look like from the photograph, but he'd always wanted his mother to be the one to confront Garth Treasure. She would demand he take care of them. Garth would, even if he didn't love Clark's mother. He could set them up in an apartment in a city, like what wealthy men did for their mistresses. Everything would be paid for and Garth would never have to tell this other family.

Except, this other family didn't mind at all.

"Let's enjoy this beautiful day." Georgette settled back against her cushion, tipped her head, and closed her eyes. "I've always loved how warm the sun is."

"Yes, ma'am." He wondered what she would think if he struck up a conversation with the driver, another Bromi slave. She probably wouldn't approve, him being a Treasure now. Clark sighed. Getting Tangled Wire over with would be the second step in his freeing himself. He could get through this…for his mother, who'd kept that letter from Garth as if it was worth a gold bar.

Judging by the top of the line steamcoach, maybe the letter was worth that much.

Wind gusted down Main Street in Tangled Wire, blowing sagebrush onto the porch of the post office. Shutters rattled over the windows and dust slapped Clark's face. He lifted his elbow to his mouth to breathe against his jacket. Holes had appeared in the roofs and windows had broken. The laughter and chatter of everyday life had faded as if his mother's destruction had dragged everything away.

He blinked, swearing dirt had gotten in his eyes and not tears. What did it matter to him if Tangled Wire collapsed? The town had never served them right.

The steamcoach passed beneath the front buildings. One had been the foreman's office, now boarded shut, and the other had been the foreman's home, still intact, but with shutters missing off the windows. Urchins had once dashed through the street, chucking rocks at stray cats or hitting barrel hoops with sticks. He'd been one of those, another fatherless wretch too young to work but too old to stay with his mother.

The smithy came next, followed by the newspaper shop. The owner had paid a nickel a day to deliver papers around Tangled Wire. Clark would sneak one away so he could help teach Mable how to read. She'd liked stroking the words, but when it came to book learning, she'd pick at a scab or wander off

He'd yearned to return for her, but coming back while the army still watched over the mine might've meant his capture. With Tangled Wire in shambles, she should've moved on, maybe to a city.

Sweat beaded across his brow. No soldiers to be seen. A black cat sat on a barrel in an alley cleaning itself. An elderly man with a long gray beard slumped on the porch outside the hotel with an empty bottle of gin knocked over beside his bare feet.

"Where did you live?" Georgette spoke from behind a lace handkerchief. Clark wondered if she did that to protect herself from filth or if the dust in the wind bothered her lungs. It left his own with a raw itch.

Clark cleared his throat. "We lived at the saloon. My mother *was* a Tarnished Silver." He shouldn't be ashamed of that. She'd done what she could to keep them alive.

Georgette stomped on the floor of the steamcoach. "Driver, take us to the saloon, please, and wait for us there."

The Bromi inclined his head and steered the vehicle toward the right-hand side. Clark scratched his cheek. The driver must've been to Tangled Wire before, since the sign had fallen off the front of the building. Clark recognized it only by size. It was still the biggest building.

Once the steamcoach stopped in front, Clark swung the door open and hopped down. Dust billowed around his feet.

"Clark, dear." Georgette fluttered her handkerchief. "We wait to be helped down."

His nerves felt as though they'd been pulled tight. He glanced around the street, but nothing moved besides the sagebrush. Perhaps no one would come.

"So the hertum was used up in the mine?" he asked for clarification. All he knew about the mineral came from newspapers.

Georgette accepted the driver's hand and stepped down from the coach. "Three years ago, yes. My husband sold the land to the government. Soon this will become a ranch, or flooded for a lake, or perhaps the train will pass through."

Clark nodded, studying one of the crumbled houses. It had been a boarding house for mineworkers with a shed in the back. He and Mable had scaled the woodpile onto the shed's roof so they could hop to the boardinghouse's roof. If they lay on their stomachs, they could watch Main Street without notice.

Georgette held out her arm, so he cupped her elbow as they headed up the porch stairs into the saloon. His heart thudded harder. The last time he'd stepped there, he'd been fleeing from the mine. He'd pummeled into the main room, pushing aside customers, and dashed to his mother's room in a fog.

Blood on the floor, on the bed. A Bromi slave lifting her body. Her hand dangling, with a trickle of red along her wrist.

"Clark?" Georgette's even tone yanked him from the memory.

"I'm fine," he grunted. The interior still reeked of booze and mold, but another scent crept in: dirt. Wind whistled through a crack somewhere in the wooden wall.

"Hello?" Georgette called.

Chairs had fallen over at the tables; a lone mug rested beside a stack of cards.

The saloon owner emerged from the back room. "Yeah?" Despite his gray whiskers and baldness, Clark recognized the bulbous red nose and pockmarked forehead. He'd never cared about the affairs of the army so long as they paid him for his goods. Good, he wouldn't mind Clark Treasure being back, if he even remembered the boy who'd lived in his attic.

Georgette stiffened. "Do you own this property?"

"Sure do." The owner dragged his gaze over her ensemble. "You wanna buy it, lady?"

She lifted her nose. "I do not. I'm here about information."

He turned his head to spit tobacco juice onto the scarred floor. "Look, I ain't a businessman. I rent rooms now that the hotel shut down and I serve meals. It's a fine location, even if things are bad now. People travelling gotta stop, and this here is the last place for a good ten miles."

Georgette leaned against the nearest chair. "We'll eat here then, and I still need some facts." Her voice purred. "What food do you offer?"

Recalling the owner's culinary skills, Clark wrinkled his nose. At least they seemed to be the only people in residence, besides the drunk in the street. Old Billy, the drunkard he remembered from way back, and been replaced by this new fellow with the matted beard.

Clark sat across from Georgette and stretched out his legs. His skin tingled with a naughty delight as if he were a child again. He'd never gotten to sit at one of the patron tables before.

The owner brought them tin plates of hard wheat bread and slices of turkey. Georgette smiled while she ate, as though it tasted divine. Under the table, Clark noticed she clenched her hand into a fist. She would make a grand actress. Clark gnawed on the gritty hunk of bread. Even the stuff he'd consumed on the run had fared better, but it reminded him of his childhood.

"Be thankful for that," his mother would say whenever he complained. Living alone, he'd learned how amazing that vulgar food had been.

"Another plate," Georgette said. The Bromi driver ate at the table beside the door so he could guard the steamcoach.

The owner brought them water-spotted glasses of ale. Georgette passed him fifty cents and sipped the drink.

"Thank you kindly. Now, for that information." She flashed her teeth.

That woman could flatter her way to the top. Clark popped the last bit of bread into his mouth. Maybe that was how she'd won a catch like Garth Treasure.

"What you want?" The shop owner wiped his hands on the stained apron that strained against his rotund beer belly.

"This is Clark Treasure." Georgette nodded to him. "His mother used to work in your establishment as a Tarnished Silver. Her name was Judith Kurjaninow."

The owner narrowed his eyes at Clark. Fresh beads of perspiration coated Clark's body. If the owner didn't remember him, he should frown, not glare.

"Might you remember Miss Kurjaninow?" Georgette asked as she finished her ale.

"I don't got no Tarnished Silvers left." The owner took her glass behind the counter. "They all moved onto other mines. The cities. Wherever. No matter to me none. People don't come here for that entertainment no more."

Clark steeled his voice. "What about Mable? She was a little girl. Should only be about fifteen now. Sixteen maybe." Old enough to have to whore, unless she found better work.

Or had died.

Ice ran over his spine. Laughing Mable, who'd chased cats to pull their tails until Clark had told her he'd slap her next time she did it. He wouldn't have, but he'd hated the screeches of the felines who had no better lot in life than they did.

"Everybody moved on. The rooms are rented out now."

Clark wondered if his mother's blood still stained the floor. Were any of her clothes packed into trunks? Maybe his old cot still rested under the eaves in the attic.

A click riveted his attention to the counter as the owner pulled a shotgun from beneath it and aimed it at Clark's head. "Said your name's Clark Treasure, huh? Judy's little by-blow?"

CHAPTER SEVEN

Clark gripped the edges of the table. Coming back had been a mistake. If he ducked, Clark would have time to draw his pistol from his belt; he could knock the older man down then. Georgette might get shot, though.

He fought away the buzz in his brain. He had to diffuse the situation. "What of it?"

"You're the one the army's after. Saw the wanted posters around. Figured they had you by now." The owner spit onto the floor again. "Never forget when one of my sluts gets shot, either. That captain never got a dismissal, the bugger. Now git up, boyo."

Those blasted wanted posters. "It can't be me the army wants. Must be a mistake." He didn't take his gaze off the shotgun.

"Sure was you. I'll be getting that reward now. Eight hundred dollars will really help me a lot. Finally get outta this dump."

A chair scraped near the door; the owner swung his gun and pulled the lever. It fired with a blast that rattled the saloon. The Bromi driver jerked and blood splattered the wall behind him as he fell.

Poor man. If he'd been with his tribe in the cliffs, he might have still been alive. He'd probably been after the gun under the steamcoach. Clark had seen the butt of it sticking out when he'd first climbed aboard back at the ranch.

The driver had perished because of Clark.

"Nobody move now!" The owner pulled a gunpowder horn from beneath the counter.

It would take him a few seconds to reload. Only a fool would be scared enough to pause.

Clark yanked the pistol from his belt, aimed it at the saloon man's heart, and fired. The owner pitched backwards, sputtering. Blood lifted in a shower. Droplets struck the bottles behind the counter, most of them empty, and dripped down the whitewashed wall. The body thumped against the floor.

Clark stared at his hands, but they didn't shake. Shit. What had the world done to him that he cowered thinking about facing his past, but didn't worry about killing another human being? He checked the pistol to confirm he had four other bullets in the cylinder and slid the weapon into its holster. Maybe the Treasures would buy him one of the zoompistols. Although they pumped steam from the holder as exhaust, the laser beams worked with more accurate precision. They cost a small fortune, too.

Would Georgette want to support him still, even after she realized he was a murderer?

"That was a good shot," she said.

"I'm sorry." He fastened the leather strap over his pistol to keep it from tumbling out.

"You've killed before?" She pulled a lace-trimmed handkerchief from her silk reticule and wiped perspiration off her brow, but her voice didn't waver.

He met her gaze. She would respect an honest answer. "Yes." He'd killed a lot since the day he'd fled the mines.

"With good reason." She flicked her handkerchief before tucking it away.

"Yes. My mother lost her life to senseless murder. I would never do that to another." He pictured Judy's large gray eyes framed by painted lashes. Her laughter had made everyone else laugh with her.

"Do you want to tell me what happened when you were here last?"

He kept his hands still at his side, his chin lifted, shoulders drawn back. "No."

Georgette nodded. "I will never ask again, but if you ever care to, I will listen. I won't judge you."

He tipped his head to the side. "Thank you." How could she accept everything? Georgette was an educated, wealthy woman. She should know better—but he *was* safe. Somehow, she saw that in him.

He would prove he deserved her respect.

She crouched beside her driver and felt his neck. "Dead. Can you find a blanket for him?"

"Yes. The saloonkeeper had kept a closet for linens, in case any of his patrons insisted on clean ones. Some of the generals had; most of the customers hadn't cared as long as they got a cheap tumble."

"We'll put him in the back of the coach. I'll drive us back."

"I can drive." He'd worked as a chauffeur for a summer, before the army caught up with his trail.

"All right. Is there anything else you want to do while we're here?"

The driver deserved respect, not to rot on the floor. The old rooms held nothing for Clark anymore. "I'll get the blanket. Come with me in case anyone else walks in."

She hovered at his back as he found the closet in the kitchen. As he opened the door on hinges that squealed, he remembered a time when his mother had been getting fresh ones because a man had ordered it.

"Don't you hate catering to them?" he'd spat as she'd handed him pillowcases.

She'd fingered the fine linen. The man had been paying extra, so the saloonkeeper ordered the best. "Sometimes you must set them up to knock them down."

"Huh?"

With sheets in her arms, she'd kicked the closet door shut. "Sometimes you have to play by their rules so you can learn them. Then, you can blow them over better." She winked one of her blue-coated eyelids. It had been the only time he'd seen a rebellious side to her, but it let him know life hadn't beaten her down.

By playing the Treasure card, he could learn those rules. He could set up his own game and knock down all the villains.

The closet smelled of mothballs and potpourri. He pulled two sheets off the top shelf. The linen didn't seem as bleached as he recalled. Awkward yellow spots made his cheeks flush as he stepped past Georgette.

"I'm not ignorant of the world," she said. "My parents were factory workers, but my father earned enough to start his own when I was fifteen. Did you know Garth was a lawyer?"

"No." He didn't know much about Garth—his father—other than

his wealth.

"My father's previous boss tried to sue him for rights to the new factory. Garth was that man's lawyer. He met me at one of the hearings. Garth won the case and left my father penniless, but Garth hadn't believed in hurting a working man. He offered my father a small fund to start a new cloth business. Garth paid court to me for a year before we married."

Clark mulled that as he carried the sheets to the driver. Garth had learned to play by the rules, even if it hurt a poor man, and then he'd turned around to knock the boss down.

They rolled the body into one sheet and knotted the other on top. Despite the Bromi man's bulk, Clark hefted him over his shoulder. The muscles in his back and shoulders pulled tight.

"I can help." Georgette lifted her arms.

"It's fine," Clark grunted. She opened the steamcoach door for him and he laid the body on the rear seat. He helped Georgette onto the driver's bench and swung up alongside her.

She rested her hand on his knee. "You're sure you're done here? It'll be easier for you to acclimate to our family if you have no regrets."

Georgette had been the one seeking answers. The rundown town, the saloon with a dead owner behind the counter, another in the coach. His mother's blood perhaps staining a floor. "I have no regrets."

The man peered through the attic window of the saloon to watch Clark Treasure drive away with that frilly bitch sitting beside him. Leave it to Clark to find himself some rich old matron. The man bared his teeth and ran his tongue through the hole where his front tooth had been knocked out in the street fight.

Woo-eee. Clark Treasure had actually come back to Tangled Wire. Idiot. What had he expected? The army had combed through Tangled Wire looking for that bastard a whole year after he'd skedaddled. If they'd been willing to pay then, they'd still be willing now. They didn't give up on a man *that* wanted.

The miner memorized the decorations on the steamcoach: gold embossed trees and horses across a white background. Each family used their own design for their vehicles. Once he described it to Captain

Greenwood, the army would know how to nab that little fool. If it weren't for Clark, the mine mightn't have closed. The miner might not be penniless in a beat up town.

Chuckling, the miner set off for the blacksmith. That old man would let him borrow the donkey so he could get to a telegraph office to find Captain Greenwood.

When they reached the Treasure ranch, the sun had begun to sink. Jeremiah marched from the stables to meet them. Clark bit back a groan. He had to be polite to his half brother, no matter how much the man irritated him.

"Why're you driving?" He narrowed his blue-gray eyes at Clark.

"There was an accident," Clark began, but Georgette stood.

"Where is your father? A despicable man shot our driver in Tangled Wire."

Jeremiah grabbed the edge of the coach. "Mother, are you hurt?"

"*We're* both fine." She allowed her son to lift her down. "We need to see him buried."

At least they would give the Bromi man a proper burial. Clark coughed for attention. "Where should I put the steamcoach?"

"Leave it there. Someone else will see it goes away," Jeremiah snapped. "Father's at the Smith farm."

"He doesn't usually call on them so late." Georgette turned to Clark. "The Smiths bought some land from Garth last summer. They hope to start a new life farming out here."

Jeremiah ground his teeth as he ran his fingers through his dark blonde hair. "The Horans threatened the Smiths if they didn't sell the land to them."

"What?" Georgette shrieked. "They mustn't. The Horans will pay them mere pennies for what they bought it. The Smiths don't have anything except that farm."

She hadn't become so flustered when her driver had been shot. The Horans had to be worth something.

"Jim Smith was over here an hour ago. The Horans said that if they didn't sell, they'd burn the farm and kill them in it." Jeremiah snorted.

"The sheriff—" Georgette gripped the lapels on her son's leather jacket.

"You know he's scared of the Horans."

Clark jumped down to the driveway. What kind of people could the Horans be if the powerful Treasures couldn't stop them?

"Father's already there with Zachariah. I'm heading over now." Jeremiah nudged his mother toward the mansion. "Stay here with Amethyst."

"Let me go too." Clark rested his hand on his pistol. "You're family now. I might not be a hired gun, but I can shoot."

"Yes, take Clark," Georgette said although Jeremiah scowled. "The more against the Horans will show better."

"You better know how to ride." Jeremiah stormed toward the stables.

"I'll bring my bike." Clark jogged after him. If he could prove himself, he wouldn't have Jeremiah's distrust. If the young man didn't accept him, he might sniff at his past, and those facts had to stay buried under the dust.

Clark had stood against enemies before. The Horans couldn't be too chilling.

CHAPTER EIGHT

Jeremiah leaned into the smooth gait of his horse. The hooves pounded the dry dirt with precision; Password never missed a step. Jeremiah grinned. Password fit his name perfectly. The one who rode him had to know the code of obedience to get the roan's respect.

A second horse followed a half-mile behind. When Jeremiah glanced over his shoulder, he saw it as a dappled speck.

Let that bastard urchin struggle with leather reins. He couldn't drive his fancy bike over unmanaged terrain. Maybe Jeremiah should've let him try. It might prove funny to see him struggle with that machine. Give Jeremiah an animal any day over steam and wires.

The field stretched toward the road and Jeremiah urged his mount to jump the fence. They flew, the wind streaking over them, lending ultimate power, and the horse struck the dirt road. Jeremiah turned him toward the right and kicked his sides to coax the animal to regain speed.

If Clark couldn't make the jump, too bad on him. He could follow the fence to the opening a mile down on the left. Jeremiah hadn't asked him to come along, so it was up to Clark to keep up.

Jeremiah's horse lengthened his strides, pounding along the deep-rutted dirt road. Soon, they might start to pave the streets with gravel or cobblestone, if more farmers moved in. Jeremiah gazed at the rushing hillside. Mountains rose in the distance, and between him and them lay fields with a few trees. The forest kept closer to the mountains.

If more farmers did move in, houses would ruin the view. Horses couldn't speed over cobblestones sleek with rain and dust. Yards would ruin the fields.

Jeremiah glanced back to where Clark followed, his mount galloping now. At least the kid could keep up. Jeremiah smirked. Kid would be a perfect name for that poser, let him know Jeremiah wouldn't accept him as a half-brother. They might share a bit of the same blood, but that didn't make them equals.

Jeremiah continued the gallop for another half-mile until the Smith barn rose into view, the sides glowing a brilliant red in the fading sunlight. Flowers lined the porch of the one-story cabin beside it. Stephen Smith stood on his front porch brandishing a pitchfork, the center tine bent sideways. His wife leaned against the porch, clasping her bonnet strings beneath her chin.

Stephen waved to Jeremiah and marched down the dirt walkway to the road. Jeremiah reined his horse and jumped down. Late spring dust puffed around his boots.

Soot smeared Stephen's face and chest. He'd taken off his shirt, so he only wore overalls. The faint scent of smoke lingered in the air.

"What happened?" Jeremiah pulled his handkerchief from his back pocket and handed it to his friend to clean himself.

"My son still at your place?" Stephen panted as if he'd been running.

"He's in the kitchen." The little boy had trekked far since that morning when his father had sent him for help. Not that Jeremiah would ever send his son to get help, but sometimes parents faced desperate situations.

"The Horans came this morning before we was up." Stephen shook his head at the handkerchief. "They done burned our outhouse. That thing stunk. Said if we don't sell, they'll burn the barn next, then the house." Stephen narrowed his eyes. "I can't sell, Jere. This here is all I've got. He only wants to buy it off me for a little bit. I can't live off that."

Jeremiah clapped his shoulder and squeezed. Even though Stephen was six years older, Jeremiah stood a foot taller. "Don't worry, chap. We'll handle this. Where's my father?" Scanning the yard, he didn't spot Garth's dappled stallion.

"He went to get help in town. Start a posse." Stephen spit at the grass, browning from lack of rain. "Why the Horans gotta mess with us? What we done to them?"

The Smiths had something they wanted. Stephen's paltry ten acres didn't stand up to the Horans' four hundred, but it was something they didn't have. Plus, Smith's pond served as a good watering hole for livestock.

"They gonna burn it down around our heads." Stephen jabbed the handle of his pitchfork into the ground.

"No one will do that." Jeremiah tightened his fist around the reins. The Horans would try, though. Without Treasure protection, no one would stand against them. The Treasures had more land, more wealth—if they fought for the Smiths, the Horans might back down. Eventually.

Clark reined his horse in beside Jeremiah. Smooth, swift motions. He might not have been raised in the saddle like Jeremiah, but he knew what he was doing. At least he wasn't a complete idiot.

Jeremiah scowled. No, he was an idiot. The idiot secret brother his father should've never recognized. How was that going to look in the news?

Clark slid to the ground. "What's the plan of action?"

Stephen nodded toward him. "Who's that?"

My father's bastard. "He's...."

"Clark Treasure." Clark pulled off his leather gloves and held out his hand.

"Stephen Smith." The farmer shook before he glanced at Jeremiah. "He your cousin?"

Maybe he could pass Clark off as that. Jeremiah opened his mouth to agree, but remembered his father would be there soon. "Brother, actually." He coughed.

"What can we do to help?" At least Clark didn't let an awkward silence develop.

Stephen shifted his pitchfork between his hands. "We fight."

"While Father gathers reinforcements, we'll start barricading the house and barn." Jeremiah pulled his horse by the reins toward the house. "They won't get to your buildings."

Darkness oozed like a slug over the fields. Jeremiah stood beside the front door, Stephen at his side. Purple and orange seeped with the sun to slip beneath the edge of the world. With the loss of day, the darkness thickened. Jeremiah wiped sweat onto his jacket sleeve; it shouldn't still be so hot that his forehead perspired.

Garth leaned against the railing. The twenty men he'd found in town scattered around the house and outbuildings. The livestock had been left in the barn, but unharnessed in case they needed to flee. Someone only needed to unlatch the double doors.

A light flickered on the road. It grew brighter into two, then three, becoming a dozen, multiplying into closer to fifty red flickers.

"Ready yourselves." Garth straightened from his crouch.

Calm froze over Jeremiah's skin. Fifty torches and lanterns. The Horans had brought a team.

Jacob Horan stopped his horse in front of the cabin. The rest of his men fanned out across the yard, surrounding the farm. They'd brought horses, so they expected terrain, not just roads. Jeremiah rested his fists over his pistols strapped to his leather belt.

"This fight isn't with you, Treasure." Jacob removed his dark glasses. Gold teeth flashed in his mouth. Gaudy fool. Chains hung from the top hat strapped to his head. More chain hung off his leather-fringed jacket and matching slacks. Polished boots reached his knees.

"It is when you threaten my friend." Garth took one step forward, hands hanging limply at his sides.

"Well now." Jacob's gray beard shifted when he spoke. "Stephen Smith, you here, boy?"

"I ain't surrenderin' to you," Stephen yelled.

Jacob laughed. "I offered you money, boy. One hundred dollars. That's more than you'll get anywhere else."

"I ain't sellin' nothin' to you or nobody," Stephen snapped. "I work this land. I'm keepin' it."

Jacob whistled. "Bad, bad move, boy."

His hired men, each dressed all in black with the Horan crest on the front of their jackets, shifted on their horses. Garth's recruits tightened their holds.

"Leave him be, Horan." Garth took another step. "He plans to stay here for quite some time, leave a happy legacy for his children."

"Here's the thing." Jacob pulled a cigarette from his jacket pocket. He held it to his lips before removing matches. He lit the tip of the cigarette, a spark flaring. "Treasure, you don't own this land. Smith does. Whatever you say, Garth, doesn't mean anything. Stephen knows what he has to do if he wants his family safe. Huh, boy?"

"There's another option." Clark's voice sounded from near the side of the house.

Jacob blew smoke into the air.

Jeremiah ground his teeth. Stupid idiot. Clark needed to shut up, let Garth handle it. Horan would back down if he knew anything about stopping a fight.

"Garth Treasure could buy the land," Clark said. "For two hundred."

Jeremiah snorted. Yup, stupid idiot. Stephen didn't want to sell. That was the whole point.

"Then Stephen rents it," Clark continued. "You could never get the land, Horan. You won't harm Treasure land. The law will stand up for that even if it doesn't care about the poor."

Jeremiah flipped the straps on his belt to free his pistols. Horan would retaliate if he knew an idiot was arguing with him.

"Well, Mr. Smith." Garth turned his back on Jacob Horan. "Looks like Mr. Horan here will keep badgering you, so I'll have to buy your land back. Three hundred dollars cash. We can discuss rent later on."

Jeremiah widened his eyes, his lips parting. His father was going along with Clark's ridiculous plan?

Stephen gulped, pale in the flickering light. "Looks like we'll have to do a deal with that."

"What?" Jeremiah snapped. "Ste—"

"Can't do that if there's nothing left." Jacob waved his cigarette overhead. His men charged, whooping.

Clark aimed his pistol at one of the men charging toward him, dust flying from around horse hooves. The man fired his assault rifle into the side of the cabin. Most of the bullets would stick in the logs, but some might have gone through to hurt someone. He didn't know if it had been abandoned.

Clark fired, his bullet ripping through the man's throat beneath his leather helmet. Fear might've flashed in the attacker's eyes, but his goggles hid it as he thumped off his horse.

"Dang," the farmer next to Clark muttered. "You killed the fellow."

Clark cocked his pistol. "He would've hurt someone else." They weren't here for niceties. Tangled Wire had raised him on gunfights. Shoot first and true, and life continued. The gunslingers who paused were the ones who fell.

"Dang," the farmer repeated in a whisper.

More of Horan's minions charged through. Bullets ripped into the buildings. Glass shattered as they struck the windows. Clark stayed crouched beside a bush in back of the cabin. A sliver of glass bumped his shoulder and fell into the dirt. Treasure's recruits fired back at the villains. Men shouted. Horses neighed. Clark swore under his breath. Horan should've brought mechanical mounts or vehicles. Real horses didn't deserve the danger or panic.

Someone whimpered from within the cabin. Clark glanced up at the broken window. "Brass glass."

"You hear that too?" the farmer asked as he aimed his rifle at an attacker. He fired, striking the man in the leg. As he rounded with his assault weapon, Clark aimed for his neck and fired. Body shots were too risky. They might wear armor underneath, or the injury might rile up their blood even more into a killing lust.

"Someone in there?" Clark dug fresh bullets from his jacket pocket and reloaded.

"Check, I'll cover you," the farmer grunted.

Trust or not? Clark pressed his lips together. The farmer wasn't the greatest shot, but he seemed sincere. He risked his life to aid the Smiths.

"Right." Clark stood, keeping his body against the cabin, and peered through the window.

A little boy lay on the dirt floor in blood.

Stephen's son must've snuck back. Clark recognized him from the quick glimpse at the Treasure ranch. A brave child wanting to be a man. Clark's heart beat faster as he used the handle of his pistol to knock in the rest of the glass. Gripping the sill with his gloved hands, he boosted himself over.

Bullets had ripped holes in the back of a chair. The rest of the furniture consisted of a trunk and a table with split log benches.

Clark lay flat on the ground beside the boy to avoid more gunfire. Blood squished against his leather jacket. The child had been shot in the belly. How long had he laid suffering in the cabin?

"Brass glass," Clark swore. Oily black hair matted around the child's pallid face. Blue eyes stared at the ceiling.

More gunfire struck the house. A bullet hit the steamer trunk.

A child didn't belong in a man's fight any more than an innocent horse did. Clark pulled off his left glove and pressed his hand over the child's mouth.

Live.

The room shifted into the desert wasteland, where the sand glowed white and the sky vibrated crimson. Smith's son faced him, a yellow glow around his stick-thin body.

"I have to help Pa," he shouted. "I don't want to die."

"You won't." Clark grabbed his hand. "Live."

The scene shifted back to the cabin. Breath emerged from the boy's mouth to heat Clark's palm, and the boy's eyelids fluttered. Clark yanked his glove back on.

"You'll be fine." He gripped the child's shoulder. "Stay down."

"I...I...." The child blinked.

"Shh. It'll be fine. You'll live." The wound would still be there, but it would shrink, and if the bullet hadn't come out his back, it would disintegrate within a few minutes. He'd gotten to save enough people since that day in the mine to know how it worked.

Since he'd brought someone back, he could take another life away.

That would require going outside and leaving the boy—keeping him safe was critical. If Clark didn't touch someone else and think about death, the ability would fade within ten minutes.

"Stay down. Keep still." Clark rolled onto his stomach.

"It hurts," the boy whimpered.

"The pain will fade." He reached out to hold the child's hand in his. "I'll keep you safe."

Jeremiah ground his teeth as Horan rode away with his five remaining hired guns. He'd left his *loyal* mercenaries to be buried by the enemy. Jeremiah gripped the porch railing to keep from punching something.

"Stephen." Garth clasped the farmer's hand that was streaked with grime and blood. "My son had a strong idea. I'll pay you a handsome price, but it will still be yours. I hate to do it, but it seems to be the only way to keep Horan away."

My son. Not Jeremiah or Zachariah. Clark. Jeremiah ground his teeth harder.

"It'll have to be." Stephen sighed. "I hate this."

Men limped around the yard. The doctor would be fetched. Garth had warned him in town, so he would have his supplies packed, awaiting the call. Garth had already sent one of the men into town.

The door to the cabin opened and they glanced at it. Who'd walked in through the back?

Clark stepped out with something in his arms. Figured Clark would be the one to go inside. Had he spent the entire fight hiding?

"Luke!" Stephen pulled away from Garth to bolt to Clark's side, taking the dark bundle from him. "Blooming gears. *Luke.*"

"Luke's…." Jeremiah trailed away. The boy should be back at the ranch. Jeremiah had left him there in the kitchen nibbling honeyed bread.

"I heard him in the house." Blood splattered on Clark's jacket and denim pants. "One of the bullets knocked some debris off the wall. I cleaned up the cut, took the wood out." Clark lifted the boy's shirt, the checkered flannel stained dark crimson. "He should be fine. Lucky thing he was unconscious."

"Luke, Luke." Tears dripped from Stephen's face as he clutched his oldest son tighter. The boy, only seven, meant more to him than that land.

The urge to punch something drained away. Clark had tended to Luke Smith. That would mean more to a father than defending his farm.

A smile tugged at the corners of Jeremiah's lips, where dirt, dust, and sweat gathered. Clark might be a bastard, a secret Jeremiah never knew, but if he was stuck with the Treasure name, at least he did it proud.

CHAPTER NINE

Amethyst widened her eyes until the corners ached and moved her mouth into an O. "That is the most beautiful dress I ever did see."

"I'm glad you approve." Her mother stood next to her outside the dress shop window. In Amethyst's mind, the phrase "dress shop" hung loosely. It reminded her more of her servant's closet back in the city.

The dress consisted of an oval neckline, straight sleeves, and a plain skirt. The bodice laced up the front, the only detail in the pale pink cloth. Amethyst pointed at the golden corset she wore over a tight white blouse. Black gears had been embroidered over the gold-hued threads. "It looks like me, doesn't it?"

Her mother's smile slipped. "Amethyst, it doesn't need sarcasm."

At least strolling the town with her mother involved looking in the shops. When her brother had brought her, he'd driven through town to show her the training station for the army, as if that shack meant anything. When she'd asked to browse the village, he'd driven home, grunting something inane about work needing to be done.

Amethyst turned to Clark, who hovered at the edge of the wooden sidewalk staring at the dirt road as a mechanical horse pulled a cart by. She grabbed his sleeve, grinning when he jumped.

"Clark, *darling*. Would you rather see me in something like this?" She pointed to her cleavage, shoved upwards by the constricting corset, bared by the opening of her blouse. "Or something like that dowdy old thing?" She hooked her thumb toward the single dress displayed in the window.

His gaze hooked on the flesh she'd powdered to make it appear creamier. So what if he was her half-brother? He could still admire her.

"It's all the rage to make your breasts look like doves," she cooed. Back in the city, she and her friends had used kohl pencils to add beaks and eyes to their mounds that peaked over corset tops.

"Amethyst," her mother snapped. "Cease. Don't make your brother uncomfortable."

Brother. Amethyst rolled her eyes. "He knows I'm joshing. You aren't mad, are you, darling?" She slid her left leg forward and the flounced black skirt rode up, revealing her fishnet stockings and ankle boots. Men loved a glimpse of leg.

"This is the dress shop." Georgette raised her voice. "We get most of our clothes here, but we can also order from the city stores for special occasions."

"*Mother.*" Amethyst pointed at the shop, squeezed between the physician's office and the bank. "I will *not* be wearing something from there. Ever. I'm a Treasure. We don't wear rags."

"You'll behave—" her mother began when the doors to the saloon banged and a young man slid into the street howling. His bowler hat rolled off into the dirt

"You'll be sorry fer dat," he slurred, waving his fist. Dirt covered his tweed jacket and slacks. "Real, real sorry." He rolled to grab his hat and staggered, hitting his chest against the road. A steambuggy swerved around him.

How disgusting. Couldn't drunks stay indoors?

"Poor man." Clark ducked around a horse and crouched beside the drunkard. "Let me help you." He slid his hands beneath the man's arms and lifted him. "Are you hurt?"

The drunkard leaned against him, brown saliva dripping from his mouth. He had to be young, around Jeremiah's age. Certainly not a friend of her brother's, though. Jeremiah tended to abhor alcohol, from what she recalled. Perhaps age had helped him change that tune.

Amethyst rolled her eyes. "Can't we just go home?" When her mother had suggested shopping, it had sounded like fun. Shopping involved browsing high-end stores where designers let her take merchandise for free just to have her be seen there. *Amethyst Treasure wearing the newest trends.*

"Fine, fine." The drunkard shoved Clark away and staggered. "Fine!" His gaze landed on them. "Brass glass, you're Treasures." He narrowed his bloodshot eyes at Clark. "I know you. You was at the Smith place."

Georgette snapped her cedar wood fan. "Charles Horan, your manners are atrocious."

"My family's in high places." Charles pawed at his chest, a grin spreading across his face. "Real high places, woman. Yer family's gonna be real sorry."

"And we are just as high. Come, Clark." Georgette kept her face smooth. "I'll show you the weapons shop. Your father loves visiting there."

Clark took a step back from Charles, his hands raised. Amethyst glanced along the street. People strolled the sidewalk around the shacks and stout buildings, but no one paid heed. Charles Horan making a spectacle had to be a common occurrence.

"Soon. Real soon!" Charles yanked a silver pistol from inside his jacket and waved it overhead.

Amethyst sucked a breath in. If he didn't know what he was doing, he could kill someone. "Mother, call the sheriff!"

Clark snapped his hand around Charles's wrist and jammed his other hand into his elbow. Charles howled, releasing the pistol. Clark caught it, aimed the barrel at the ground, and snapped open the gears. Scowling, he threw the weapon into the dirt. "Empty."

Amethyst's jaw dropped. Clark had disarmed the fiend in mere seconds.

"It'll be today," Charles slurred. "You'll see."

Clark rested his hand on the small of Amethyst's back to turn her away from the drunkard.

"He isn't worth it. You mentioned a gun shop?" Clark asked Georgette.

Clark scratched the back of his head as he studied the street. No wonder being shot at in Tangled Wire didn't rile Georgette. She went through it daily, even if she was a Treasure.

Could the Treasure name offer him enough protection?

Georgette patted his arm. "Not quite what you expected Cogton to be?"

Not quite what I expected you to be. He forced himself to chuckle. "Just getting used to it all."

"Getting used to having it all?" Amethyst winked at him, her lips parted to show her bleached teeth.

If he had to have a sister, why did she have to be like that? Amethyst Treasure would've made a topnotch Tarnished Silver back in Tangled Wire. Why couldn't she be more like Mable, up for innocent fun? He was Amethyst's brother, not her suitor.

Georgette cupped his elbow as she steered him down the sidewalk. "We have accounts at every store in Cogton. Whatever you want, ask to have it put on the Treasure account. My husband—your father—already informed the shop keepers to add your name."

Clark gulped. Endless cash. He'd never dreamed of that. "You can't. I could never pay that back."

"That's the point." Amethyst laughed from five steps behind them. "Father pays for everything. He has mines. A ranch. Stock in trains, banks. Your wildest dreams come true."

He glanced back at her. "You have no idea what my dreams are." An edge crept into his voice and he could've punched himself for it. Georgette was wonderful. He owed her to be nice to Amethyst. Besides, she was still his half-sister no matter how she acted.

Amethyst glowered at a passing wagon. "Don't all men dream of wealth?"

"Some of us fantasize about staying alive and free." He steeled his voice against that edge.

She met his gaze and the mirth slipped from hers. The corners of her painted lips turned downward. "Then you'll get that."

"It's challenging when the world gives you poverty," Georgette said.

A cowboy hovered behind Georgette, his skin shimmering with white light. Death. Clark hesitated as the spirit pointed toward the sky. Another horror from the concoction he'd drunk: sometimes, the dead appeared. A red hole soaked through the spirit's chest where his heart had been. He must've been shot.

A siren whirled overhead and a gust of wind tore through Main Street. People around the shops yelped and the horses tied to hitching posts whinnied, stomping their hooves. A purr started in the distance, growing louder.

Georgette gripped the edges of her straw bonnet. "What in the name of the queen?"

"Is it a blimp?" Amethyst dashed to the edge of the sidewalk.

A silver disk suspended by an airship balloon zoomed over the village. Crimson lights blinked along the metal rim as the purr grew to a deafening drone.

"What is that?" Throughout his travels, Clark had never come across something like that. "New type of farm equipment?"

A thick wire shot out from the bottom and three prongs appeared on the end. They wrapped around a man standing near a watering trough; he bellowed as the prongs enfolded his belly.

With a whoosh, the wire yanked him into the airship's underbelly. Not farm equipment then.

Clark's heartbeat sped. Could it be after him? The army had the ability to power machines like that.

"Run, get back," a man hollered from the saloon.

Another wire grabbed a woman outside the dress shop. Her green skirt fluttered as she disappeared after the first victim.

The spirit kept pointing toward the sky.

Clark grabbed Georgette's arm to shove her backward toward the nearest building, the train station. "We have to find shelter." He turned, flinging out his hand for Amethyst, but she'd left the sidewalk for the road.

Her mouth agape, she gawked at the silver disk. The wind from the propellers on the disk sent her hair tumbling down and her skirt whipping around her legs. Dust blew about her ankle boots.

"Amethyst," Georgette called. "Hurry!"

Clark shoved Georgette into the doorway and leapt toward Amethyst. Stupid girl. Didn't she realize how dangerous it was? The airship had already snared two victims.

The wire shot back down and the prongs closed around Amethyst's waist. The pearl buttons on her shoes glistened as the machine wrenched her off the ground into its belly.

CHAPTER TEN

A methyst!" Clark yanked his pistol from its holster to fire at the flying craft and the bullet pinged off the smooth blimp. Clark fired again, this time toward the balloon. The wire swung down, empty, and swooped toward him.

If it caught him too, he wouldn't be able to save her.

Clark leapt from its path and rolled through the dust, missing a neighing horse. The prongs dug a hunk of dirt from the road before recoiling. On his back, he aimed at the opening in the blimp's underside where the wire emerged and fired again. The bullet pinged off something inside. With a hiss, the wire disappeared into the interior, and the airship shot over the town, the wind from its propellers rattling the shutters on the windows and shaking the buildings.

"Brass glass." Clark somersaulted to his feet, a short curl falling over his forehead. "What was that thing?" If they didn't know, they couldn't find Amethyst.

Of course his new sibling would be kidnapped by a flying machine. *Of course.*

"That thing took my son," a man yelled from the saloon entrance. "Somebody go get him."

Another spirit appeared beside Clark. Along with a bullet hole in his chest, blood smeared around his mouth. He carried a top hat and wore a suit, unlike the usual ghosts Clark met on his travels.

Clark ground his teeth. He didn't have time for the dead to pester him.

"It's a Markay," the spirit said in a smooth voice. The accent reminded him of Garth's, where the a's were pronounced as long a's.

"Clark, where is she?" Georgette staggered through the spirit to grab

Clark's jacket. The ghost shimmered before it solidified again.

"I don't know." Clark wrapped his arm around her trembling back so she could press her face into his neck. At least he could provide her a strong arm to lean on while they planned.

"We'll get Garth." Her breath smelled of peppermint tea. Amethyst had smelled like that. His heart constricted.

His own mother had smelled of alcohol and the rags she'd rubbed on soap to clean her teeth.

"Garth will fix this." Georgette's voice wobbled.

What if it had been the army? They might have been trying for Clark and missed.

Being a Treasure didn't come with a safety seal. Only, he couldn't leave them now, especially if Amethyst's kidnapping was his fault.

Garth slammed his fist into his desk. "When one of those things flew over the ranch, I sent some of the helpers for the sheriff. He doesn't know anything."

"He'll call the army," Zachariah said from beside the fireplace. "They'll figure this out."

Clark stiffened as the office air closed around him. Someone from the army might recognize him. They had to hate how they couldn't arrest him for experimentation a little more each day. "You've never seen anything like that craft?" There must have been two of the airships, if one hit Cogton and the other attacked the ranch. The wire from that one had torn up fencing and rammed a hole in one of the barn roofs.

"Never." Jeremiah slammed the door to the office gun cabinet and rammed bullets into a rifle. "When I find that thing, I'm gonna fix it good."

"Garth," Georgette shrieked. "They have our daughter. We can't wait for the bloody army to come along."

Yes, exactly. "We need to act before they get too far." Clark raised his fist. "We can follow the tracks. They blew enough dust around; we should be able to find something."

Find them before the army arrived. Save Amethyst before anything deadly happened to her.

Nolan, the Bromi from the kitchen, knocked on the open office door. "Master Treasure, there's a feller here to see you. Master Horan."

"Blooming gears." Garth wiped his hand across his flushed face. "What the dickens does he want? Send him in. I don't have time for any more games."

"Maybe they attacked his ranch, too," Zachariah said.

Clark rested his hand on his pistol. Jacob Horan couldn't be there to offer help.

"Have to see." Garth stormed around his desk as Horan entered with his top hat in hand. The man grinned to reveal golden front teeth.

"Howdy, neighbor. Heard you had a bit of trouble."

"So did Cogton." Garth inclined his head in what might have been a greeting—or a threat, if his narrowed eyes counted for anything.

"Would be a real pity if that girl of yours got hurt." Horan patted the pocket in his pinstriped suit. "A crying shame, you could say."

It had happened an hour ago. Clark stepped away from the wall. "How'd you know the thing took Amethyst?" He and Georgette hadn't been able to report it to the sheriff, since he'd been on his way to the Treasure Ranch. They hadn't told anyone until they'd arrived, when the sheriff was leaving.

Horan chuckled. His beer belly bounced, straining beneath the jacket's single diamond button. "Is this the surprise bastard? I'm shocked, Garth. Thought you flaunted your morals too high for a quick romp."

Georgette gasped and Jeremiah aimed his rifle at Jacob Horan's head. "Careful what you say about my family."

"Lower that," Garth snapped. "What do you want, Horan?"

Whom did Jeremiah protect against Horan's slander—his father, his mother, the Treasure name, or Clark? Clark squeezed his eyes shut. Everyone who heard about him had to consider the same thing: Garth's little mistake.

When Clark caught whoever took Amethyst, he'd show how *little* he was.

"It's a funny coincidence about the flying machine," Jacob drawled. "It's called a Markay, if anyone is interested in using proper terms."

Clark's lids lifted. The spirit in Cogton had called it a Markay, too. "How would you know?"

Jacob pulled a pocket watch from his suit jacket pocket and flipped open the brass cover. "You might not know this, boy, but my brother is the senator for the state of Hedlund. He happens to have two of those Markays in his airship hangar. They're new, getting ready for government use. I'd say in about an hour, two of those Markays will be landing back there. Out for flying practice, of course."

Clark snapped his jaw shut when he realized he gaped. Jacob couldn't mean—

"You *brute*." Georgette lunged forward, but Zachariah seized her wrist. "You took Amethyst. You attacked our ranch."

"Now, ma'am, it weren't me." He tucked his watch away. "Didn't say it was my brother, either. Only commented as how he has two just like that contraption you folks saw flying about."

"Horan." Garth's voice sliced through the office. If it had been a dagger, it would've shredded the wallpaper. Clark imagined the blade digging into Jacob Horan's gullet.

"Yes?" Jacob lifted his eyebrows.

"You wanted revenge for what happened at the Smith farm. A rampage on a poor farmer is nothing compared with taking my daughter and," he glanced at Georgette, "two people from Cogton. This brutality is beneath you."

Jacob had ordered his minions to open fire on innocents protecting a poverty-stricken man's land and income. How could Garth think kidnapping and vandalism was beneath him?

Jacob flared his nostrils. "My brother's been in court—safe as a bunny in a hole all day. He's a senator. He keeps to the government. Now, if someone took out his Markays, that's not his fault."

"What do you want?" Jeremiah aimed the rifle at Jacob's head again.

Jacob lifted a corner of his upper lip in a smirk. His graying goatee brushed against his black cravat. "You must realize I'm a man who likes to win. Family sticks together, eh? Everyone knows how important family is to Senator Horan."

"The army will know it was your brother who did it." Garth rested his hands on his belt where two pistols hung. "How would that look for the senator's reputation?"

Jacob snorted. "Funny, but I don't think anyone will find my brother's airship hangar. That particular one, I mean. He has five others, and the military knows about those."

"You've gone beyond threats." Garth stepped forward. "I want my daughter back."

They could bicker all day. Jacob Horan had won with the secret weapon. He had Amethyst. He might not kill her—she was a woman, after all—but he'd keep her there. Even if Garth gave him Smith's land, Horan might not surrender Amethyst. When the army came to fix things, they would need to strategize, play by the rules in regards to Senator Horan. They might not care about Clark, the mine-working son of a Tarnished Silver, but they would care about a government official.

Clark nodded at Jeremiah to catch his eye. When the older man glanced at him, Clark hooked his thumb toward the door and, keeping against the wall, edged from the office. In the drawing room, he waited near the window for Jeremiah to join him.

"We're wasting time," Clark whispered.

Jeremiah panted, his fists tight around his rifle. "That son of a—"

"We'll get her ourselves." They could avoid the army. Soldiers wouldn't need to see Clark.

"We don't know where the bloody hangar is." Jeremiah kicked the wall. The plaster cracked, leaving a hole the size of his boot heel.

Clark rested his hand on his half-brother's shoulder. "We'll follow the wind trail as best we can."

"You ever been in this wilderness? How you figuring to follow a nonexistent trail to a hangar nobody knows about."

Some people did know about it. Clark grinned. Since fleeing Tangled Wire, the open prairie had been his solstice. "Trust me. I've got some friends out there who can help."

CHAPTER ELEVEN

lark's steamcycle roared over the dirt, dust billowing behind his tire. Hot wind slapped his cheeks and pushed against his helmet, forcing his head back and straining his neck. The strap pressed into the underside of his chin with that familiar bite. Behind him, Jeremiah followed on the ranch's only steamcycle, a newer model than Clark's, with the Treasure emblem on the sides. Jeremiah's loose, brown coat flapped behind him, and extra bullets were slung on a belt across his chest. A red whip of braided leather bounced against his thigh.

The wind from the airship had blown a weak path. Clark assumed they were headed in the correct direction, but it wouldn't matter after tomorrow. He knew who could find anything in the desert.

The cloudless sky purpled with twilight as the sun sank. The more dangerous animals emerged at night. They should find shelter and rest until morning.

At the next ridge, Clark steered to the right and Jeremiah followed. They passed skeleton trees shriveling in the dry dirt, cactuses, and bushes.

As the beige land whirled by, he sensed his mother beside him, as though she could run as fast as a steamcycle—more a memory than a spirit. She wore her sequined dress, the one without straps and the hem that ended at her knees. The saloon owner had given it to her to wear when she danced on the bar, but as she aged, she'd done that less. The old man had still made her wear it at holidays, even though her waist had thickened. Without enough food, the rest of her body remained skin over bones. As a child, he'd dreamt about bringing her enough food that she'd grow as plump as the generals. She wouldn't have to look as if his hug might break her.

Beneath the bandana he'd wrapped over his mouth to keep the dust out, he smiled. She would be proud of him. He'd survived by honest means. *Mostly* honest counted. She would be thrilled that he wanted to save Amethyst. Family meant everything.

"We must stay together," she had told him. "Without family, you have nothing."

The shadows crept over an abandoned monastery in the next ridge. He turned his steamcycle into the path overgrown with desert weeds and drove through the wrought iron archway. Metal words read *McKinley Monastery of Saints.*

Gravestones, with the words weathered off, lined the pathway and covered the front yard. Clark parked beside the front door and slid his leg off the seat, stretching the cramp from the small of his back.

Jeremiah stopped in front of him and pushed down his dirt-encrusted bandana. "Why're we here? You think this is the place?"

The wooden door that sagged off the hinges. The broken windows, some without glass. The holes in the wooden roof. The chips in the stone walls. Did Jeremiah really think it was the airship hangar?

"We should rest here."

A vein leapt in Jeremiah's jaw. "We have to get Amethyst. What do you want to do? Run off? Hide at this dump?"

Clark pulled down his bandana. "I'm not stupid. We won't reach the hangar before dark. You want to get picked off by a cactus cat?"

"We're on cycles," Jeremiah spat. "A cactus cat won't yank you off one."

Clark blinked at him from beneath his goggles. Did Jeremiah really think a cycle could keep him safe? Clark had seen too many people ripped off by a cactus cat's powerful jaws. The creature could outrun a cycle if it tried hard enough. "Trust me. I've lived out here."

"You lived here?" Jeremiah waved at the dilapidated building.

"Yes." Clark pushed open the door. It had become a refuge more times than he could count. "You take shelter when you find it." He gripped his handlebars and pushed the steamcycle inside. "We don't want anyone taking off with our rides."

"We're alone out here." Jeremiah glanced at the desert.

Clark headed to the room to the right of the entrance hall. It had been a meeting chamber with a table and benches. Dirt littered the floor and someone had chopped a bench in half. Clark kicked the other half of the bench, splitting it down the middle. As Jeremiah entered with his cycle, Clark tossed the broken wood into the hearth. Since desert dwellers kept the monastery as a haven, the fireplace was kept clean. You didn't screw over other thieves, a law of survival when you didn't have anyone else to watch your back.

He fished through his jacket pocket for his lighter and held it against the dry bush someone had left in the hearth. It caught, the flame transferring to other brush.

"We'll leave at first light." Jeremiah crossed his arms as if the room would attack him. Unbuttoned, his jacket revealed the white shirt underneath, the linen speckled with grime from the road.

Clark set his helmet on the table. "The fire will keep animals away if they come to the doorway and it will provide us with some heat. We'll take turns sleeping." He popped the back compartment of his cycle and pulled out the bread Jeremiah had taken from the kitchen. He'd wrapped it in a cloth and added two jars of peaches. One jar he set on the shelf near the door. "That will be for the next straggler."

How odd to actually have food in the refuge. When he'd come before, he'd huddled near the hearth burning furniture from other rooms, ignoring the growls in his stomach.

"You're wasting our food?" Jeremiah reached for the jar, but Clark seized his wrist. Jeremiah had grown up without feeling dizzy from lack of nourishment, without ever staying awake for fear of starving.

Clark's mother had appeared beside him, once, when he'd wept from hunger.

"Don't fear, my darling boy," she'd cooed, be she hallucination or spirit, perhaps a memory. "Your own pains can be ignored so long as you don't inflict them on others."

She didn't appear often, but when she did, he crumbled.

"There's more than enough back at the ranch," Clark growled at his half-brother. "The people who come here need it."

"Outlaws?" Scowling, Jeremiah jerked away.

Would he call Clark an outlaw now? "Men who would be honest if

73

they could, but instead, they survive."

Jeremiah bared his teeth. "What do we do tomorrow?"

"We find some of those people." Clark grinned when Jeremiah gulped.

By midmorning, Clark and Jeremiah had reached the Spindle Pass, where two ridges pressed together. Rocks had fallen along the edges and the path down the middle appeared bumpy, unused. As Clark headed toward the left, Jeremiah waved for him to stop.

Clark halted and his half-brother pulled up alongside. "Yeah?" Had Jeremiah ever left the ranch?

"You know what this is?" Jeremiah pointed at the ridges.

Clark pulled down his bandana. "Spindle's Pass." He refrained from adding "duh." Jeremiah might not understand the slang term.

"We can't go through here," Jeremiah yelled. "The gangs prey on these people."

Clark rolled his eyes. Before the railroad, Spindle's Pass had been one of the few paths to Hedlund from the rest of the country. Outlaws had lurked at the top shooting arrows and guns at passersby. They would charge down the rocks to accost them. With the railroad, though, fewer people passed through and the gangs had moved on. "That was over twenty years ago."

Jeremiah scratched his thigh. "But it happened."

"The outlaws built caves and shelters," Clark explained. The perfect hideouts for misfits. Some people still passed through, so action did still happen, but fewer. Instead, Spindle's Pass had become another refuge for those who didn't want to be found. "This way."

A narrow edge provided enough room for a steamcycle, or a horse, and led to the top. The tires bumped over rocks and some of the path had crumbled. Clark held his breath as he maneuvered his cycle close to the wall.

"Bloody gears," Jeremiah swore from behind him, but he kept the cycle steady.

Why hadn't anyone accosted them yet? Clark bit back a scowl. The gangs had better still be there. He'd come from the pass to the Treasure Ranch. The misfits couldn't have moved on that fast.

An arrow pinged into the dirt beside Clark's front tire as he rode on to the top. He stopped, leaving enough room for Jeremiah to drive off the ledge onto steady ground, and removed his helmet so the gang could see who intruded. He held out his arm to keep Jeremiah at his side.

"Gears," Jeremiah breathed.

The cycles had made enough commotion to rouse the inhabitants from the thirty lean-tos sprinkled across the ridge. Young men and women stepped forward with weapons drawn, a mix of archery and guns. The youngest occupant, a boy of thirteen, wielded a hatchet.

Misfits cast from society: orphans expelled from the religious orphanages for being too unruly, Tarnished Silvers who chose not to whore their bodies, men wanted by the law for a mistake they regretted. Their number also included Bromi natives who had chosen freedom over slavery—or death.

"Hello." Clark turned off his cycle's engine. "Didn't expect me so soon, huh?"

A Bromi man around Clark's age stepped forward with his arrow aimed at Jeremiah. "Who you bring?"

Clark switched to the Bromi language; the misfits used it in case anyone outside the pact overheard. "This is my brother. I have been accepted into my family."

"You speak that?" Jeremiah yelped. "That's the slave tongue."

Clark winced. Of course Jeremiah would have to insult their helpers.

The Bromi man continued forward with measured steps, but he nodded. The sun had turned his bare skin the color of mud, his chest and arms corded with muscles. A deerskin loincloth hung around his narrow waist and a copper necklace dangled from his thick neck. His naked toes dug into the rock as he paused. "Why you bring him?"

"My family has been attacked." Clark pushed his goggles up so he could study the crowd's expressions. Most of them had poor luck with family. The girl behind the Bromi man, younger than Clark by a year, had been kicked out of her home when a drifter raped her in her father's cornfield. She'd turned to prostitution as a Tarnished Silver before fleeing from a cruel brothel master. She would have no passion for family.

Yet, those who remained at the ridge, and those who visited before moving on, were a family. They stuck together because they had no one else.

"Who attacked you?" the Bromi asked.

"Senator Horan's brother has a vendetta against my family." Clark jutted his chin. "Senator Horan has an airship that looks like a metal disk. He used it to kidnap my sister."

"How old is she?" asked a man with a rifle. Closer to Jeremiah's age, he'd been forced to rob banks with his father until a sheriff shot the man.

"Sixteen," Clark said.

"We saw what you speak of." The Bromi nodded. Wind tugged on his shoulder-length black hair. "It was far in the distance, a silver flying machine."

"Senator Horan keeps it in a hangar secret from the government. We need to find that hangar." Clark saluted the crowd. "Has one of you seen the building? I bow to your wisdom." A Bromi saying that worked well to show respect and homage.

Another Bromi warrior glided forward, his steps silent despite the loose stones. "Before my tribe was enslaved, we lived near where it was built. I can take you."

"I will accompany," said the first Bromi man. "A sister is precious. You will need assistance."

Clark turned to Jeremiah with a chuckle. "They'll help us. Robin Flight knows where the hangar is."

"Robin Flight?" Jeremiah repeated.

He'd be more familiar if the slaves weren't given "normal" names in captivity.

Jeremiah removed his helmet as he faced the group. "We will pay whoever wishes to help."

The first Bromi man lowered his bow and slid his arrow into his quiver. "It is honor we choose, not money."

"And to ruin a senator," Robin Flight said in Bromi. Jeremiah didn't need to know that until Clark knew where his feelings lay in regards to the government.

CHAPTER TWELVE

Amethyst kicked the wall. Metal jolted against her bare foot and she gritted her teeth. "Give me back my bloody shoes!"

The guard's laughter drifted through the tin shed where they'd locked her. A padlock sealed the door and rope bound her wrists. The brown linen dress they'd given her to wear scratched against her skin.

"You could've left me underwear," she added.

The guard laughed outside. The one who'd brought her in had shoved her into the shed, tossed in the dress, and commanded she change out of everything. When he returned, he'd pulled down a corner of her sleeve to check her bare shoulder to make sure she wasn't wearing anything.

"You want me naked?" she'd shrieked.

He'd chuckled, his goggles making his eyes appear to bug. "You won't go nowhere without proper clothes."

Day had turned into night, marked by the darkness outside the shed. When dawn came, the tin seemed to glow. Now, heat vibrated within. Sweat beaded along her skin to run down, soaking into the dress. At least it was thin enough to keep her from overheating.

"Idiots," she snarled. The shed, with its dirt floor, was empty except for her. The criminals had to want a ransom. Sure, her father would pay it, and then he'd sic the army after them. They wouldn't go without punishment for dragging her into that contraption and leaving her to melt in a tool shed. "I'm not a shovel!"

When the army freed her, she would be in every newspaper across the country. *Treasure daughter found* and *Treasure heiress rescued*. People would send her gifts of sympathy. Her parents would let her go back to her great-uncle in the city where the worst thing to happen was being mugged at the docks when they watched ships sail into port. At least one positive thing would occur if it meant going home.

"You hear that?" came the muffled voice of the guard. No, "guard" sounded too professional. He was a villain.

"Like a steamcycle?" asked another villain. His voice seemed softer, as if coming from farther away.

"The army will rescue me," she yelled.

"Honey," said the first villain, "the army don't care about you."

Her eyes widened. "My father is *the* Garth Treasure. My brother is a general. Of course they'll care!"

"It stopped," the second villain said. "Must've moved on. Horan should come by later."

Horan. Amethyst bit her lower lip. The crook didn't want a ransom then. He wanted revenge.

Clark sat back on his cycle's seat and folded his arms. Below the outcrop, sunlight reflected off the tin hangars. Two were side-by-side and long enough to house three airships each. A wooden cabin rested behind, probably for Senator Horan to use when he arrived, and beside that, a tin shed. Two men in fringed pants, button up skirts, and leather vests stood outside it.

"Amethyst must be in there." Clark pointed at the shed. They wouldn't guard it for nothing, with their rifles slung across their backs and pistols at their waists.

"Let's ride down." Jeremiah snapped his goggles in place over his eyes. "We'll take them when they don't expect us."

"No, we plan," Clark snapped to his half-brother beside him. Riding down might turn into a massacre. They needed to scope the site more to determine how many guards Senator Horan had posted altogether.

"Your brother is right," Robin Flight said. He'd gathered twenty of the misfits, all those with steamcycles; innocent horses didn't belong amongst bloodshed. The gang stretched across the edge of the outcrop like a ribbon of metal upon rock. "They think this is secret. The government doesn't know. They won't expect you to have us."

Clark frowned at the hangar. A faint path led toward the east, probably to the main road. "Nothing can be a secret forever." *Except for mine*. Despite the baking sun, he shivered.

"We kill everyone we see," a man down the line barked. He'd been an accountant at a bank until the manager accused him of stealing to cover up his own crimes. An accountant wouldn't be believed over a manager; the man had taken off to live free.

"We ruin the airships." Jeremiah pumped his fist. Maybe he didn't make such a bad misfit.

"I'll get Amethyst and the other two people from Cogton," Clark called. "You do the rest." Jeremiah's hotheadedness would fuel his bloodlust. Let him take it out on machines and villains. Clark would get Amethyst away. His mother would want her to be the top priority.

"Attack," Robin Flight shouted. The warriors switched on their steamcycles in a unison rumble that seemed to shake the rocks beneath them. They gunned their vehicles forward fast enough to jump the jagged edge. The rubber tires bounced against rocks and the riders swayed to keep the cycles upright. Jeremiah whooped as he followed the crowd.

Clark grinned despite the dust slapping his face. Grit crunched between his teeth. If he had to have an older brother, Jeremiah didn't make such a bad one.

The guards ran toward them, rifles aimed. One of the riders drew a pistol and shot it at the closest guard. Blood blossomed on the front of his plaid button-up shirt. His body jerked before he fell backwards into the hangar's wall. The other guards paused to fire and the misfits retaliated with bullets and arrows. The four Bromi in the group parked their cycles to handle their bows. Bullets ricocheted off rocks and buried into the ground. Dust rose into the still air. Arrows with hawk feathers attached to the ends buried themselves into the guards' arms and legs. Men shouted in pain, bellowing curses. Explosions from rifles and pistols drowned out the roar of the cycles.

Clark swerved around the group and drove to the shed. He parked in the back so a stray bullet wouldn't hit his cycle and darted around to the door in the side. A padlock sealed a chain to the wall and through the handle, leaving the door open a sliver, as though to let air circulate through.

"Amethyst?" He banged his fist against the door, his leather padding his hand.

The bang vibrated through the shed and a softened voice called, "Clark?"

She recognized him, despite the cycles and gunshots. Something within him tightened.

"Get back." He pulled his pistol from his belt and fired into the padlock. Metal crunched, but when he yanked, it still held. "Brass glass." If blowing it up didn't work, he'd have to cut through the tin. It would take a while, but it would work. He held the barrel against the keyhole and fired again. The bullet crushed gears inside with a crack. When he yanked, the latch gave. He tossed the padlock behind him and worked the chain out.

Clark kicked the door, revealing Amethyst huddling against the back wall. A brown dress hung off her left shoulder and puckered around the lacing that trailed from collar to waist. Bare feet protruded from the long hem.

Her nipples showed through the linen.

Something else he recognized well tightened in his pants. Blooming gears, he couldn't think like that. She was his sister! He started to pull off his leather jacket for her to use as a covering, but scowled. Heat had turned her face and neck as red as ripe apples. Her skin shone with sweat and her unbound hair stuck to her forehead. The thick jacket might cause her to pass out.

"Did you bring the army?" Her dry lips stuck together with each word.

Last thing he'd bring. "No. Where are the others from Cogton?"

"They let them go once we reached the desert. They only wanted me."

That made things easier. Sort of. "You mean they're wandering in the desert?"

She tried to lick her lips, but panted, as if her saliva had dried. "We dropped them outside a town. They should've made it there safely."

He held out his hand for her. "We're getting you home."

She staggered toward him, her arms behind her back. "Is Father here?"

"Just Jeremiah. I'll explain." He grabbed her shoulder and realized someone had bound her wrists. "Hold still." He pulled out his pocketknife and switched the blade out, then sawed through the ropes. The shouts grew louder outside, followed by thumps against metal. The gang had to be destroying the airships, or at least trying. How much damage did they think they would do against layers of metal?

When the ropes fell to the dirt, he flexed her fingers and grimaced. They appeared stiff, whitened.

"The idiots tied the knots too tight," she grunted.

Clark snickered. Despite being kidnapped and held captive in an oven, she could call them names. Other girls from her background might be whimpering.

With his arm around her waist, he helped her onto his steamcycle, lifting her skirt around her waist so she could get her legs over each side, and swung ahead of her. "Hold me tight." He had to ignore the cream-colored skin that covered her calves, her blue painted toenails, her legs waxed of hair to appear as smooth as satin. Where the skirt crumpled, he caught a glimpse of her thighs.

Her arms slid around his waist and she pressed her front against his back. Her breath brushed his neck where the onyx helmet didn't cover.

"If you want a hug, just ask," she purred.

Minx. He set his jaw as he revved the engine and steered his steamcycle away from the fighting. She might get hit if he drove through the middle. He would follow the ridge before boarding it.

Jeremiah struck the airship with a hammer he'd found on shelves in the back of the hangar. The tool bounced off, jolting his arm. "Bloody thing!"

One of Clark's friends stabbed the airship with a screwdriver and swore when that bounced off too. "We need a sledgehammer."

"See one around here?" Jeremiah scowled. "We've got to destroy this thing." He stalked around the airship, straw crunching beneath his boots. "Stupid, bloody piece of shit."

The other man threw the screwdriver at the tool shelves. "This ain't working."

"We'll figure out how to drive this thing and crash it."

"And die." The man wiped sweat off his forehead. He'd left his helmet hanging from his handlebars. "I'm out. Do whatever you want."

"Sure." Jeremiah kicked the airship. He should've worn his spurs to scratch the thing. When they returned to Cogton, he'd sic the army on this place. Senator Horan wouldn't get away with having secret equipment or attacking Amethyst. The Treasure name wouldn't tarnish.

Clark popped the seat on his cycle to remove the canteen. He shook it before handing it to Amethyst. "It's warm, but it'll keep you hydrated."

She unscrewed the lid and took a long gulp. A trickle of water appeared at the corner of her lips. "When I get home, I'm ordering a glass of lemonade. With ice. Lots of ice."

"Did they rape you?"

She took another gulp. "That's not very decent to say. You should be more delicate with your words."

"I wasn't raised with manners." His mother had done the best to teach him the correct way to be a gentleman, but they hadn't been gifted tutors. The best thing for him had been the library of classics the seamstress in Tangled Wire had kept in her shanty. "Did they hurt you?"

Amethyst wiped her wet lips on her sleeve. "I feel like I should use a handkerchief, but I'm practically naked." She laughed. "When I first got in the airship, one of the idiots tried to touch my bosom. I bit his nose. They didn't try that again." She sipped the water. "Can I finish this?"

"If you need the water, yes. If you don't, we'll share it with Jeremiah."

She screwed on the lid. "I'll save it."

Amethyst sat in the dirt beside his cycle, so he crouched beside her. "Do you need anything else?"

"Actually yes." She rolled to her knees and rested her hands on his shoulders, gazing into his eyes. "So many times, I could've grabbed one of their pistols and shot them in the chest. I would've, too. I'm not afraid of killing."

"You should be." He gripped her wrists, but didn't push her away. Her skin felt as soft as he'd imagined.

She shook her head, lips parted. "Teach me how to shoot. Jeremiah won't. My father would forbid it. Zachariah won't, of course. He has too much honor. Will you? We can go out at night."

"You want to kill." He should look away from the gap in the front of her dress, at the shadow between her breasts.

"I want to protect myself." She sat back on her heels. "Please, Clark?"

His mother had believed everyone should know how to defend against evil. She'd kept a derringer in her garter and a handgun in her top dresser drawer.

Steamcycles approached from the east, billowing dust like a cape. He cupped her chin as he stared into her eyes as clear blue as his. "Yes."

CHAPTER THIRTEEN

lark stood beside Amethyst's chair in the front parlor of the Treasure mansion. She sat against the emerald velvet, the red fading from her face to be replaced by whiteness. Her eyes seemed too bright. Silent, she sipped from a decanter of blackberry wine. Georgette hovered behind, resting her hands upon the back of the chair.

"You don't need anything else?" Georgette patted Amethyst's hair. She'd braided and pinned it and exchanged the linen dress for a dressing robe. Clark would've preferred she'd put on one of her gowns. The dressing robe hung too open in the front. His gaze kept falling to her collarbone and, once, the shadow between her breasts. They might not care how revealing she kept her attire since she was family, and they didn't want to lift her skirt, but his stupid mind kept straying.

Garth glared out the window near the settee. Darkness had fallen over the ranch. Light from the gas lamps caused his reflection to glare back.

Zachariah sat on the settee with his elbows resting on his knees. "I say when the army arrives, we send them after Senator Horan. This is outlandish. The army will fix it all. He won't get away."

"I vote we go back ourselves." Jeremiah drained a goblet of wine at the liquor cabinet. "Let them know Treasure men aren't scared."

"You already proved that," Garth said. "We will never be able to thank you enough, Clark."

Clark inclined his head. "Family must protect each other. My mother said that every day."

"Honorable words you've proven thrice now." Georgette squeezed his shoulder. "You've done us so proud."

Amethyst slid her hand off her lap to clasp Clark's. Their fingers interlaced and he sensed a tremor in her skin. The ordeal must have finally sunken into her mind. He tightened his grip to let her know she didn't need to suffer alone.

Garth coughed before turning to the crowd. "When the army arrives to ask what they must do, I vote we tell them nothing. We pretend it was a joke in town that we misunderstood."

"That's lying," Zachariah sputtered. "You can't tell falsehoods to the army!"

Clark winced. Did Zachariah really think the troops were so golden?

"To get the upper hand over Horan, we will pretend nothing happened. No one got ransom money. No one was hurt and you boys tell me Horan's men were killed at the hangars. When he arrives to view the site, he'll find his followers dead and his captives gone. He won't know how. She'll be home acting as if nothing occurred. It'll peeve him to no end."

The plan did ensure the misfits from the desert would remain hidden. If they stayed out of the light, it meant Clark could too. "I agree."

Jeremiah snorted. "I'll go with that. Let Horan wonder how we did it all."

As Clark nodded at him, a picture above Jeremiah's head snared his attention. The small portrait, framed by engraved wood, depicted a young Garth with a man, similar in age and looks. They both wore suits, but the other man held a silver-headed cane shaped like an eagle.

It was the spirit he'd observed in town, the one who'd known what the airships were called. Ice seemed to form over Clark's skin.

"We have to tell the army," Zachariah whined. "They'll know what to do."

"Obey your father," Georgette snapped. At least she too had grown tired of his government worshipping.

Clark crouched to whisper to Amethyst. "Who is that fellow in the painting by Jeremiah?"

She licked the rim of her glass to catch a red droplet. "Father and an old friend of his. I don't recall his name. They did business together. Oh, Eric something-or-other. Why?"

"Feeling better?" Clark asked to change the subject. *His ghost told me the name of the airship* sounded insane.

Without moving her head, she rolled her eyes to study him. "I will after tonight."

That special place tightened again. Too bad she didn't mean what else that statement could entail.

Brass glass, he couldn't think like that about his *sister*.

She winked. That didn't help at all.

"Father." Amethyst set the decanter on the table in front of her seat. "I wish to go for a walk. I feel very nervous and I know that would calm me. Clark, will you accompany me?"

"It might not be safe," Jeremiah started.

"If Clark is with her, it will be fine," Garth interrupted. "It will ruin our farce if she never ventures outside."

Clark lifted her from the chair and rested her hand in the crook of his arm. "Around the gardens, then?" They would have to go farther than that to avoid discovery.

"We'll see where it takes us. Let me change and I'll be right down."

When she joined him on the front porch, she'd put on a blue dress with sleeves that hung off the shoulders and a black corseted vest embroidered with silver leaves. He held out his arm again, even though the ranch hands had retired to their bunks and the others had stayed in the parlor.

"You've got it?" she whispered.

"What?" She couldn't mean the bulge in his pants. It hadn't lessened since she'd licked the wine glass.

Amethyst rolled her eyes. "A pistol. Rifle. Handgun. Whatever."

"Of course, I always keep rifles under my shirt." He tugged her down the stairs into the lawn. They'd walk down the road until they were far enough away. "I've got my pistols on my belt always. We'll work with the one that has the silencer."

"It's silent?"

"Yeah. It's a special device you can attach to the barrel."

"The ranch must have some of those too."

"Shh." He let his breath brush her ear. "They're illegal."

"Oh." She pursed her lips, but her eyes glowed.

As they rounded an apple tree, the spirit from town shimmered into existence. *Eric.* Clark stumbled. Why would the spirit return to him? They stayed where they died unless they had a mission, like his mother, when she wanted to comfort him.

"Did you trip?" Amethyst asked.

"A loose stone." He frowned at Eric's blackened eyes. Some spirits did attach to an object they'd owned, but Clark didn't have anything new. Amethyst might have something if Eric had been friends with her father.

Clark glanced back at the house. Lights glowed in a few of the windows, but most of the ranch remained dark. "Here should be good. We can aim at that pear tree."

"Won't it hurt the tree?"

How innocent, that she would worry about the plant. He ruffled her hair, as he'd once done to Mable, but Amethyst's hair felt far silkier. A curl had come free of her bun and it slid over his thumb. Coughing, he stepped back. "The tree will be fine as long as we don't chop it up."

"What do we do first?"

He removed the pistol and handled it to her, showing her how to hold it without resting her finger on the trigger. "I haven't loaded it yet, so don't worry. First we'll practice the proper stance."

"Great." She leaned against his body. "You smell nice. Like hot earth."

Blooming gears. Did she have to say that?

Eric shimmered in front of them, as though Amethyst had been the one to shoot the hole in his chest.

"Don't fret over liking her," the spirit said. "She isn't your sister."

Clark coughed again. Spirits repeated the same thing: *he killed me; she stole my money; I need you to find my daughter.* They kept whatever pressing thought they'd died with, and repeated that until Clark walked away.

Eric spoke too coherently, as though he still knew his thoughts. What a strange mantra, too.

"Keep your legs hip-width apart," Clark explained to Amethyst. With her present, he couldn't confront the ghost, and this one might be able to carry on a conversation. Brass glass. "There will be some recoil when you shoot. With a stance like this, you'll keep your balance better."

She rocked her bottom into his hips. "Like this?"

"You don't have the same parents," Eric said as Clark jumped back.

"P-perfect," he stuttered.

Could Eric be right? Perhaps Garth had fooled around with a third woman and she'd begotten Amethyst. The family might only pretend Georgette was her mother. But that would make Garth her father still as well. Perhaps Georgette had met another man.

"Garth Treasure isn't your father." Eric hovered closer. "I am."

Clark slammed his bedroom door and Eric shimmered into existence beside the bed.

"What do you mean?" Clark snapped. "Garth Treasure admitted to my parentage."

"To protect me." The ghost's unblinking black eyes made Clark shudder. "We were friends since childhood. That was my picture you showed him from your mother. He knew you had to be mine. We could've been twins to those who didn't know us well."

Clark sank onto the floor, his back against the door, and rubbed his mouth. He couldn't be listening to a spirit. "Garth Treasure—"

"Would protect any child of mine. This is how he's doing it. He gave you his name, his money. He'll never tell you."

"You screwed my mother?" Clark ground his teeth.

"I loved her."

"You left her—*us*." His mother, weeping at night because she had to be alone. She yearned for an honest man. After he'd grown old enough to sleep in the attic of the saloon with Mable, he'd wondered if his mother had tried speaking to his father.

"Garth and I started our business adventures together. We bought up mines and land, and we supported the railroad. He owned Tangled Wire, but I went with him and met your mother. Judy amazed me. I promised her I'd get her away, and if she ever needed help, she could rely on Garth Treasure."

Clark clenched his fists. "You both slept with her?" Garth hadn't denied knowing her, and the saloon owner sometimes forced his Tarnished Silvers to take two men, or more, at once. His father—or fathers—should've had more decency than that.

"Only me. I couldn't go back for her, never knew about you. Senator Horan shot me the next month."

Horan again. The spirit could be preying on the recent troubles. "Why would he want you dead?"

"I was an inventor more than an investor. Eric Clark Grisham the Third."

Grisham, Clark's middle name. Clark's mother must've named him after his father. She had known he wasn't Garth Treasure, but with Eric dead, she would've relied on Garth...who hadn't helped her.

"Why didn't Treasure help her?"

"She must've been embarrassed, figured he'd think she was trying to trick him."

Maybe the spirit didn't lie and he was his true father. An inventor. "Horan wanted something you made?"

"Lots of things, like the Markays. I regret them all now. He wants to use them for warfare. I was stupid. I wanted money and I loved to make things. I didn't think about what they could be used for."

"Is my mother with you?"

"Sometimes. The spirit world is clouded. She's forgiven me and we're happy."

"Why didn't you show up before now? I can see spirits, you know," Clark hissed.

"You were doing well. Now I think it's time for you to get back those inventions."

Clark blinked. "Huh? How?" Could this man really be his father?

Did it matter so long as he took weapons from Horan?

"I'll tell you where they are and how to work them. You'll do it?"

Garth Treasure had taken him in out of loyalty to Eric Grisham. No wonder Georgette wasn't upset about her husband's infidelity—he *had* been faithful to her.

Amethyst wasn't his sister. He didn't need to feel guilty for finding her attractive.

The Treasures had welcomed him, made him a part of their family even though his bastard status besmirched their name. He should punish Horan for them and avenge his father, help heal his mother, who'd suffered from Eric's death. "I will."

Chapter Fourteen

The door to Clark's bedroom opened in a smooth whoosh. He stiffened beneath the blankets. Night remained in the room, but from the corner of his eye he spotted a figure slip inside. A skirt swept her legs. Amethyst?

He slid his hand beneath his pillow to grip the knife he'd left there.

Heels clicked the floor in quick steps before the figure paused at his nightstand. Amethyst always skipped.

He whipped around, kicking the blankets off, and seized the figure's arm. He twisted the intruder around and pressed the knife against her throat. "Explain yourself."

She screamed. "Saints protect me! Master Clark, I beg your pardon."

Desiree, the young Bromi slave who helped Georgette and Amethyst with their wardrobes. She had enough to worry about without him attacking her. Her throat moved beneath her black velvet choker as she gulped.

He stepped back, wishing he'd stayed in bed rather than leap up in his cotton long johns. "I beg your pardon," he said in Bromi. "I didn't recognize you."

She coughed, fidgeting with her white apron. "Miss Amethyst wanted me to bring you cologne as a surprise."

He accepted the glass vial she handed him as she went to his window to fling back the curtains. The bottle had a green tint, with a styled stopper. He set down his knife to pull out the stopper, sniffing sandalwood.

"She brought it with her from New Addison City," Desiree added. "Said she meant to give it to Zachariah, but thought you deserved it more. It was supposed to be a surprise for when you woke up."

He'd never worn cologne—it cost too much. At least sandalwood was a gentle odor. "Tell her thank you."

Desiree nodded before backing from the room.

"Amethyst is nice." Eric shimmered into existence in front of the door Desiree had shut. "She reminds me of her mother. Strong. Kind."

"You're not going to follow me into the washroom?" Clark set the bottle on his bedside table. She must've gotten up early to give it to Desiree for him.

"Today we start taking back my inventions."

Clark opened his wardrobe doors. The clothes Georgette had ordered for him would arrive soon. Would he feel uncomfortable wearing them? "What are the first?"

"I invented helmets that would let you talk to each other. Riders could communicate."

Clark pulled a black and red plaid shirt from the wardrobe. That actually sounded interesting. "Where is it?"

"Horan's brother keeps them at his ranch."

Clark forked the last bite of sausage off his plate into his mouth. It would seem impolite to leave during the meal, but once he finished, he could skedaddle.

"You shouldn't eat that." Amethyst's voice cut to him from across the table.

He looked up mid-chew, remembered to close his mouth, and gulped a hunk of the sausage flavored with hot peppers.

She sipped her apple juice and lifted her waxed eyebrows. "A poor little animal died for that, you realize."

Garth, sitting at the head of the table, ceased his conversation with Jeremiah beside him. Across from Jeremiah, Zachariah set down his newspaper. Georgette, seated at the other head of the table, rested her spoon against her bowl of oatmeal.

"Amethyst," she said. "Please refrain from improper dinner conversation."

"This isn't dinner. It's breakfast." Amethyst smirked over her drink. "Besides, Clark won't know if he doesn't learn."

Clark wiped his mouth on his linen napkin in case food stuck to his lips. "Won't know what?" The morning meal had been progressing smoothly. Of course she would have to set everyone on edge—but it made the day come to life. She was always so…unexpected.

"That an innocent creature died in the making of that disgusting sausage." She wrinkled her nose. "You people are vulgar. You think you're wonderful as you eat your pets."

Jeremiah snorted. "We have to eat meat. Why else do we raise pigs?"

She tossed a curl over her shoulder. Her crimson bodice hung low in the front, causing the swells of her bosom to bounce. She wasn't his sister. Clark imagined kissing the pale swells to sense their softness. That stray curl tumbled back over her bare shoulder. "People in New Addison City have pigs as pets."

"People in the city don't have to work," Jeremiah snarled. "I need the energy."

Clark ran his tongue along the inside of his mouth. He'd often wondered the same thing: what gave a human the right to eat an animal? Animals had feelings, families. He'd never be able to surrender to her morals, though, when all that stood between him and starvation was a hunk of beef jerky.

"I can never reason with you." Amethyst rolled her eyes.

"You don't know what ranch life is like," Jeremiah hissed.

"Clark." Georgette lifted her voice. "You seem to be in a hurry this morning."

He folded his napkin beside his plate. "I was hoping to explore the countryside." Namely, the Horan Ranch. "If I'm going to live here, I need to know everything I can." That shouldn't sound too much as if he overstepped his boundaries. They had offered him their home. "When I return, I'll help anyway I can," he added to Garth.

Garth lifted his hand. "Please. Take your time. It *is* important you know the landscape better."

Superb, a word he'd learned in one of the seamstress's novels back when he'd read them aloud to Mable. "If I may be excused?" Clark nodded to his empty plate. If he could, he would've licked it. His stomach hadn't felt that full since the holidays back in Tangled Wire.

"By all means." Garth extended his hand toward the window. "It looks like a wonderful day for exploring."

With the sun bright and the sky cloudless, it would be wonderful for exacting revenge.

His hands in the pockets of his new denim slacks, Clark hastened his steps through the Treasure apple orchard. On the other side, lay the Horan Ranch. Sunlight baked through his clothes. The leather satchels he'd brought bounced against his legs. Huge, empty satchels didn't appear suspicious. He snorted.

His father, Eric Clark Grisham the Third, floated beside him. "Stay in the orchard. It won't look suspicious. You'll be overlooking your new inheritance."

"I'm not stupid. I know how to look inconspicuous." Brass glass, he smirked. Blast it all. Clark tried to rub the smirk away, but it clung to his lips. For his entire life, he'd wanted a father to give him advice. Sure, Garth had been his father for a short while, but Garth had been calmer, serene. Garth knew he wasn't Clark's blood relation, so he oversaw rather than guided. This Eric Grisham *guided*.

"This must be done with precision." Eric flapped his pallid hands. "Study the trees while looking at the ranch. There shouldn't be too many people near the orchard."

A man actually wanted to teach him. A folly on it all. Clark grinned broader.

Soil crunched beneath his thick boots. Weeds had been plucked from around the apple trees, spaced to avoid the branches from mingling too close together. Workers in denim slacks cuffed to the knees and white blouses with the sleeves rolled to the elbows strolled a few rows down inspecting the trees. They placed mechanical beetles the size of fingernails on the leaves that had been nibbled by real bugs. The machines would kill the bugs to keep the trees healthy.

He'd helped in a harvest once, a year ago, up north. The harvesters played a high-pitched note on a special flute that called the beetles back into leather satchels. The harvesters then plucked off the fruit to place into baskets. Despite the heat and aches in his back, Clark had loved seeing the fresh fruit, feeling the supple flesh.

"You'll be fetching my helmets," Eric said.

"Sure thing." Clark glanced at him. Had Eric mentioned more while his thoughts wandered?

"This is important," Eric snapped. He must've repeated himself a few times. Clark shrugged to make it seem as if he didn't care. Shoot, his father deserved more respect. Eric hadn't chosen to abandon them. Sure, he could've shown up in his ghostly form, but he hadn't picked death.

"What does Horan plan to do with the helmets?" Clark asked. "Talking to each other while you ride doesn't seem that dire."

"It does when you're planning heists. A plan crumbles when you can't communicate freely." Eric floated close. "Wouldn't you rather own the helmets?"

A new cycle helmet would be helpful. His had a crack in the back from when he'd been thrown in a chase. If it weren't for his mates, the army might've caught him.

"They should be yours by right of inheritance," Eric whispered, as if he could be overheard.

Clark licked his lips, wishing he'd brought along a canteen. "You tell me where they are and I'll get them."

Eric grinned. The dimples in his cheeks made breath catch in Clark's throat. He had those same dimples.

The orchard ended with a wooden fence. Below the sloping hill lay a pasture with grazing horses and a four-story brick mansion. Beyond that stretched fields and fences.

"Horan Ranch?" Clark guessed. The building itself reminded him of the Treasure home, but Georgette kept flowers along the pathway and the garden in the back. This mansion's yard had only a colored patch, probably of herbs.

"See that brick shed out by the barn?"

Clark squinted until he located the outbuilding. "Gotcha."

"Horan keeps the helmets in there with his other riding gear."

"Locked?"

"Do you know how to pick locks?" Eric countered.

Clark didn't blink. "Of course."

Eric grinned. "Me too. I love obscure hobbies."

Loved. Clark winced. If Eric still lived, they would've had a different relationship than what Garth shared with his sons. They wouldn't carry on casual conversation at the eating table. They would *do things*.

"Since its morning, most of the hands will be working around. Tell anyone who sees you that you're hired to fix Horan's cycles. You can tinker, can't you, if anyone looks on?"

"I can keep 'em running."

"I've built cycles, so I'll walk you through any difficult steps."

"Awesome." Clark glanced over his shoulder, but the harvesters with the beetles strolled onward. He grasped the top of the fence and swung his legs over. The unkempt grasses reached his shins and the horses glanced his way. A dappled gray whinnied. They would be used to people and he knew how to handle livestock.

"You sure no one will look this way?" Clark kept his voice low. "I can come back on my cycle with some tools. Make it look more realistic."

"If you show up on a cycle, it'll draw too much attention," Eric said. "This way, you have a chance of slipping in and out without anyone seeing you."

A brown mare nickered. Sometimes spirits upset animals.

"They better not shoot me." Clark scanned the ranch as he lumbered through the weeds, avoiding pockets of manure. As long as he didn't hurry, he wouldn't look too out of place.

Clark hopped the fence and rested his hands on his sacks, one hanging off each shoulder, as if they weren't empty. The four helmets Eric claimed existed better fit inside them. Eric had promised they would be sufficient.

Clark kept his eyes forward and whistled his mother's favorite saloon song as he headed toward the shed. A woman in a green dress weeded the patch of herb garden without looking up, and a stable hand walked a calf across the yard by a rope. The other workers would be in the main fields or herding the cattle to a new grazing patch. Far away. Hopefully.

The man with the calf glanced his way and Clark nodded, smiling. He widened his eyes to appear innocent. The man nodded back without pausing.

Clark reached the brick shed and dropped his bags as if they were heavy. He studied the area, but the woman weeding appeared to be the only one. Clark tried the doorknob, but it wouldn't budge. He ran his finger over the lock; he would have to pick it. Still whistling, Clark peered over his shoulder as he slipped the lock picking kit from his jacket pocket.

The weeding woman stood at the fence staring at him, wiping her hands on her apron. Brown streaks smeared the white linen.

"Can I help ya?" she called in a thick, Bromi accent.

Clark waved with his free hand and caught himself before he answered in Bromi. "Just fixin' the cycles, ma'am!"

She shook her head. "Door's locked. I'll go get Pete."

CHAPTER FIFTEEN

Clark parted his lips to look dopey. People considered a dopey person innocent. Inside, his heart beat faster. Brass glass, he didn't need help. He couldn't tell the Bromi woman he could get into the shed, though. It would take him a few minutes to pick the lock.

"I'll just be a moment." She scurried into the house through the backdoor, still wiping her hands on her apron.

Clark leaned against the door and folded his arms to look bored. This couldn't take too long. The more he lingered, the more his chances of being caught by Horan, or another authority figure, increased. Who was Pete, anyway? An important man, if he had keys. Clark steeled his face against scowling. Pete better not know the cycles weren't being fixed. If he were the overseer, he should know what happened on his ranch.

Clark scanned the yard of well-packed dirt. Chickens clucked around the nearby barn. Cows mooed in the field behind the shed, grazing on weeds. The back door of the mansion opened. A Bromi man in denim overalls and a plaid shirt exited, the Bromi woman behind him. Good. A Bromi might not report the cycle fixing. Most Bromis Clark knew hated being slaves. It kept a level of disloyalty in regards to their masters. They loathed being taken from their lands, forced to work without pay, husbands and wives sold to other ranches, all Bromis in captivity forced to wear a cravat around their necks to hide their tattoo branding them for their tribe.

"Need to get inside?" The Bromi man pulled a wide-brimmed straw hat over his balding forehead.

"Gotta fix the cycles. Ain't runnin' too smooth." A common

complaint among cycle owners. Making the engine purr had been the first thing Clark learned. People didn't notice you as much if the engine didn't roar like a puma in attack.

"You from the cycle shop in town?" The Bromi removed a silver key ring from his pocket and fit a long key into the lock on the door. No accent, so he would've been captured as a child, or born to a slave mother.

"Yeah." Clark shrugged. "New. Hope I can make a living this way."

"Sure, sure." The Bromi turned the key and pushed the door open. "Need anything?"

Clark patted his saddle bags as if they were full. "Got it all right here." Spotting the darkness inside, he whistled. It wouldn't impede his mission—Eric would tell him what to steal—but it wouldn't do for the ruse. "Could you get me a light? Looks mighty dark in here."

"Light's in the ceiling." The Bromi pulled a step ladder away from the wall and stood in the center of the shed to fiddle with a hanging lamp. A flame sparked to life. "That enough?"

"That'll do. I'll let you know if I need more." That should sound realistic. If he were too polite to a Bromi, it would cause questions.

Wooden shelves of tools and cycle accessories lined the walls with four cycles in the center of the dirt floor. Gold buffalo adorned the sides of the cycles.

"These are Master Horan's own," the Bromi said. "The cycles for the workers be in the barn. Ya want his private ones, right?"

"The ones he wants in tiptop shape." Clark grinned. Of course Horan would own four for himself. Did Garth keep as many wasted goods sitting around rotting?

"Since you ain't been here before, the gold buffalo be his crest. He strong and big, like buffalo. Buffalo he hunts." The Bromi snorted. Clark turned his head aside to hide his smile. The wealthy idolized the buffalo that roamed across the fields and plains of the west, but they also killed them in massive hunting sprees, as if there would be an endless supply. The Bromis had once lived off following buffalo trails. Of course the man would be snippy.

"I'll let you know when I'm done so you can lock up," Clark said. Horan better not punish the Bromi slave. If the heist succeeded, Horan wouldn't notice the missing helmets until it was too late to remember the Bromi who'd unlocked the door. According to Eric, Horan only rode the cycles when he went on hunting sprees or to threaten his neighbors.

The Bromi man nodded before heading back to the house. Since the woman still pruned the herb garden, Clark shut the door behind him. Eric appeared above the cycles.

"You know your way around a situation," the ghost said.

Clark averted his gaze from the black, empty eyes. "I've survived this long."

If he sought deep enough, he could blame Eric for not marrying his mother sooner. They might all be a family. Those thoughts wouldn't be fair, though.

"Where are they?" He coughed in the musty air. The flame in the gas lamp flickered.

"Top shelf in the back." Did Clark sense regret in Eric's words?

Clark eased around the cycles toward the indicated shelf. Leather bags to attach to the sides of the cycles, leather gloves to protect the rider's hands…four brass helmets. "Bravo." Clark dropped his saddle bags and grabbed the stepladder the Bromi slave had used. Stepping on it, Clark reached the first helmet. "This is a lot lighter than a regular helmet." It couldn't have been heavier than a pair of strong denim pants.

Pale yellow silk adorned the cushioned interior of the helmet. When he set it on his head and pulled the visor down, lights flashed across the glass.

"That's not glass," Eric said as though he'd sensed Clark's thoughts. "It's a substance I designed myself. It won't shatter, so you'll be safer. It can crack, but pieces will never fly off to stab you."

"Awesome." His voice sounded muffled from the piece of material that went over his mouth. A normal helmet only covered the top of the rider's head or, on the more expensive models, used a glass visor to keep dust and bugs from the rider's eyes.

Clark pulled off the helmet and fitted it into the bag. Taking down another helmet, he squeezed it in beside the first and buckled the bag's flap into place. He filled the other bag, turned off the gas lamp, and set the stepladder back.

"The Bromi is coming," Eric said.

Clark dropped to his knees beside the nearest cycle and rubbed his chin as if pondering. The Bromi woman's shadow danced across the floor.

"You need me get one of the Horan boys?" she asked. "Master Horan out in the back fields, but the boys closer."

The last thing he needed were one of them. "I'm fine. Each cycle is different. I need to find which wires need tweaking. Sometimes they loosen when the cycle is ridden over rough terrain." More information than necessary might make her retire to her plants.

"Last time someone from your shop come, he need Mr. Horan to start the cycle to hear it."

Brass glass, of course. Clark hadn't planned to stay that long, but it would look suspicious if he didn't hear the problem. "Sometimes I can tell by looking at it."

The Bromi woman tugged on her apron. "Don't want Master Horan mad if his cycle ain't fixed right."

Clark stood and brushed off his pants. Brass glass, the slave had to be good and fearful. "I'll go get them if you tell me where they are."

"It ain't trouble. You work and I go. The boys are out by the watering hole."

"Thank you." The watering hole would be out in a field for the cattle to drink. It would take her a while to fetch them while he broke away.

Clark watched from the shed's doorway until the Bromi woman disappeared around the barn. His hands resting on his bags and a whistle on his lips, Clark headed across the yard toward the horse pasture. He kept his steps deliberate, unhurried, as if he belonged.

The bags weighed on his shoulders, but at least the helmets weren't heavy. Clark checked to make sure no one looked before he hopped the fence. The horses glanced at him before they resumed eating. A black mare cantered away. Clark continued up the field, whistling. They would find the shed abandoned, the helmets gone. The Bromi slaves would describe him as coming from town. Horan would check with the cycle shop, and the owner wouldn't know who he was.

Clark reached the top fence and sighed. "I made it."

"Good job, son," Eric said.

Clark laughed as he dropped the bags over the fence and hopped onto the other side. "That was fun." Eric had called him "son." His father, his real father, felt pride for him.

"How come I don't get any fun?" Amethyst's voice drifted from the orchard. Clark froze, his hand clenching on the top bar of the wooden fence.

She stepped out from behind an apple tree and sauntered toward him, swinging her hips. "I like fun." She wore her dark brown riding suit, the pant legs wide enough to look like a skirt. She'd buttoned the tight bodice so that it revealed a glimpse of her white lace camisole.

"Brass glass." Clark shut his eyes. She would tell Garth. The Treasures would question why he'd been on Jacob Horan's land. "You followed me?"

"I didn't walk through the orchard because I'm addicted to apples. Apple flavored liquor...now *that* I do love." She'd painted her lips with fresh crimson rouge, as bright as any fresh apple. Clark dragged his gaze up to her kohl-lined eyes.

"Why would you follow me?" Her answer would gain him time. "Your parents trust me to go off on my own." They were way too trusting.

She laughed, plucking a leaf off the tree. "Of course I *trust* you. I'm bored. This is a horrible area. There's nothing to do." She tore a section of the leaf off the vein. "You're just so interesting."

Clark crouched to rest his hands on his fallen bags. If she demanded to see inside, what could he tell her? She would recognize the buffalo symbol painted on the sides as belonging to Horan. "We can go for a cycle ride."

"Really?" She blew the leaf off her palm.

He coughed. "Would your parents let you?" Girls he'd run with had owned cycles, but they hadn't been heiresses. Irritating Garth and Georgette wouldn't help him.

"Your parents too." She sashayed over to him and tapped his head. "I'm sure they would agree as long as we were careful."

"Hey!" A man's bark seared through the pasture behind him and horse hooves pounded the dirt. Clark's blood seemed to freeze in his veins. Leaving the bags, he rose and turned, lifting his arms to block Amethyst.

He could grab her hand and they could run through the orchard, but men on horseback could jump the fence and chase them down.

Two young men drew their horses to a stop on the other side of the fence, glaring down at Clark.

They'd discovered his trickery. Clark lowered his hands to rest them at the pistols hanging from his belt.

"Hello. I'm Amethyst." She bounced forward to lean against the fence, the sunlight reflecting in her blue eyes.

The man atop the brown horse with a white star on its forehead tipped his leather hat. "I'm Adam Horan, ma'am. This here's one of my brothers, Jeff."

"You're mighty pretty for a Treasure." Jeff whistled. They both had dark hair that curled beneath their hats. Clark guessed they were in their mid-twenties. Adam appeared older, with a few lines around his gray eyes. The front and cuffs of his white shirt laced, the collar undone to reveal a tanned chest and tight black curls. A green cloth scarf looped around his neck.

"I'm mighty pretty for a lot of things." She winked, adopting their western drawl.

Clark rested his hand on her arm. "We'd best get back for that ride."

"Here's the thing." Adam pulled a pistol from his belt and aimed the barrel at the sky. "I sure hate Treasures near my land. You recognize what I mean?" Sunlight glinted off the goggles snapped to his brown cowboy hat.

Clark closed his fingers around Amethyst. "We're not on your land. This is Garth's orchard."

"Be our fence, though." Adam shifted the gun toward Amethyst. She gulped, sliding her hands off and stepping backward into Clark. An honorable man should know better than to threaten a woman, especially a lady.

"We ain't never liked us a Treasure." Jeff snickered. Sweat stained the armpits of his blue and white striped shirt. "You hear?"

"We hear," Clark said. Jeremiah would defend the Treasure honor— Clark could tell that from talking to Jeremiah for ten minutes. It was the time to get away, not fight. Good thing he wasn't there, or maybe he'd learned to avoid the Horan sons. "Come on, Amethyst."

"I can go where I want." She puckered her lips. "It might be your fence, but this is my father's orchard. It's praised across the territory. Mother wrote to say when the queen herself passed through, she stopped to eat with my parents and praised the apple pie. I've never heard anyone praise something that came from *your* ranch."

"Bitch." Adam pulled the trigger. The gun fired with a boom and Amethyst jerked. She took a step back into Clark and slumped forward.

"Amethyst!" He caught her under the arms and lowered her as her eyes rolled back in her head, jaw slackened. Crimson soaked across the front of her bodice.

CHAPTER SIXTEEN

W hat'd you do?" Jeff slapped his brother's arm. "You
think Treasure will let this go?"

"Self-defense," Adam growled. "The fellow here
attacked us first. He shoved the girl forward." Adam
waved the pistol at Clark.

They didn't recognize him. They probably thought he was an orchard
worker. Workers held no say with the ranch owner once a wealthy
woman died.

"You shot the Treasure girl," Jeff rasped. His skin paled beneath his
sunburned cheeks and dark tan. The red bandana around his neck
matched the color soaking across Amethyst.

"Weren't us." Adam cocked his pistol at Clark's face. "You tell
Garth who did it and we'll blow your brains out. We'll hunt you down.
We can. Our uncle is Senator Horan. You won't smear our name with
your shit."

Heartless bastards. Clark set his jaw and nodded.

He would kill them himself.

The sons turned their horses away and charged across the pasture.

Clark pressed his two fingers against Amethyst's throat. Although he
wore leather gloves, he couldn't feel a pulse. Her chest didn't stir with
breath and she stared without seeing at the cloudless sky above.

"Blooming gears," Clark muttered. The bullet must've hit her heart or
lungs, most likely her heart since she'd died so fast. Painless.

Death was better. She might've died slowly in a doctor's care. He
could fix this.

Clark bit the fingertip of his glove to pull it off, cradling her head with his other arm. He spit the glove into the dirt and pressed his bare hand over her mouth.

The orchard flashed to the desert of death. An orange sun glowed in a sky as crimson as Amethyst's blood. She stood in the black sand, circling, her arms waving, naked but for a white glow that blurred her features.

"Amethyst." Clark stepped toward her, lifting his hand. He could pretend she'd blacked out. The gunshot had only grazed her. She would heal after he brought her back.

"Clark?" Her voice wavered. "Where am I?"

"Dreaming." He took her glowing hand. "I'll lead you back."

She shimmered as he concentrated on life, but then she pulled back. The glow around her solidified, taking her farther from life. "He shot me!"

"I'll take care of you." He grabbed her hand and interlaced their fingers. She felt like nothing, no more than a wisp. Life. They needed life.

The orchard reappeared and Amethyst jerked in his arms. She gasped, arching her back, and flailed her arms. He clamped his hands over her shoulders.

"I'm dead," she shrieked.

"You're fine, I swear!"

"I felt the pain. I *died*." The ashen pallor clung to her face. "I can't be alive right now."

He helped her sit up and turned her to face him, pulling her close until their noses almost touched. "Shh, you're fine. It was a mistake. The bullet hit…." What could he say it hit that would result in so much blood? "The bullet hit the horse. That's where all this blood comes from."

Amethyst panted, her breath hot against his mouth and scented with peppermint tea. Usually the risen smelled of spoiled eggs. "No, no, no. It was *me*."

"You blocked it out."

"Then where's the horse?" She knotted her hands in his jacket.

"They walked it off to tend to the wounded flank. It was a graze, but must've hit a vein." He didn't know too much about horses, but that had to sound plausible.

She leaned her forehead against his shoulder as her body shook. "Tell me the truth, Clark. I know I died. I felt the pain. There was happiness, whiteness. My grandfather *welcomed me*. Then I was in the desert. You pulled me back." She drew a deep breath that rattled in her lungs. "My grandfather is quite dead, Clark."

He closed his eyes and draped his arms over her back. Brass glass—he tightened his grip on her. He'd saved her. She should be grateful enough for that. "I...brought you back."

"How?" she whispered into his leather jacket.

"I have no idea." He chuckled, but the false humor tightened in his throat. She wouldn't let it go, she would keep pestering. She might go to anyone for answers and the questions would lead smack into him. "Years ago, I lived in Tangled Wire."

She nodded.

Did he dare trust her with the truth? "A general in the army...visited...my mother. Sometimes I would...." Bloody stools. "We were very poor so I would go through the customer's pockets."

She nodded again. Rich little Amethyst must've never stolen in her life.

"I hated doing it," he added. Sure, he felt guilty every time he took something, but he'd never wanted to prove himself honorable before. Her opinion mattered somehow, like how he still wanted to make his mother proud.

"Some of my friends in the city steal from stores. Just for fun." She turned her face into his neck and he felt tears dampen his skin.

He held her so tight he hoped she didn't still hurt. Her injuries would be healed within a few minutes. "They must have money that they wouldn't have to steal." He'd loathed every second of it, and his mother had too, judging by the hollow look she'd get when they reviewed his spoils.

"What happened after that?" She pressed her nose into his neck and breathed inward, as if she loved his scent.

His groin tightened. Bugger it. She'd just died. He shouldn't imagine sleeping with her, their flesh pressed together, her mouth on him in a kiss.

"I took a vial. The liquid was green, so I figured it was the general's absinthe. My mother didn't let me touch the real stuff. I swigged it down and went to work. The stuff really had mechanical micro bodies in it. They mixed with the hertum in the air."

"Why was hertum there?"

"I worked in a hertum mine." He'd never gone to another mine. No telling what the micro bodies would do if he got near more hertum.

"Aren't those dangerous?" She looped her arms around his waist and settled into his lap.

He stroked her hair. "Sure, but it was all I could do. The micro bodies had been designed to work with hertum to change the user's body. I can touch someone who's dead and bring them back to life. I have to touch someone else, and they'll die, or that will go away."

"I've never heard of that."

"It's a government secret. I overheard the army discussing it." Clark squeezed his eyes shut as his heartbeat sped up. The general discussing hertum with a fellow soldier, irritated that Judy was dead and he still didn't have the vial; Clark had heard it as he dashed from the mine.

"Got to find whoever took it," the general had said. "Them at the brothel reckon it was her bastard. Didn't know she had a whelp."

Clark shuddered. "When they find me, they'll use me for experiments. I'll become a weapon." They'd never found him under the shed back in Tangled Wire. They would never find him if he could manage it.

"They can't force you," said the girl whose brother idolized the army.

Clark stiffened. "They can. I'm a nobody." In her sheltered world, she would have no idea what those in power could force others into—and him explaining it wouldn't help.

"You're a Treasure..."

"That's why I finally came here. I'd hoped the family name would protect me."

"We'll tell Father and—"

"No!" Clark pushed her away to stare into her eyes. "This is my secret. I saved your life." He hated to lord that over her, but if he had to, so be it. "Do me this favor."

Amethyst narrowed her eyes. "Thank you, then. I won't tell anyone."

"Can I trust you?" She might be loud and flighty, a troublemaker, but he'd never caught her in a lie. She'd admitted that the wealthy in the city stole when he hadn't even asked.

"Always. Do you save a lot of people?"

"Whoever I can. I have to use this as a gift. Otherwise, it's a curse."

She glanced over her shoulder. "What were you doing at the Horan Ranch?"

Of course Amethyst would go from death to curiosity. Anyone else might have still been shaken.

"I have to have something to do." Eric had vanished. Where was he with his advice? That was what fathers were supposed to do. His mother would've had an earful for him.

She pulled away and grabbed one of the bags. "With luggage?"

He seized the strap. "I don't go through your things. Respect my privacy."

"Sisters always poke around brothers' things." Grinning, she pulled back a corner of the flap. The smile slipped from her lips. "A helmet?"

"To go riding later." He yanked the strap until the bag ripped away from her.

She frowned. "The Horan buffalo is on top. You stole a helmet. I thought you disapproved of stealing." Ice tinged her voice.

Clark groaned. She could already have him arrested for the first part—he was wanted by the army—so why not the second? "After I got here, a ghost approached me."

"You can see ghosts, too." She pawed at the bag, so he slapped it behind him. Darn it—he smiled at her dramatic gestations.

"If they want me to help them. Most of the time I can't, but this ghost told me about his inventions." Clark exhaled through his nose. "The ghost is my father."

"Father isn't dead." She rubbed at her blood-soaked shirt.

Clark stood to help her up. "I need to take these bags back to my room. I'll tell you along the way."

CHAPTER SEVENTEEN

Amethyst pressed the heels of her slippers into the plush, maroon carpet. Ugly yellow triangles decorated the edges. The city would have consumed something that hideous, but it fit the western atmosphere of empty spaces and dry dirt.

She rested her elbows on the table in the back eating nook overlooking her mother's garden and smiled at Clark. "Your real father was quite rich."

Clark tapped his silver fork against the edge of his plate, the potato salad and watercress sandwich untouched. "He was an inventor."

Having a rich father must not have meant much, considering he always thought himself her father's offspring. She nibbled a hunk of potato. At least the cook had gotten her favorite summer meal correct, although the city had more spices to add to the flavors.

She swallowed. "I remember Father mentioning him a few times, just in passing. Eric Grisham was a friend. Is he here now?" She glanced around the nook, sectioned off from the main eating hall by a white lace curtain. Through the holes, she could view the empty room: no one to overhear them. Her mother ate in her room at noon, her father in his office while looking over paperwork, and her brothers had gone horseback riding to check the fields.

"No, and I don't know how to call him." Clark took a sip of his ice water. At least the ranch had an ice box like in the city. Westerners weren't altogether primitive.

His Adam's apple jumped as he swallowed. For living on the run, he didn't seem scrawny, like the homeless beggars in the city. His biceps pressed against the sleeves of his crimson button-up shirt. What would he look like with that shirt off, his skin tanned and glistening with the sweat of the hot day?

Amethyst wiggled her eyebrows at him. He wasn't her brother. She'd wondered why she found him so irresistible when her parents claimed he was her half-sibling. Staying at the ranch wouldn't be dull at all. He spoke to ghosts, for steam's sake.

"Perhaps he has wealth somewhere you can use. You should ask him."

Clark took another sip. "He's been dead my whole life. I'm sure he doesn't."

"He might."

"I'm safer if I stay Treasure's son." He met her gaze, his eyes wide, pleading.

She nodded. "I won't betray you." The secret might be juicy, but she knew when to back away. Gossiping about this left more at stake than whether society knew which girl had lost her virginity over the weekend. "You could be two people, though. Clark Grisham and Clark Treasure. We could dye your hair."

"I've tried changing my appearance, but short of breaking my nose and gouging out an eye, different colored hair doesn't help much. The army wants me. If I'm a dead man's son, they'd be more powerful. Your family's name can protect me."

"Like what my parents must want." They had seen Clark's photograph of his real father. They knew his parentage – they'd offered him this regardless.

"And my father wants me to get back his inventions." Clark bit into his sandwich. She wondered if he'd eaten watercress before. She could introduce him to a new palate of tastes and textures. How exciting!

"So do it. Honor his wishes."

"Find his inventions." Clark finished off the sandwich. His throat worked with each swallow…how would he taste if she licked those muscles? She dragged her gaze up to his face.

"He'll tell me where they are," Clark continued. "I already got the helmets. There can't be that many more."

"Horan has them all?"

"He worked with Senator Horan, so him or his brother. I've never met the Senator."

She clapped. "This will be so much fun. Next time you see him, ask your father where we go first." It should be soon, if Eric wanted him to do this.

Clark wiped his mouth on his linen napkin. What manners for being a street urchin! "Are you going to blackmail me into taking you along?"

"You don't want me?" She blinked. People loved to do things with her. No one excluded Amethyst Treasure from a gala.

"If it's dangerous…." His voice trailed off. Something dark glimmered in his eyes. Could it be lust? "I'll let you know what he says."

He did want her, too. Amethyst licked the prongs of her fork. If he were a prospective suitor in the city, she would call him by name and stroke his arm whenever they conversed. She would ignore him in crowds, but then catch his attention and smile. He would go to her and she would wait until he brought her gifts, until he ignored the other girls. It might take a few weeks, but he would be hers and she would use him until she tired of his attentions.

This wasn't the city. He wasn't a prospective suitor. Clark was…a secret. She slid back her chair and sashayed around the table. Just because they were stuck together as supposed siblings didn't mean she had to give up all the games.

Amethyst bent at the waist so her corset would push her breasts high and pressed her lips against his cheek. His skin smelled of earth, heat, and the cologne she'd sent him. A giggle bubbled in her throat as she trailed her fingernail over his chin.

"We'll have fun," she whispered.

He turned his head and clamped his hand at the nape of her neck, shoving her closer. His lips closed over hers, hard, forcing them apart so his tongue could poke the tip of hers. No man in the city had ever been that bold. Her eyes widened and she jerked back, but he held her harder, his other hand slipping around her waist.

She slid into his lap, guided by his arm, and clenched his shoulders as his head tipped, the kiss deepening. His lips shut over her tongue, he drew back to inhale through his nose, and he kissed her again, slower. She moaned. He tasted of lunch, and she must have too. The flesh of his shoulders felt hard with muscle. Did she dare unbutton the top of his shirt? She'd seen men shirtless—the most she'd done had been lying in undergarments on her last beau's settee in his bedroom.

Her stomach clenched. If Clark tried to unlace her petticoats, she'd let him. He kept one hand behind her head and the other at her waist, though.

Clark leaned his head back. When she leaned forward for another kiss, he closed his fist around her single braid, pinning her in place.

"I'll let you know," he repeated.

She nodded, slipping off his lap. Her hands trembled and her legs shivered. She hadn't felt that weak since she'd been thirteen and had her first suitor.

"Thank you." She yanked the curtain aside and stumbled through before she begged him to kiss her again.

Blast it all, he controlled the game—and this made her tremble with delight.

Clark shut his bedroom door and leaned against it, breathing through his clenched teeth. The steam take it all, she had to have wanted the affection. She'd started it, with her cheek kiss. Sure, he could have left it at that, but the vanilla smell on her clothes had been too much. Stopping it wouldn't have been any fun. He'd fooled around with girls before, even if they weren't the same social level as her.

"You should marry her." Eric shimmered into existence beside the bed.

Clark pushed off the door. "I can't marry her." He'd never felt strongly enough about a girl to offer her his name. His false name, apparently.

"I would be pleased to know my son married Treasure's daughter. You would treat her like a princess."

"She's already treated like that." Clark fought down a smile. They couldn't marry, but it would be fun to kiss her again and feel her body through the corset. "Where's the next invention?"

"I invented a hypnotizing organ."

Clark pictured a beating heart that could make people do anything just by hearing the beats. He wiped his hand over his mouth; Eric had to kid. "That's ridiculous."

"It's not." Eric swung his hands, the translucent outlines blurring. "The different tones and changing lights work with your mind. I designed

110

it to make people happy when they heard the music."

Not a heart then, a music organ. What a strange invention, but a nice gesture. "So Horan uses it to make himself look like a great musician?"

Eric flapped his hands harder. "Senator Horan uses it to hypnotize people into voting for him. He reworked the configurations."

Clark scowled. "That's how he always wins the elections?" He'd never voted—outlaws didn't matter to the government—but he'd assumed from the victories that Senator Horan was well-liked, not casting magic over people.

"That's exactly how he wins. We'll stop him yet." Eric pumped his fist in the air.

"Do I have to go to him to get it?" He could travel that far by cycle, but he would need to explain it to the Treasures.

"He travels the countryside with it. I'll find it and report back." A tinge of amusement toyed with his voice. "Bring Amethyst."

CHAPTER EIGHTEEN

A methyst rubbed the rag over the side of Clark's new helmet. Paint remover scented the air until her eyes watered, but she rubbed the Horan buffalo harder.

"Would you believe I've never scrubbed paint off before?" Her fingers tingled from the liquid, but she hadn't wanted to ruin a pair of gloves. Who knew where she could get another fine pair?

Across from her, Clark reclined on the mudroom bench. "I can do it."

She leaned against the wall. Heavy coats dangled from hooks and headwear decorated upper shelves. "I don't mind." Back in the city, she didn't do manual labor because she never got the chance. Things were done for her, so she could chat with her friends or shop. Here, there was no one to gossip with or a place to shop at. "Want me to paint a new design on it?"

"You can paint?"

"Every proper young lady takes a few years of painting lessons." Not to say her paintings looked like anything when she finished. A mountain landscape and a green blob could look similar. "I can look through Father's desk to see if I can find the Grisham symbol."

Clark dipped his rag into the jar of paint remover. "That would be too noticeable."

"Grisham's been gone for almost twenty years. I doubt anyone would remember."

"Horan would."

Amethyst shrugged. She'd find the symbol anyway and paint something nice for him. As best she could paint, anyway.

Clark settled onto the plush seat of the cycle and adjusted the straps of his new helmet, courtesy of Horan Ranch. The cushioned interior felt much softer than his last headgear.

"You're sure you don't want a new cycle?" Garth asked. "I don't mind purchasing one. I know it would be put to regular use."

"I prefer this one, sir." Clark pulled on his black leather gloves to protect his hands from the handlebars. "I'm familiar with how she runs and the distribution of weight."

"And we have these nice new helmets I bought in town," Amethyst sang. Her blonde braid thumped against her back, long enough for the ribbon at the end to reach her bottom.

"You didn't need to," Garth said. "We have plenty of helmets."

"These *matched*." She pitched her voice into a whine.

Clark bit his cheek to keep from snickering.

"What's the point in having a new brother if I can't spoil him?" She batted her painted black lashes and giggled. The servant who sewed had tightened the legs on her navy blue traveling pants until they fit almost as snug as stockings, accentuating her round behind and slender legs. The bodice buttoned up the front like her other suit, now ruined with blood stains, but she'd fastened even the top button at the collar. A crimson lace scarf poked out from around her neck.

"It would be best if you rode in the coach." Jeremiah hooked his thumbs through his belt loops and scowled at Clark.

"Then it wouldn't be brother-sister bonding time. Duh." Amethyst twirled with her helmet outstretched. Flashing her brother a smile, she set it over her head. "This will be so much fun."

"The open buggy wouldn't require an extra rider," Garth said.

"Father," Jeremiah snapped. "They should be chaperoned. Amethyst is an innocent—"

"Pish posh!" Amethyst waved her hands at her older brother. "You wouldn't insist upon a chaperone if you were taking me. You'll hurt Clark's feelings."

Clark ducked his head to hide his grin. A chaperone would ruin the scheme—he'd have to go without her, then. It would also ruin his chance to steal kisses. They believed he thought he was her sister, and she thought him her brother. Garth and Georgette wouldn't expect Clark to act in any way except brotherly toward Amethyst. The taste of her lemon lip balm tweaked his memory.

Georgette bustled from the front door carrying a leather saddlebag. "I had them pack you a lunch. The saloon may not be suitable in Reynolds."

"Goodness, I would hate to go into a shady establishment," Amethyst squealed before she winked at Jeremiah, who scowled deeper.

"Be very careful at Mitchell Steam." Garth fastened the saddlebag over the back of the cycle. "It does have a picturesque waterway, but not much else."

"How did you hear about it?" Jeremiah folded his arms.

"I thought you wanted me to become more interested in this area." Amethyst ignored her father's outstretched hand to swing her leg over the cycle. Her warm weight pressed against Clark's back.

"I'll take good care of her, sir." He twisted in the seat to adjust her helmet and position the bar across her mouth. His thumb flicked the switch inside that allowed them to communicate together.

"I know you will. We trust you." Garth clapped him on the shoulder.

"Where should I place my hands?" Amethyst cooed into her helmet's speaker, too soft for their audience to overhear.

"If you don't mind, you can hold onto my jacket pockets." Clark patted the front of his leather jacket and turned to grab the handlebars.

Amethyst kept her distance as she slid her hands around his waist to clench his pockets.

"Drive safe," Georgette called. Jeremiah, still scowling, stomped toward the stables.

Clark nodded to the group, adjusted his mouthpiece, and started the cycle. By the time they were out of sight of the ranch, Amethyst had slid forward until her front pressed against his back, her gloved hands looped around his hips.

"Teach me how to drive?" she asked into her speaker.

Clark laughed, careful to keep his voice low so it wouldn't be too loud in her helmet's earpiece. "Whatever you say." Despite her sheltered life, she was way too willing. Maybe it was *because* of that sheltered life she wanted to try things. He'd seen proper men and women flaunting themselves through the slums whenever they could snare a moment of freedom. Those outings usually involved maiming or death. He wouldn't allow anything like that to happen to her.

"It takes an hour to get there. Can I drive some of the way?"

Clark steered around a hole in the dirt road. "Not on my cycle. It's older and not so steady. I can teach you on one of your father's."

"He'd never let me ride." Amethyst squeezed Clark's waist. "Please? You can hold on to me."

Clark imagined sitting behind her, his arms around her softness, resting against her back while holding his hands over hers on the handlebars. "Maybe."

"Yay," she breathed into her speaker. "You're the best, Clark."

He chuckled. "I'll have to show you what else my best applies to." Blooming gears, why had he said that? It made him sound like a pig.

She giggled, though. "I can't wait."

Clark steered the cycle into the main street of Mitchell Steam. Miles back, they'd ridden past a few farms. Here, clapboard houses and shops rose alongside the dirt road. Farmers in overalls and straw hats spoke outside the Mitchell Steam Public House. Horses tied to sidewalk posts tugged on their reigns.

"Why so many horses?" Amethyst mused.

"Farmers can't afford mechanical gear." He scanned the sidewalks for officers, but only saw one speaking to a woman at the bank entrance: a simple cavalry man judging by the plain blue slacks and matching jacket, unadorned. Higher officers preferred wearing their medals and pins. A cavalry man wouldn't care about a renegade mine worker and he might not be aware of all the wanted posters in the western territories.

Clark parked his cycle outside the public house. The men peered his way, and the tallest spat tobacco juice into the dust. At least Clark's cycle was battered. A fancy Treasure vehicle would've garnered distrust.

"Howdy." Clark affected a more southern drawl. "My lady and I heard about the Organ Man. They said he's passing through this way."

A man in a plaid shirt tipped his straw hat to Amethyst. "He's out by Miller's Gulf now. My wife took the kids to see him yesterday. Real nice music. We don't get a lot of music 'round here."

Clark swung off the seat and lifted Amethyst by the waist. She leaned into him a moment before he set her down.

"Why are we stopping?" she whispered.

"We'll grab a bite to eat."

"Mother packed us a lunch—"

"We can hear more about the organ player if we stay here." He pulled off his helmet and rested it under his arm, grinning for the men's benefit.

"Real nice cycle," the plaid man said.

"Thanks." Clark helped Amethyst pull off her helmet. She shook her hair to make her braid bounce, but the top of her hair remained flattened to her skull.

"Where you folks from?" the only man in the group to wear gloves asked.

"The city." Clark shrugged. "Would've preferred a horse, but it's easier having a cycle there." He swung his arm through Amethyst's and led her up the step onto the sidewalk, then pushed open the swinging half door to the public house.

A bartender polished glasses behind the counter. A group of men talked at one table, the others empty. Clark set his helmet on the table closest to the door and took Amethyst's helmet.

"We can sit here."

She pulled back a chair and dropped into it. "This is so exciting! Do you think they have wine?"

Clark lifted his eyebrows. Having Amethyst inebriated would make the journey a lot more difficult. "We'll take water."

The bartender stepped over, wiping his hands on a rag. "What do you need, folks?"

"We're here to see the organ player. Thought we'd have some food first." Clark sat and rested his hand on his helmet. "What time does he give shows?"

"Every morning, noon, and supper time. Round five o'clock or so."

Clark checked his dented pocket watch. "We'll catch the noon show, then. Should be able to eat in forty-five minutes?"

"Sure thing. Today we have boiled cabbage with chicken and vinegar."

"And water to drink," Clark added before Amethyst could ask for alcohol. The meal might not suit her elevated tastes, but if she picked at her food, he could finish it and she could eat whatever Georgette had packed.

"You a couple?" the bartender asked.

Clark started to say they were siblings, when Amethyst clapped her hands. "Indeed we are. My sweetheart wanted to surprise me with an outing. Isn't he adorable?"

She leaned over to loop her arms around his neck and slammed her mouth into his.

CHAPTER NINETEEN

lark closed his eyes, slipping his hand up her back to grab her braid while he nipped her lower lip. She giggled as she leaned back.

"Be right back from the kitchen." The bartender headed toward a door near the stairs.

"Minx," Clark whispered. It seemed a far nicer name than the things he'd grown up hearing.

Amethyst smoothed her bodice, her fingers lingering beneath her breasts. "You're not my brother. We can have fun."

He rested his arm on the table. "How far do you want to take this?" They could fool around as long as they weren't caught—it would ruin the sibling façade and the Treasures wouldn't want their heiress compromised. He owed Garth and Georgette more than that.

Amethyst lifted her gaze off her bosom. Her eyes widened and her lips parted, the flush creeping from her cheeks. "You mean… intercourse?"

Clark bit his cheek to avoid chuckling. How innocent for her to use that formal word. "You play this game with men a lot, don't you?"

Amethyst coughed as though to clear her throat. "I don't *play*…I…in the city we—"

"I've worked in enough places to know your kind." He kept his voice soft so it wouldn't sound cruel. On ranches across the west, the privileged daughters played with the hired hands and strung suitors along to see how much of a clutch they could gather. In the end, they kept their prized virginity and married the man their father chose.

"I'm not…." She studied her crimson-painted fingernails as if they fascinated her.

"I don't mind a good time," he whispered. "I can't offer you more than that."

She licked her lips as though nervous, her gaze glued to her hands. "Then we'll do that."

The bartender pushed through the kitchen door, carrying two tin plates. He set them on the table. "Be right back with your water, folks."

"Thanks." Clark nodded. "Am, I can eat yours—"

"I don't mind." She picked up the tin fork and stabbed a hunk of cabbage. "It's all part of the experience." She smiled at him from beneath her painted lashes, then ducked her gaze back to the plate and stuffed the vinegar-drenched hunk into her mouth.

Clark drummed his fingertips against the table. The act hadn't seemed coy, but sincere. Could it be more than a game to her?

Amethyst squeezed her arms tighter around Clark. The helmet would be perfect if it still allowed her to smell him. Instead, the odor of metal slapped her nose. It wasn't overpowering, but Clark's musk made her heart race. The metal just annoyed her.

Her stomach rumbled from the plain fare at the public house. Phooey on Clark for not letting her have wine, or whiskey, or whatever strong spirits the establishment offered. One drink wouldn't make her tipsy.

The dirt road followed wooden fences, past which grew fields and orchards. Cows and horses grazed in pastures. Clark veered toward a farm where blankets had been laid on the grass. One of the men who'd sat near them during lunch had explained that farmers offered land for the organ player's use.

An organ on a wooden wagon, painted red with yellow stags, rested beside the barn. People sat on the blankets, some with picnic baskets. Small children darted between the groups.

"Women can't vote," Amethyst said into her speaker. "That's mostly all that's here."

"Men must come more in the morning or afternoon, when there's less work to be done." Clark slowed his cycle as they neared the pedestrians. "Women might not be able to vote in the elections, but they have their husbands' ears. I'm sure that contributes to it. Women have escorts too."

Some men sat with the women, but most of the females flocked with others of their own gender. Amethyst leaned her helmet against his shoulder, hoping it didn't hurt him. Wagons and buggies parked along the roadside. Clark stopped his cycle next to the only other of its kind, a beaten-up version with rust on the metal edges. He swung his leg off and lifted Amethyst down.

She closed her eyes as she leaned into his hands. Even with gloves on, their strength reached her. They weren't pale and skinny like Zachariah's, not ink-stained like her father's, and not stubby like Jeremiah's; these were long and muscled. Callused and tan.

"Man fingers," she whispered.

He pulled off her helmet. "What was that?"

Amethyst coughed. "Nothing." Rusty gears, she never acted the fool around men.

He set their helmets on the cycle and took her arm. "I apologize for not thinking to bring a blanket. It never crossed my mind how we would sit. Eric should've mentioned that." He grumbled the last sentence and she smiled.

"It's fine. I don't mind sitting on the grass." One of the Bromi slaves could wash out the stains later. "Aren't you afraid someone will steal the helmets?"

"Most farmers are honest. They wouldn't need the helmets, anyway."

People in the city didn't steal because they needed the goods. They stole for fun, to see if they could get away with it. Amethyst smoothed her bodice to avoid looking at Clark. Despite his wretched life, he hadn't resorted to petty crimes.

Clark pressed his hand against her hip to steer her between the blankets to the back of the gathering. "We'll stay here so we can talk."

She settled beside him and ran her fingers across the grass. The last time she'd sat on the ground had been with Clark when she'd been shot. Amethyst shuddered. The time before that had been a year ago when a suitor took her to the park. They'd sat on a blanket while his servant fed them fruit and cheese cubes.

"There're quite a few people," Clark whispered.

Amethyst leaned her head against his shoulder. "I noticed." A little boy wearing only denim overalls tripped over her leg and fell onto his front, sliding in the grass. He rolled back to his feet and darted across the blankets.

"Eric wants me to take it back to your ranch."

Amethyst rubbed her leg where the boy had kicked her. Other than leaving a speck of dirt on her slacks, he hadn't given her a mark. "How would that work? Father will ask where you got an organ from, and how would we even take it away from here? You can't hook that wagon to your cycle." She might not know much about vehicles, but the wagon was as long as her walk-in closet. His small cycle wouldn't have enough power to pull it. "Plus, there are so many people here. We would have to trick them into thinking we were fixing it." She widened her eyes. "We could tell them our father owns an organ shop."

He brushed his fingers over her cheek and kissed the top of her head. "Hush, dear."

Her heartbeat thudded. He'd called her "dear." Was it part of their façade or did he mean it?

"We're not going to take it," Clark murmured. "We're going to destroy it."

CHAPTER TWENTY

Clark leaned back on his elbows and tipped his head toward the sky to keep appearing calm. No one seemed to notice them, and the few stares sent their way had to be due to seeing strangers.

Amethyst folded her hands in her lap. "How will that work?"

Eric appeared above her. "You can't! That's my invention."

"We'll see how things go." Clark shrugged and closed his eyes so he wouldn't have to observe Eric.

"I'm your father," the ghost howled. "Don't ruin my invention! I spent years creating that."

"He's your father," Amethyst snapped. "How can you want to destroy something he created?"

Clark winced.

"She understands," Eric screamed. "Listen to her. The organ belongs to me."

Clark kept his eyes shut. "We can't steal it. It would be too obvious and the senator might be able to track it. We can make destroying it look like an accident. Eric will have to decide if he wants to leave it in the senator's stash or if he wants it gone."

Amethyst sucked in a breath. "I...is he here?"

Clark nodded. "He thinks the same as you do."

"Where is he?" When she scrambled, he opened his eyes. She'd twisted to her knees as she studied the surroundings.

"Above you." Clark lifted his gaze to his father.

Eric nodded, defeated. "Do what you have to. It shouldn't be used for coercing votes."

"We'll destroy it." Clark tipped his head back. "We wait and watch for an opportunity."

A man strode from the barn and lifted his hands to the crowd. He wore a black suit with a red bow tied at the collar of his white shirt, his hair slicked back with oil. The crowd clapped, children stood, and a man toward the front whistled. Clark clapped with them, and hooted, to seem as excited.

Amethyst giggled as she clapped. "Good job becoming involved, *my dear.*"

He nodded to her. If he'd worn a hat, he could've tipped it. "Thank you, miss."

Her smile slipped and her hands stilled. Did she feel overwhelmed? He couldn't send her back to the cycle. She might ride off, knowing her. Did he know her that well yet?

"I am pleased to have come here," the organ player called. The clapping stilled. "This town has been remarkable. Thank you all. Any requests?"

"Old Steamer's gone to Pasture," a man called.

"Load up the Gears," a woman suggested.

"I've never heard of these songs," Amethyst whispered.

"They're working songs," Clark whispered back. "Farmers sing them in the fields to make the time go by. Your father's workers sing them, too." Garth had taken him on a tour of the ranch, with Jeremiah pouting behind.

"Aren't you a lively group?" The organ player slapped his leg. "I'll play more tonight. Don't want to keep you folks too long from your work. I'll start with Old Steamer and see where it goes." Flicking his wrists, he swung onto the wagon and sat at the bench. He cracked his knuckles and set his fingers to the keys. Strong music blasted from the organ, peeling into the air with a grace Clark had never heard before. He frowned, leaning forward. The beat seemed to enter his soul.

"Don't listen," Eric said. "Horan has it tuned to turn your mind."

"It's beautiful," Clark admitted. "I've never heard music so smooth." Usually, an instrument hadn't been tuned in ages, or was too old to sound correct. He recognized the tune as Old Steamer, but it had never sounded so sweet.

123

"He could be a professional musician," Amethyst breathed.

"Tell her not to listen," Eric squawked.

"Eric said not to listen." Clark shook his head to clear his mind.

"How can I not? He's amazing."

Clark grabbed her hand and squeezed it. "Think about something else or plug your ears."

She blinked at him before that smile emerged on her lips. "Maybe I'll think about you, then."

"How can I destroy it?" Clark glanced over his shoulder at Eric.

The ghost wavered, flapping his hands. "You can't break it unless you use a sledgehammer. I made it strong. You'll have to burn it."

Clark gazed into Amethyst's eyes to keep his mind off the tantalizing melody. "We need fire." A better way to stay distracted: he linked his hands behind her head to kiss her.

After an hour, the organ player rose and bowed to the crowd from the wagon. "Thank you, my wonderful audience. You have done me proud. I am pleased to know that my music has brought you joy."

The crowd clapped and whistled. Men and women stood. The children waved. Clark grasped Amethyst's hand to help her up. The gathered group had been too mesmerized by the music to notice the couple in the back. Clark lips had dried from kissing her. Hers appeared dark and swollen. The bite mark on her neck showed above her scarf. Chuckling, Clark adjusted the silk to hide it.

"That...is the most I've ever kissed someone." She blinked at him as though dazed.

For all her flirting, she wasn't experienced enough. He pecked her forehead before turning back to the organ player.

"At least we didn't get lost in the music." The sweetness of her voice had become hoarse. His lips curled into a smile. He'd done that.

"I'll be back at suppertime." The player saluted the group. "I hope to see many of you again. If you'd like to donate to my cause—that I may continue traveling the west sharing my music—there is a collection box here in the wagon." The player hopped off and bowed again.

The group hurried forward, pulling coins from purses and pockets to place into the slot on the box attached to the side of the wagon. Clark kept his arm around Amethyst's shoulders to keep her in the back. The player shook hands with his fans, laughing with them.

"He seems very sincere," Clark murmured to Amethyst. "Do you suppose he knows what Horan is using the organ for?"

"He must know who's letting him use the organ. Senator Horan wouldn't give it away if he wants it used in his territory."

"I don't want an honest man out of a job." If the organ player were innocent, Clark would hate to know he suddenly had to steal or cheat to make a living.

Amethyst rested her head against him. "I'll recommend he see my great-uncle in the city. He knows many musicians and music halls. They can help him to find work."

"Thank you." That would have to be enough.

The viewers drifted to their horses to head back to their farms. Clark drew Amethyst forward and held out his hand to the organ player to shake.

"Pleased to meet you. My wife," she would have to be that to avoid their love play appearing awkward, "enjoyed this tremendously."

The organ player kissed her hand. "I'm glad to be of service to you both. It is by the grace of our good Senator Horan that I bring you this entertainment. Make sure to vote for him in the next election to ensure this continues."

That in itself sealed Clark's mind: the organ player had to know a bit of what he did.

"Of course." Clark slapped his knee. "Wouldn't think of it otherwise. May I see the organ? It's a wonderful piece."

"I'm thinking of buying my husband one for his birthday." Amethyst stroked his back, sending tingles across his skin.

"You, an organ player?" The man slicked back his hair. "It is a noble pursuit to share music with others."

Oiled words. Senator Horan must've taught him well. Clark tugged on Amethyst's braid—the sign.

Amethyst held out her hands to the player. "Please, sir. I would love to see the river that runs through here. They say it is black, since the river bottom is made entirely of slate."

"Yes, ma'am. Amazing river to behold."

125

"Is it that way?" Amethyst pointed to the west, the opposite direction.

"No, ma'am. It lies in the east."

"All the way back east?" She covered her mouth as though to hide a gasp. "Will you point the way?"

"Here, ma'am." He stepped around the bar and waved toward the east. "A few miles that way. There's a bridge that crosses it. I've seen children fishing from there."

Clark pulled his electronic lighter from his jacket pocket and flipped the switch. A tiny flame blazed on the tip. While Amethyst led the organ player around the barn, he hopped onto the wagon's wheel and set the lighter near the edge of the organ.

It had better catch soon.

He pulled out the flask of whiskey from his other jacket pocket—used for wounds, not drinking so much—and trickled it nearby. The flames spread fast, catching the wagon and the organ.

"Look," Clark yelped when he heard their voices approaching. "There's some sort of fire!"

The organ player bolted around, gasping and yelping. "Not the organ! Put it out. Find me water. We have to stop it. Horan will...."

The flames crept up the sides to lick the air. Through them, Eric shimmered, his head downturned. If the elder Grisham weren't dead, Clark knew he would see tears on his father's face.

Clark parked his cycle in the back of the vehicle garage. Garth had offered to build Clark his own garage for other vehicles and tools he would accumulate, a place only he would have access to.

"I'm sure you like to fix things yourself," Garth had said.

To have his own place, something just for him—but not his—because it was Garth's land, his money for the labor and supplies. He could accept gifts from Garth to fill a garage.

Amethyst slid off the back. "Can you take me riding again tomorrow?"

He hung his helmet on the hook in the back and reached for hers. "If your parents let us. Don't we have work to do?" There had to be something he could help with on the ranch. Charity wasn't for the likes of him. He already owed them more than his share of free labor for a year.

"That's what the servants and ranch hands are for." She stepped up behind him and slid her hands over his back, trailing her fingers toward his waist. "I promise we'll have fun."

He turned in the circle of her arms to tap her chin. "I need to see what Eric wants next." At least investigating the inventions served as something constructive to do. For as long as he could remember, he'd never had to *not* work. There had been moments of play, such as with Mable back at the saloon, but then there had been stealing for his mother, working at the mine, helping in the establishment.

Footsteps crunched in the dirt outside the open garage door. Clark stepped backward as Jeremiah appeared in the doorway, framed by the orange dusk.

"You were to be back sooner." His words ground through clenched teeth.

"It was such a lovely day," Amethyst sang. "Who cares how late we are?"

Clark bowed. That might appease her brother. "I shall apologize to your parents immediately."

Jeremiah snorted. "Look—"

"Is supper ready yet?" Amethyst pranced by Jeremiah and patted his arm. "I can't wait to eat. We nibbled on Mother's food along the way, but I'm starving. Let me tell you about the river. It really does look black."

Jeremiah sent a final glare at Clark before following Amethyst.

Eric glimmered by the doorway. "Thank you...son."

CHAPTER TWENTY-ONE

Amethyst flopped backward onto her bed and spread out her arms. "If I were back in New Addison City, we'd be going on picnics and shopping. The stores have wonderful summer merchandise."

"And the city smells with all the heat and garbage." Her mother continued sorting through the clothes in her cedar wardrobe. "You promised us you'd spend the summer here. You can go back in the fall."

Amethyst lifted her wrist overhead to study her silver charm bracelet, a gift from a suitor years ago. If she went back, she wouldn't be near Clark. "Can Clark come with me?"

Georgette paused with a wooden hanger in her hand. "I'm not sure he would like that. He's grown up in the west."

"So?" She sat up on her elbows. "He's part of the family." That was what her parents wanted them to believe. She would have so much fun showing him around the city. They could visit her favorite cafes and take the buggy ride through the park. At the clubs, she could show him off as her newest beau.

As her new *brother*. Amethyst winced.

"Clark belongs here. We're not hiding him, but it would be best if he stayed at the ranch."

In the city, someone might recognize him as Eric's son. That might be why her mother was hesitant. "I'm sure Clark would enjoy it."

Georgette smoothed her hands over the clothes and shut the wardrobe drawer. "They seem appropriate enough for this terrain. I don't foresee needing to buy you anything new."

"I can't go shopping?" Amethyst wrinkled her nose. "Mother, that isn't fair. I know the shops here are wretched, but I can order from back east. We're not poor."

Georgette sat beside her on the bed and sighed. "There are other things to do besides shopping."

Like cycle riding and pistol shooting. "Mother—"

A knock sounded at the door. "Am, are you decent?"

Her heartbeat sped. "Enter. Mother and I are discussing how I have been forbidden the wonderful joy of owning a new dress," Amethyst wailed.

Georgette frowned. "That's not the point."

The door opened enough for Clark to enter. He bowed to the bed and removed his cowboy hat, the beaten rim proving it a castoff.

"I'll take Clark shopping." Amethyst whirled off the bed to grab his hat. "He deserves a stunning wardrobe."

He snatched it back and bopped her head, laughing. "I've already been spoiled beyond belief."

"Clark?" Georgette rose and smoothed her skirt. "I hope you're feeling welcomed. I understand this is all very new. Never feel out of place, please. I also understand you and Amethyst are both adjusting to the ranch. I'm glad you have each other now."

Amethyst ducked her head to stifle a blush. They were both new to Treasure Ranch, but it had become more than that.

"You've been unbelievable." Clark's voice croaked. Could he be choked with emotion?

"Will you take me riding?" Amethyst asked. "I enjoyed seeing the area from a cycle."

"I was hoping you could teach me manners."

Amethyst blinked. "You're not a bumpkin."

"That's an excellent idea." Georgette patted his arm. "I'm sure Amethyst will prove an appropriate teacher."

He nodded. "I don't want to embarrass you or Garth."

"Your father and I could never be embarrassed by you." Georgette stepped into the hallway.

Clark lowered his voice. "Eric told me about a new assignment we need to work out. An old friend of Eric's has special handguns. They don't require bullets. They have lasers that self-charge over time."

"Aren't those already used?" Clark wanted to keep her on his team!

She clasped her hands behind her back to refrain from clapping.

"They have handguns with lasers that you can wind to recharge or buy new cartridges for. These recharge over time slowly, but faster if in the sun. The old friend has them stored in a hidden cellar."

"Certainly I'll go with you."

Clark kicked the heel of his boot against the floor. "Here's the thing. He lives about two days away, so we would have to spend the night somewhere."

"So? That would be a fun trip." Curled up in bed together. Her cheeks reddened.

"Your parents wouldn't approve. We'll have to take someone else with us."

"Like a servant?" A Bromi could be bribed.

"I was thinking Jeremiah or Zachariah. Zachariah doesn't do much."

Her brother went to the army station in town every day, leaving in the morning and returning at supper. "He would be best. What's our excuse for going to…?"

"Hawk Valley. Eric said he's an old friend of your father's, too. I think you should pretend to recall his name and suggest paying him a visit. Can you do that?"

Amethyst set her hand on her hip. "Of course. My friends and I put on dramas in the city."

"Donald Boroughaghans," Amethyst stumbled over the name, "would certainly love to hear from us." Rusted gears, she should've practiced that.

"Burrows," her mother supplied. "Donald Burrows."

"That's right." Amethyst tipped her head, grinning. "Him."

Georgette's silver needle slid through her cross-stitch pattern. "How did you remember that name?"

"It came to me."

"We haven't mentioned Donald Burrows in years. I lost touch with him after his wife died."

"So we should get to know him again. I can tell him about what he's missing in the city."

"I'm sure he's perfectly happy being a lawyer out here. He never liked the bustle of cities."

"We can visit him, right?"

"That's a two-day trip." Georgette kept her gaze on her needlepoint.

"Clark and I will go. We can see the scenery. We can take Zachariah, too," she added. It might look suspicious if everything she did involved just Clark.

Georgette glanced at Clark, who stood in the parlor doorway. "I'm sure he doesn't want to run all over the west. Let him settle down. You need to relax—"

"I'm bored," Amethyst whined. Her parents wouldn't want her to suffer. "It will be such a fun trip, and Donald whatever-his-last-name-is can meet Clark. We don't want to hide him." The secret love-child.

"I don't mind traveling to meet someone close to the family," Clark said. How smooth he spoke. On the outside he appeared calm, but he had to be as nervous as she was on the inside.

Georgette sighed. "I'll send Donald a telegram asking if we can visit."

"We?" She couldn't mean the entire family. That might make it harder to steal the laser handguns—more people around to see what was happening.

"Your father can't get away, but it might be nice to take a trip." Georgette picked up her needle. "I'm sure Donald will enjoy meeting Clark."

Amethyst twirled her charm bracelet. Donald probably would, especially after Georgette explained he was Eric's child, not theirs. Georgette would have to go, too.

A Bromi servant strapped Amethyst's trunk to the top of the Treasure coach.

"Do you need that much?" Clark nudged her. "We'll only be there a week." He'd packed a valise, even though Garth had offered to purchase him a steamer trunk.

"A proper girl must always look nice." How easily she acted. Only half the trunk contained items. The rest of the room would be used for the weapons. Eric hadn't explained how big they would be, but it wouldn't hurt to be prepared.

"Clark, it wouldn't be right for you to drive." Georgette tugged on her leather traveling gloves.

"I wouldn't mind." Driving a coach would give him fresh air. He wouldn't need to be careful not to ogle Amethyst in front of her mother.

"You don't know the way, either." Georgette smiled. "We'll have plenty to chat about inside the coach, and any time you feel stifled, you can ride up there. Learn the countryside."

The Bromi servant opened the coach door and took her hand to help her up.

Clark winked at Amethyst, who blushed. "I may take you up on that. I like knowing where I'm going and how to get back."

By seven at night, the coach slowed in the town of Rusty Port on the river. People bustled around the clapboard buildings.

"We stop here," the Bromi told Clark in his language. "It's halfway to Hawk Valley. This is also the only place with a proper inn for Mistress Treasure. It's busy since it's on the river."

Clark nodded, mentally inserting the directions into his brain. "I'll help the ladies if you get the luggage."

The inn had three floors, with a downstairs restaurant and separate saloon. Georgette had telegraphed ahead with reservations for four rooms, three on the second floor and one in the cottage house out back for the Bromi.

"I have my own space?" Clark dropped his valise in the doorway of his bedroom.

"Of course." Georgette rested her hand on the doorframe. "As my son, you deserve the same amenities as we do."

Clark gazed at the dresser with a mirror and washbasin, at the bed with a quilt and two pillows. This mere inn room was far better than anywhere he'd ever stayed, apart from at the Treasure ranch. "Ma'am, I can't...thank you."

"Please, call me Georgette." She crossed the door to a card hanging near the window from the ceiling. "If you need anything, pull on this and it will notify a servant in the kitchen that you requite assistance. This is one of the best riverside inns."

"Remarkable." The bedrooms at the ranch had the same system, but with a smaller cord near the doorway.

Georgette stepped into the hallway. "We'll rest for an hour and meet for supper at my room. We can all walk down together. Amethyst?"

Clark peered after Georgette. Amethyst's trunk rested just inside her door, but the rented room and hallway lay empty.

CHAPTER TWENTY-TWO

Amethyst?" Georgette stepped into the room. "Are you in here?"
"She can't be." Gripping the doorframe, Clark leaned back
to study the hallway over his shoulders. "Did she go in
another room?"

"I don't see why she would have." Georgette straightened her hat.
"She must have gone back downstairs to get something."

Leave it to Amethyst to wander off without saying anything. Hadn't
she thought her mother would worry, or was she too used to doing as she
pleased? Georgette had wanted to rest before supper—she had to be
tired, and concerned of how her daughter would feel.

"I'll get her." Clark patted Georgette's arm. "You can lie down."

She glanced toward the stairs with her lips parted before she smiled at
him. "Thank you, dear."

Clark pushed their luggage into their rooms and shut the door. Let
Amethyst find whatever she'd wanted. It had probably been a drink so
she could embarrass her mother by hanging over a stranger at the bar.
Things might be looser in her city, but a woman without morals in the
west would bring shame. He'd seen his mother frown at her reflection
every day in the commode mirror.

"Don't you think you're pretty?" he'd asked her. She would have him
sit on the dresser while she applied her cosmetics and fastened her hair.
The other girls would tell her she looked fine, no matter how the product
came out, since it worked in their favor if they stayed more appealing.

"I wish I was a different kinda pretty." She'd had to apply thicker
creams and powders to hide the wrinkles and sun spots. "I wanna be the
kinda pretty that comes from having a family—a husband and my boy.

134

Other boys to look up to you. Some girls I can teach home stuff to. I wanna have my own garden and my own bed."

He'd vowed to give her that, and he'd failed. Scowling, Clark marched toward the stairs. Laughter rose from the first floor where the revelers clanked tankards. Most of the men wore torn shirts and stained denim overalls. A few wore the fringed deerskin of the Bromi tribes. Some men wore proper clothes—captains from the river boats. Amethyst could've gone to any in the crowd. She might find a rogue dashing.

Clark stood on the stairs to scan the crowd, spotting a few tarnished silvers. Their breasts popped from bright corsets and skirts had been hiked up to waists, revealing fishnet stockings. The regal women would've headed to the dining hall. He ducked through the double doors in the back and checked the tables, but couples sat in the chairs, along with a group of four businessmen in black suits.

She had to have gotten somewhere. He wandered to the street, but didn't see her amongst the sparse wanderers and passing vehicles.

Clark leaned his elbows against the counter to appear casual. "Excuse me, sir?"

The clerk looked up from his tally book, squinting through wire-rimmed spectacles. "Yes?"

"I'm Clark Treasure—"

"Treasure," the clerk repeated. His skin paled beneath his ginger beard.

Clark refrained from smiling. So, the prestigious name preceded them. "Did you notice my sister come back down? I was supposed to meet her. She's wearing—"

"You didn't come with a sister."

Clark set his jaw. A clerk should know better than to interrupt. It created bad feelings amongst the customers, ruining business. "She was with us when my mother signed in."

"Saw your mother and you. No one else."

Rude and unobservant. "Check the list. Our mother would've signed her name." He'd seen Georgette use her fancy scrawl on the smudged sheet.

The clerk's hands shook as he passed the tally book across the counter. "Ain't in there."

Clark turned the book to face him. Toward the top of the page, he spotted **Georgette Treasure**, followed by an ink smear, then **Clark**

Treasure. He stretched his fingers to keep from clenching them. "Someone crossed off my sister's name." The clerk hadn't done it then. His hands shook too hard to make an even line.

"Y-your mother missed. She marked up."

"My mother," Clark said slowly, "does not mess up her handwriting. She attended a private school for calligraphy from when she was seven to eighteen." Such a school might not even exist, but it would make sense for a wealthy woman to have attended one.

"She...musta been tired from the trip." The man gulped and tugged on the collar of white button-up shirt. Nervousness.

He wasn't just a bad employee.

He knew something he didn't want to tell.

Amethyst bit at the hand clamped over her mouth, but the captor held tighter.

Shaggy hair beneath a cowboy hat. He looked so familiar. The rugged cow smell marked him as someone not from the city. Had she seen him at the ranch?

He'd clamped something cold around her wrists, pinning them behind her back. The more she wriggled, the tighter they became.

He pulled a bandana from his pocket and shoved it into her mouth. Sweat and something gritty coated her tongue. Her throat threatened to gag as she twisted her head aside. Laughing, he pushed her onto the bed. She stared at the ceiling, at a water stain near the window. Staying overnight should've been fun. Once her mother fell asleep, she'd planned to sneak into Clark's room. He had to be fantasizing about the same thing. She wasn't supposed to be assaulted. Did the fool think he'd get money from her?

Amethyst twisted to kick her heels against the wall, but he grabbed her ankle. "We can't have you making noise. That would arouse too much suspicion."

She swung her other foot forward to knock off his grip, but he seized that with his other hand and shoved her into the bed. The brown quilt bunched beneath her head, jabbing into her neck.

"You just don't want to behave, do you, Treasure?" When he spoke, she saw his teeth. They were too white and even to belong to a common cowman. Her mother and Clark would find her. She was only two hotel rooms away.

"How're you still alive?" he continued. "I know I shot you dead. If you were still breathing, you should be lying somewhere, all bloody."

Her eyes widened. The Horan boy, whatever his name was. Hadn't that first shot been a careless accident?

"What's so special about you, girl?" He leaned forward to rub his thumb over her cheek. "You're not very observant. Never saw me coming in behind you folks. See now, here's the thing. I know the army wants you."

She shook her head, but he slammed his hand into her shoulder. Pain dashed through her nerves and she winced. Why would the army want her?

"We come here to trade on the river," he drawled. "Maybe you didn't know that. I was heading here with an army fellow, and he got to talking about this other fellow they're looking for. Said he can bring back the dead. When I saw you outside, I knew what fellow the army wanted."

Clark. The Horan man was going to use her as bait for Clark. She shrank into the feather mattress to escape his glare.

"You," he said.

If anyone hurt Amethyst, he would kill him or her. Clark rested both of his fists on the counter to avoid grabbing his pistol. Threatening bodily harm wouldn't work in a crowded inn.

"I know you've got something to do with this," Clark growled through clenched teeth. "The Treasure name is one of the most predominant in the country. This act won't get you anywhere."

The man backed against the wall and paled further. "I...I don't know what you mean. I...I haven't done anything."

"Then there's me." Clark smiled. "I'll make you regret ever coming to work here. The law won't know. I'll be able to do anything I want." His gaze caught on a name written beneath Georgette's.

Adam Horan. The idiot who'd shot Amethyst.

It couldn't be a coincidence.

"Were you bribed?" Clark hissed. The clerk might not know anything other than to cross off her name and pretend he hadn't seen her.

If Adam Horan took Amethyst, he couldn't have gotten far. Clark darted toward the stairs. He'd start with the top floor and work his way down. If he pretended to be a disgruntled brother seeking his errant sister, he might get into the rooms.

The Horan idiot heaved her over his shoulder. She tried to buck against him with her legs, but he laughed.

"Can't keep you here while I get the army. Someone might come looking." He worked the window open. "We'll just head on down and see what we have in the cellar. Once it gets dark, I'll take you to my warehouse. You'll be nice and safe, little dead speaker."

She caught a glimpse of a fire escape out his window and swallowed hard. Clark wouldn't be able to find her in a warehouse.

CHAPTER TWENTY-THREE

Clark leaned against the last door on the third floor and whistled a tune. With no one in sight still, he'd be free to pick the final lock. If anyone did come along, he could shield the picks with his body to make it look as if he was getting into his own room.

He'd knocked first at each door and only found one couple inside. The man had answered the door, and beyond him, Clark had seen a woman fixing her hat in the vanity mirror.

"My sister said she was visiting a friend up here," Clark had said. "I beg your pardon."

"No trouble." The older man had smiled as he shut the door. Definitely not Adam Horan.

The lock clicked and Clark pushed the final door open. Someone had left a leather trunk near the bed and a jacket spread over the pillow. Amethyst and Adam didn't hide in the shadows of the empty room.

Clark scowled and slammed his fist into the wall hard enough to jerk his knuckles, but not dent the wood. When he found Adam, there wouldn't be much left of that bastard.

Adam tossed Amethyst onto a sack of grain behind a closed barrel. Breath whooshed from her lungs as her body jerked against the hardness. The gag slipped down her lips enough for her to spit it out.

"You idiot," she panted. The only light in the cellar came from the doors to the outside that Adam had left open. "You don't think someone's going to find me in the bloody cellar?"

Adam snorted. "My father owns plenty of inns. The cellars are storage. They aren't frequented that often. *Your* father doesn't own inns?"

Not that she knew of. Amethyst wriggled around to face him from the floor. Dust tickled her nose, so she pressed her tongue into the roof of her mouth to keep from sneezing. Feet stomped upstairs and someone played a violin. Men laughed and shouted.

They wouldn't hear her—or care—if she screamed from below.

Her heart raced. "Don't do this, Adam." She'd never been kidnapped in the city. Since moving to the west, it had happened twice.

"I'll move you to the warehouse once things calm down outside. Can't have anybody seeing you."

"You really think this will work?" Pressure beat at her skull. If he got her to the warehouse, he could hide her body where no one would find it. The Horans would go unpunished. "A ransom—"

"I have more than enough money," Adam interrupted. "Won't it put a kink in Treasure's gears to lose his little honey?"

"They'll know it was you!" Somehow.

"I paid that clerk enough to keep him living large. He won't squeal. No one saw me. No one's knowing anything, sugar." He leaned against the barrel. "Let's adjust that gag now. We'll sit here nice and quiet for a while, just you and me."

The raw heat in his gaze made her body stiffen.

Clark stepped into the stable and kicked his boots against the dirt floor for attention. Dust motes hung in the air.

A boy in breeches looked up from grooming a dappled horse. "Can I help you, sir?"

"Looking for my sister." The five horses glanced at him from their stables. They would look more panicked if Adam had dragged Amethyst inside. Knowing her, she wouldn't have gone like a placid young woman. Clark could picture her digging her heels into the floor and thrashing.

"Haven't seen her." The boy switched the currycomb to his other hand. "Most girls don't come out here."

"Where are the servants and coaches? She might've gotten something left behind."

"The building out back." The groom nodded over his shoulder. "The servants sleep over the motorcar garage."

"Thank you. If you see her, please let her know she's needed inside." He backed out from the stable. If the groom saw something, he might report it.

Heading toward the yard behind, Clark glanced at the inn, noticing the closed storm cellar doors.

He hadn't realized the inn had a basement.

Amethyst wiggled to escape Adam's fingers as he worked at the latches on her corset. In the darkness with the doors shut, she couldn't make out his expression. No one had ever touched her so intimately without her permission. How dare he? She would have kicked him if he hadn't bound her ankles.

"Where you going, sugar?" His breath stank of garlic. "We'll just have a little fun. You'll like it."

One of the doors creaked open, followed by the other. She twisted her head to see who stepped on the stairs with a light tread. Adam stilled above her, his breath suddenly rasping. The offensive hand slapped over her gagged mouth.

"Keep still," he hissed in her ear.

Right, as if she would listen to her captor. Amethyst thrashed hard enough to knock the barrel with her heels before his hand bit into her thigh. It didn't tip—darn it. She bucked to knock him off, but he gripped harder. His other hand clamped around her throat. Lights exploded in her vision.

He would choke her if she didn't draw enough attention.

Panting around his vice, she wiggled her hips to roll away. He tightened his grip on her throat. No more breath. Her lungs burned. The lights faded into blackness. She stilled. There would be another chance once he released her.

"You're dead." He bit her ear and the pain snapped down her nerves.

What, he would kill her now? Had she irritated him that much?

Something ripped the barrel aside and it struck the floor, rolling. Someone yanked Adam up. Since he held her, she went with him. With her ankles bound, her knees gave out and she slumped forward. A fist connected with flesh and Adam's head jerked to the side. His hands released her and she thumped back onto the sack bag.

"Adam Horan," Clark snarled.

Amethyst coughed around her gag as she fought for fresh breath. He'd come. He wouldn't let Adam kill her.

"The Treasure bastard." In the light through the cellar doors, she could see Adam rubbing the side of his face where Clark must've struck.

Clark lunged forward with his fist. Adam sidestepped and blocked with his forearm. Amethyst wriggled around on the sack and craned her head to see better, the muscles in her neck on fire and her heartbeat racing. Would Adam kill Clark? Maybe Clark couldn't die.

"You don't really belong with the Treasures." Adam paced backward as Clark came at him again. She noticed his eyebrows drawn and his mouth parted, as if about to snap the Horan son's head off.

"Clark." The word emerged muffled and broken from behind the gag.

"This girl's wanted by the military," Adam panted. Good, he should be out of breath like the state he'd forced on her. "We can get a nice old reward. She should be dead anyway."

Clark jumped into a roundhouse kick and caught Adam's shoulder, knocking the older boy into a stack of crates. Wood cracked and splintered. Adam waved his arms and legs as he fought to stand. Clark pulled the pistol from his belt and fired two bullets into Adam's chest. He jerked, and blood darkened the wood.

Adam slumped into the floor.

Clark shoved his pistol into the holster and lifted her against his chest while he sawed off the ropes around her wrists using a pocketknife. She squeezed her eyes shut. He'd killed Horan's son.

Adam had tried to murder her twice.

Could she ever be strong enough to shoot someone?

He worked at her ankle bounds. "You're fine? He didn't cut you?"

She shook her head against his neck. Although her hands were free, her arms felt numb. They were too heavy, as if leaden. Clark pushed the gag down to her neck.

"What did he do?" She couldn't make out his face with the light behind him.

"He was…." She gulped, her mouth dry. "Someone will come."

People still laughed upstairs. Boots thumped the floor and music played. They might not have heard the bullets, or cared, but someone would go into the cellar at some point.

"They'll know you did it," she whispered. "Horan won't stop until you're hung for murder. We have to bury him. Burn him!" Someone might dig up the body, but ashes…

Clark grabbed the side of her head and kissed her; his tongue forced through her lips to coil around hers. He bit her lower lip and trailed kisses across her cheek.

She lay limp against him, her body still immovable.

"I'll take you upstairs. I'll tell your mother you have a headache and don't feel like eating. We'll bring you something back." His kisses continued across her throat. She couldn't taste good. Adam had been rolling her on the floor.

Someone had died in front of her. She had died before.

"We'll leave before anyone comes." He lifted her into his arms and she leaned against his shoulder.

He would take care of her, and she would do anything for him.

Clark rolled onto his back and stared at the hotel room's ceiling. Someone would find the broken crates in the cellar, Adam Horan's body next to them. The stable boy knew Clark had been looking for his sister, but no one else had paid attention to him. The clerk might voice an opinion, but that would expose his role in a kidnapping. The proof lay in the crossed off name.

A knock came to the hotel room door. Clark shifted onto his side and peered through the darkness; the only light came the full moon outside the window. Adam Horan might've had an accomplice. Willing his heartbeat to slow, Clark slid his legs from beneath the sheets and pressed his bare feet against the floor. He'd slept in his silk shorts, so he adjusted the drawstring waist to keep it tied and lifted his pistol off the bedside table.

He cocked the weapon and slid his finger over the trigger. It might be nothing, or something serious. Clark tiptoed to the door and reached it as the knock sounded again.

"Yes?" He coughed when his voice sounded hoarse.

Another knock. He unhooked the inner latch and eased the door open a crack.

Amethyst's pale face turned up at him. A brocade robe tied around her, the sash knotted. A lace camisole peeked up from the top.

"I don't want to be alone," she whispered.

He pulled her against his chest and shut the door, keeping one arm around her back. For a month after the army had killed his mother, he had wanted someone near him, anyone he could trust. A companion, a hero. After that month, he'd preferred solitude. Being alone kept him safe.

"I know," he said against her unbound hair. She'd sent for a bath, and her skin smelled of lemon balm.

Clark eased her back to the bed and set his pistol on the table. She shouldn't be alone. Adam Horan was gone, they *thought*. She'd told Clark how Adam had thought she had Clark's ability. Adam might've told someone else, although that was doubtful. He wouldn't have wanted to share the information.

Amethyst dropped her hands to her sash as though to undress.

"No." He kissed her forehead. "Stay clothed." She might think he'd rather have her naked, might want to pay him with sex.

"Just the robe?" The plea emerged so plaintive, it could have come from a child. The flirtatious tease had passed from her.

He untied it from her. "If it doesn't make you too uncomfortable." With the moonlight behind her, he could make out the curve of her thighs through the silk skirt that ended at her knees.

She crawled to the far side of the bed and rested her head against his pillow. He stretched beside her and pulled the blankets up to their shoulders. Clark stroked the hair away from her face.

"Sleep," he murmured. "I'll look after you."

She nodded and pressed closer to curl against his chest. He wrapped his arms around her to hold her tighter.

He might not have a hero, but he could be hers.

CHAPTER TWENTY-FOUR

"At last," Georgette sighed as she stepped down from the coach. "I never used to hate traveling so much. It makes my bones feel weary now."

Clark averted his gaze to the sky. If his father hadn't given him the task, Georgette wouldn't have been dragged into visiting Donald Burrows. "The weather is pleasant." That should count for a bit.

"Agreed," Georgette murmured.

"And I'm sure Mr. Burrows will enjoy the visit." Amethyst reached for Clark's hand so he could help her hop down. "I do so love traveling."

"You should come home more often," Georgette said with ice in her voice. "We miss you when you're forever in the east."

Clark bit the inside of his cheek to keep from laughing at Amethyst's scowl.

The gravel driveway led to a brick mansion with five stories. A vineyard spread beyond that, with outbuildings and a long stable.

"The wine business?" Clark questioned. He would need Eric to tell him where the guns were kept. "The basement" didn't provide enough details. Workers in white blouses and flowing slacks moved amongst the grape vines in the field. Good—they could stay out there and be less of a hindrance.

"Donald Burrows has always loved wine." Georgette smiled as she rested her hand on Clark's arm. "Your father and I were friends with him when we lived in the city. He always had a glass with every meal. His entire home was covered in wine bottles and cork furniture. Such a sight!"

Clark kissed her cheek to hide his grin. She hadn't been lying when she referenced his father. According to Eric, they'd all been friends in the city.

"I couldn't wait to come out here to start my own vineyard," a man's voice drifted from the mansion. Clark turned toward him, instinct forcing his arm across Georgette's path. Without faltering, she brushed it aside and stepped forward, lifting her hands.

"Donald," she cooed. "I'm glad this visit had been suggested. It really has been too long."

A tall man with a short gray beard and thick eyebrows strolled down the stone steps, the front double doors open behind him. He wore a top hat with a peacock feather protruding from the brim and a suit that shone with silk. The silver head of an eagle flashed on his cane.

He kissed both of Georgette's gloved hands. "As soon as you and Garth mentioned moving west, I knew I had to join in. I've never regretted leaving the city."

Georgette laughed. "Tell that to my daughter."

"I can never have enough of the city." Amethyst swung her arm through Clark's and leaned against his side. "This is a beautiful vineyard, though."

Georgette narrowed her eyes and Clark bit the inside of his cheek to avoid snickering. Where was Amethyst's biting remark? Could she be as nervous as he was in stealing the weapons?

Donald pecked Georgette's lips before extending his hands to Clark and Amethyst. "I remember you from your childhood, Amethyst. You've become a striking young woman." He tapped his cane against his shoe. "Clark. I'm pleased to meet you. Georgette and Garth both sent me letters in regards to this trip, so I understand your background. I won't bring it up again."

Of course he understood the background. The Treasures would've mentioned the fact he was Eric's bastard, not Garth's. "I appreciate that."

Once, he'd considered the wealthy to be pompous fools who took every chance to beat the poor down, Garth Treasure included, although slightly above the pact. His father could've stayed to help his mother. Now, seeing the Treasures for their kindness, and Donald for his genuine smile, Clark's mind wavered. They'd made the best of their circumstances and it had brought them wealth. They might have had a head start through family privilege, but they hadn't squandered their good luck.

"I hope my dear friends aren't too tired for tonight's celebration." Donald headed toward his house.

"What celebration might that be?" Georgette asked as she followed.

Donald paused in his doorway. "To welcome all of you to Hawk Valley. No visit can start right without a party."

That would be a perfect time to sneak away. Clark squeezed Amethyst's elbow.

"Sir?" she sang on cue. "May we have a tour of the vineyard? I've never been to one before. Your house looks amazing, as well."

"You were here many times as a child, but you were so small, I'm sure you don't remember." He pointed his cane at Clark. "Clark deserves to see all the land. We can eat the noon meal and get started."

Clark started toward the stairs, Amethyst still leaning against him and humming, with a skip in her step, when his father shimmered into existence beside Donald.

"Son." Eric stared at him with his blackened eyes. "This man was one of my dearest friends. Be kind to him and show him the most respect you can."

Clark nodded. Eric had trusted Donald to keep his weapons. He would give this man his due.

After a luncheon in the garden, Donald took Amethyst and Clark on a tour of the yard—Georgette chose to freshen—and the main rooms of the mansion.

"Tomorrow morning, we can ride through the vineyards. I have wonderful thoroughbreds. Racehorses are one of my hobbies. I can't work on wine all the time." Donald laughed, his cane clicking the parlor floor. "Should we retire now until the festivities tonight? They start at six."

Clark shook the man's hand. "Thank you for the tour." He could explore the cellar that night. Since Donald hadn't shown him, it would be a good excuse if he were caught.

"What about the cellar?" Amethyst asked.

Clark gritted his teeth. The question seemed too obvious.

Donald narrowed his eyes for a second before his smile took reign again. "It wouldn't interest you. My prized wines I keep up here in my closet—you can pick one for supper. The cellar is more for storage."

"I'm sure we'd still enjoy seeing it—" Amethyst began.

Clark coughed to hide her squeak as he pinched her arm. "A man's privacy is sacred. I'm sure we'll both enjoy some time to relax. I'll help my sister to her bedroom."

"Do that." A coldness crept into Donald's voice. He couldn't suspect anything. It had to be Clark's imagination.

The hallway on the second floor lay empty of servants. Clark had only counted seven, and Donald had said he'd hired extra for the evening. Fewer help would mean an easier chance to steal the guns.

Amethyst jutted her lower lip. "I was trying to help."

"And you're excellent at it." He slid his hands around her waist and backed her into the wall, pressing his hips into hers. When she gasped, he kissed her mouth. "Such a good little girl you are."

She turned her head away so his lips descended on her neck. She tasted of lavender soap, the scent toying with his nose.

"Tonight," he murmured against her ear, "you'll be the star of the ball. Make yourself into a spectacle. Make sure everyone notices you and not me. I'll sneak into the cellar."

Amethyst sashayed into the garden. Lanterns had been hung between the trees to light up the stone pathways. People mingled around the fountains and benches. Her mother stood near the eatery table sipping a glass of champagne.

Hmm, no photographer in the crowd. The men wore suits and top hats, pocket watches hanging by chains on their jackets. The women had sleeveless gowns and feather fasteners in their hair. While everyone looked presentable, no one stood out. These would be people in the neighboring towns who might not be well off. They could be ranchers or bankers or shopkeepers or lawyers, but not wealthy per se.

Amethyst lifted her hands. White lace gloves decorated with pearl beads stretched up to her elbows. She'd added rings over her fingers and three silver bracelets per wrist. Her white skirt had six layers of lace and two of silk; no need for a hoop. The beaded bustle in the back bounced each time she swayed her hips. On top, she'd chosen a black corset decorated with miniature key charms. Without a shirt underneath, it made more of a statement.

She could be the one to stand out.

"Hello," she sang as loud as she could. Without wind, her unbound hair, teased with sugar water to make it poof, didn't stir. "Who would like to bring me a drink?"

Her mother glanced her way with raised eyebrows. She would have to be careful to refrain from the wild edge. Georgette would stop it and ruin things for Clark.

"I'm just making friends, Mother." Amethyst sauntered to the eatery table. The heels of her gold slippers clicked on the stones. "You love it when I'm like that." She would have to find someone to talk to, loudly, and make it extra exciting to lure others over. That should cause enough distraction to keep people from noticing Clark's absence. "Who would like to hear about my life in the city?"

Clark eased the cellar door open and lifted the lantern to spill light across the narrow wooden steps. His father floated ahead of him, past the kegs and crates. Clark shut the door and hurried after. Violin music drifted from the garden. He couldn't be too long. If he had to, he would just scope the scene and return later.

Eric headed to a wall in the back and pointed. "Wiggle that panel open."

Clark set the lantern on the dirt floor and pressed the wall. The wood shifted where his father pointed. Frowning, Clark worked it open to reveal a panel with buttons labeled with numbers.

"I invented that." Eric beamed. "The code is 35-41. Push it."

Clark pressed on the buttons in that code and the door shifted sideways. He pushed it the rest of the way and used the lantern to fill the space with light.

A table stretched across the far wall, covered by a lumpy sheet. No other furniture decorated the closet-sized room.

"I should call you Clark Grisham, shouldn't I?" Donald stepped out from behind a keg and clapped, his cane slung over his arm.

149

CHAPTER TWENTY-FIVE

lark set his lantern beside his feet and rested his hands at his side in case he had to grab his pistol. "Sir."

Donald whistled. "I can't rightly decide what game you're playing. There's no need to lie to the Treasures. They'd take you in just knowing you're Eric's son. Bloody gears, I'd take you in too for that alone."

Clark shifted his stance. In the flickering light, Donald frowned at him. If he told the man too much, he might report him to the army.

"How do you even know the code?" Donald nodded at the door panel. "Eric and I are the only ones. I watched you, boy, and you didn't try different combinations. You didn't hesitate."

"Trust him," Eric said from behind. "He won't hurt you."

"Eric's been dead eighteen years about," Donald continued. "He couldn't have told you."

Clark drew a deep breath. If he didn't admit it, the consequences might hurt worse. "Did you know that Eric was working on a powder that would react with hertum?"

Donald rolled his shoulders. "Make it so the person could maneuver the dead."

Maneuver. Right. "My mother and I lived in Tangled Wire. I worked in the mine. She always told me Garth Treasure was my father, never mentioned Eric." For better or for worse. "I got exposed to the powder and hertum. Sir, the army wants to use me. I've been running since then. They can't get me." An edge crept into his voice. "I'm not for them to play with."

Donald took a step back, but he kept his arms down. "You and the dead...?"

Clark nodded. A breeze trickled through the cellar to make his skin tingle. "I can talk to them. Bring people back if they just died. If I bring someone back, I can take someone away."

"That's how Eric…." Donald turned in a circle. "Is he here now?"

"There." Clark pointed at the ghost shimmering near a casket of wine.

"Tell him I say thank you," Eric murmured.

"He wants to say thanks," Clark offered. The man had kept his father's secret for eighteen years. He could be trusted.

He had to be trusted.

"What does he want with the weapons?" Donald shook his head as though trying to focus.

"Me to take them. To protect them. Keep them from Horan."

"They're safe here." Donald glanced at the casket.

"I want them for my son." Eric shimmered. "I never wanted to involve too many people in this. The less, the safer we are."

Clark licked his lips. "Eric said he wants me to have them. I'll protect them, sir. He wants me to collect all of his belongings."

Donald stepped toward the hidden room while watching the casket. "You can tell me more about what's been happening with you while we pack up."

He might mean Clark or Eric, but Clark sighed. It wouldn't hurt to have someone as strong in society and honor as Donald as an ally.

Amethyst leaned over the bar table and held out her glass. "More wine, suh. Keep it flowing!" She bit back a giggle. It had only been two glasses so far. She couldn't be too tipsy.

The bartender took her glass and silently filled it from a bottle of red wine. Yum, the rich stuff. If she were in the city, she and her friends would be dancing on the table. She might take off her shoes to have better balance, or make it fun by spilling into a stranger's lap.

Amethyst tipped the glass to her lips and a girl from town bumped her elbow. Wine sloshed over her chin.

"Sorry," the girl said.

Amethyst narrowed her eyes as she wiped her mouth with her handkerchief. In the city, the wretch would be begging her forgiveness.

151

Instead, the girl pursed her lips as though she disapproved.

Of drinking?

"Do you know who I am?" Amethyst wadded the linen in her hand.

"Sorry, *Miss Treasure*." Sarcasm. The nerve!

The Treasure name had to still count for something. Her father owned most of the shipping companies, almost all of the mines, a great deal of farmland… She'd never paid attention to those things, but the list had to go on.

A hand brushed across her back and she turned, her mouth open to scold.

The other Horan brother stood with a glass tipped forward. "To meeting again." When he smiled, she noticed a gold tooth in his mouth.

The linen dropped from her hand. He shouldn't be there. His brother had said he was back at the ranch.

"No," she whispered as her heartbeat thudded. A pain stitched in her side. If he was there….

He gripped her elbow and shifted her toward the back of the garden, where the landscape gave way into the fields. Amethyst grabbed the edge of the table and leaned away from him.

"I'm entertaining." Her smile had better look genuine while her heart raced. "We can go for a walk later." As with flirting, if she gave him a little, it would keep him thinking there would be more to come later.

She would find Clark to warn him.

The Horan boy tightened his grip and tugged her just hard enough to make her stumble. "We won't be gone long. I just want to talk."

Amethyst glanced at the people, but no one looked at her. In the city, *everyone* looked at her. She could scream and that would get attention.

He swayed close enough to leave his hot breath against her jawline. "What happened to my brother?"

Her legs wobbled as he directed her toward the vineyard. She would have to twist away without throwing a fuss. She had to make it seem as if she didn't understand. "Surely back at your home. I didn't realize you'd be invited to this. Donald must be good friends with your father."

"You should be dead." He nodded to a group of men smoking cigars. That sickening smile on his face made her belly clench. He wanted her gone.

"Evening, Jeff," one of the men said.

"I'm alive as ever." She laughed to make it seem unimportant. "I'm still a young woman."

"Who Adam shot. That bullet should've taken your life, but here you are." They'd reached the edge of the patio. The Horan boy, Jeff, kept along the brick-edged path. Amethyst glanced over her shoulder, but everyone talked and chortled together, while the music played a sweet melody.

Gravel crunched beneath their shoes.

"I don't know what you're talking about." If she made too much of a fuss, Jeff might report on Clark. She would have to see how much he knew. If she screamed, they were still close enough to garner assistance.

"Where is my brother?" Jeff pulled her closer to his side.

"How should I know?"

"We were both at the river, little girl. You're the bitch who can talk to the dead."

She laughed to be loud, hoping someone would notice and follow to be part of the fun. "I told you. I'm still young. No need to be dead." How could Jeff know? Adam couldn't have notified him that fast.

"My brother was supposed to bring you to the warehouse. He never showed." Jeff's fingers bruised her elbow. She twisted, but he only tightened. She bit back a yelp.

"He said it was only—"

"Why would he tell you everything?" Jeff snarled. He turned them down another path where the darkness of night drifted over the vineyard. Behind them, the sounds of the party faded.

"I'm not who you think."

He seized her shoulders and shoved her against a wooden archway. To the left lay the backyard and to the right, the wild tameness of the orchard, neat rows of grapevines crawling over wooden poles. A gold broach flashed at the knot in his crimson cravat.

"Where is my brother?"

"I don't know!" She lifted her voice in a scream. It wouldn't work to weasel her way free. Help would need to come.

His thumbs beat into her throat. She clawed at his wrists as she gasped. He would strangle her?

"Bitch," he growled. "You had something to do with his disappearance? Did you kill him?"

Darkness stung the edges of her vision. She tipped her head back, rasping, her legs kicking and her muscles twitching. Would Clark come? He was in the cellar...would anyone come? Would they find her body?

If he came quickly, Clark could bring her back again...

The murdering hands shifted to her hair. She tumbled forward and Jeff clenched his arms around her back.

"You're such a spoiled bitch." Keeping her pinned against him, he headed into the vineyard. "Let's just watch you come back. Can you do that? Save yourself?"

"You won't know...what happened...to him," she rasped, "if you...hurt me." That knowledge might be her only leverage.

He laughed. "I'm not stupid. I'll figure it out. If you've killed him, I'll haunt you in death. Father will give me some of the potion and I'll have your same powers."

She sagged against his chest as she panted. Her hand fell against his waist, brushing against his holster.

Amethyst seized the handle of his pistol and kneed his groin. He sputtered, staggering back.

"Bitch!" His arms flailed at her.

"Adam died." She aimed the pistol at his skull and pulled the trigger.

CHAPTER TWENTY-SIX

Amethyst's hands trembled around the handgun as it butted into her thumb. The barrel wavered up and down, to the side. Jeff pitched forward, clasping his shoulder. Blood ran through his fingers and stained the front of his pale shirt. Had it been white in the backyard's firelight?

"Get away from me." Her voice shook. "I won't let you hurt me." People in the city didn't want to kill her. They wanted to be photographed with her, to *be* her. Here, she hadn't paid attention and been murdered and kidnapped. Never again.

"Bitch!" Didn't he have anything else to say?

She stepped back and her heel crunched on the ground. Someone would come from the party. "Someone will have heard that. You'll be arrested."

Jeff swung toward her, his hand out and the fingers curled like claws. "Did you hear a gunshot?"

She kept stepping back, stumbling on the uneven dirt alongside the path. Had she? Her blood still pounded in her ears.

"I always use a silencer." He leered at her, blood on his cheeks. "No one's going to come rescue you." The hand not holding his wound pulled another pistol from his belt.

Rusty gears! She hadn't considered he'd have two! She'd been practicing with Clark, but Jeff would've grown up with guns. He wouldn't miss like she had.

Amethyst aimed the weapon and pulled the trigger. The bullet jerked from the barrel, past the silencer, with a hiss. Right, no bang. She pulled it again, and again, squeezing her eyes shut as Jeff jerked. Something hot and wet struck her cheek.

After four rounds, the gun clicked, but no other bullets fired. Amethyst's eyelids flew open and she panted, a pain coursing through her side toward her thudding heart.

Jeff lay in the path with his head back, legs bent, one arm thrown over his chest and the other stretched to the side. Darkness covered him, blending with the dirt.

"Jeff?" she whispered in a hoarse voice. "Are you all right?"

Music reverberated from the party and an owl hooted farther off in the other direction. Jeff didn't move. She dropped to her knees, her fingers refusing to loosen on the pistol. He'd meant to kill her. She'd taken his life instead.

"Amethyst!" Footsteps pounded on the dirt. Her name came again through the haze in her mind and Clark's arms wrapped around her. She gasped. When had she taken to holding her breath?

"I…I killed him." She stared at the grapes instead of at the body, Jeff no longer.

"Shh, its fine." Clark wiped a handkerchief over her face. The man's blood must've gotten on her.

"He was going to kill me." Her voice held steady. How odd. She almost laughed, but a sob lodged in her throat.

"I know." Clark's lips touched her forehead. "I can bring him back—"

"No!" She dropped the gun and whipped sideways to seize his arm. With the moon behind him, his face lay in shadow. "He's evil." She could say so many other things about him, but that summed it well. Maybe when her nerves slowed, she'd be more articulate.

Someone else stood behind Clark, a tall man with a top hat.

"What happened?" Donald's voice, calm and deliberate.

Amethyst stared at him, hoping she met his gaze since she couldn't see his eyes. "His brother tried to kidnap me. This one wanted to kill me." If he wanted details, she wouldn't know what to provide without giving away Clark's secret. Donald would press for answers. Clark could make up something.

"I have loyal servants," Donald said. "I'll see the body buried where no one will notice a fresh mound."

Clark eased his hands under her armpits to lift her. "I'll say that you've developed a headache."

"No." Amethyst shook her head while leaning into him. "We'll go back. Nothing will be amiss." No one should suspect anything. They shouldn't give anything away. "How did you know to find me?"

"Eric said you were in danger."

She glanced at Donald, his expression still hidden. "He...knows?"

"I'll talk to you at the party. We'll smile. We'll laugh." Clark cupped her face between his hands. "We'll be fine."

In the morning, Donald faced them across the desk in his study. Clark leaned back in the chair, the plush seat welcoming his bottom, and kept one hand clasped around Amethyst's. She sat beside him, tugging on a curl. She'd left her hair down in waves, no ribbons or beads. He'd never seen it so unbound. As long as he held on to her, she would know he protected her.

He could do some good.

"Are you sure this is the life you want?" Donald stared at her.

She could go home to her city, or hide on the ranch. Clark would never fault her. She hadn't grown up in the hardened lifestyle he'd known.

"There're dangers," he began, but she shook her head.

"It's not a life," she said. "It's an adventure. We'll go home after we get everything and everything will be fine." She licked her lips, unpainted for the first time. "Everything will go back to normal."

Clark squeezed her hand. Nothing would be normal for him. He'd be the Treasure bastard and, if he survived, he'd be free. He might work on the ranch or attend a college. Amethyst...well, she would go back to normal, as normal as possible after killing someone.

Donald pulled back his sleeve to reveal a key hanging from a chain. He fitted it into the top drawer of his desk and slid it open. Clark leaned back in his chair. The air smelled of spiced rum. What odor had clung to Eric? Perhaps his real father had been flavored with sandalwood cologne like Garth Treasure, or maybe it had been more of an oil stench since he worked with machines.

Donald lifted out a leather billfold and set it on the top of his desk. "Eric gave me this. It had all of his banking cards. If you need a place of refuge, you'll find it in his estates."

"What?" Clark forced himself to keep still. "My father still has estates? They would've been confiscated by the government since he didn't have an heir. Eric told me that. I'm his only heir."

"Parents or a cousin?" Amethyst suggested.

Donald pulled out a notebook and set it beside the billfold. "Eric's parents died in a steamcoach accident. He finished his childhood in a boarding school. The closest relatives would be distant cousins."

Clark turned his attention to the window behind Donald. No family on his father's side, and none on his mother's. Hers had perished in native attacks after first arriving in the west; she was the only survivor of their newly settled town.

"He left me everything so the government couldn't touch it." Donald rested his hands over the billfold and notebook. "By law, all of this is yours. You're his heir."

"What is it?" His mouth dried as though he sucked on cotton.

Donald smiled. "A house in the east and a house in Hedlund City here in the west. Mines. Some land. An abandoned ranch. After he died, I closed the doors. A few banks. Bank accounts. Eric tended not to spend more than was necessary. He didn't need much other than supplies for his inventions."

Clark realized he squeezed her too hard when she yelped. He rested his hands on his knees and leaned forward. "You mean I actually own something more than my cycle?"

Donald chuckled. "Dear boy, Eric was one of the top ten wealthiest men in the country. He's fallen a bit behind in that now that he hasn't been inventing or investing, but his riches are still quite up there."

"So you're saying," Clark ran his fingers through his hair, "I actually have money? Honest money?"

"And quite a lot of it."

CHAPTER TWENTY-SEVEN

Clark faced the oval mirror on the staircase landing. He should join Eric, waiting at the bottom as a shimmering spirit, and find Donald on the patio. Georgette would be with him, twirling her lace parasol. She clutched it like a weapon—a woman like her deserved a real tool against evil. She'd look smart with a pearl-handled derringer.

Clark rubbed the blond stubble on his chin. Donald hadn't provided shaving equipment, so the half-inch-long shadow stretched across the lower portion of his face. He'd gone like that in the desert when he'd run with the Bromis and his gang, had once grown it five inches long to match his shoulder-length hair.

Clean shaven worked best. It made him feel like the type his mother would approve of, with his baby-blue eyes she always called 'her sapphires'. *"I don't need real gems, since I've got you, my Clark."*

Since Garth hadn't commented on it, Clark had left in his silver loop earring. His gang had used them as a symbol of status. Once you were fully initiated—having proven you weren't yellow-bellied enough to skedaddle—everyone pitched in to buy you an earring.

He owned land. Money. A house. That man in the mirror, who had once been a Tarnished Silver's brat and then a runaway, had become a gentleman. Sort of. Clark fixed the collar of his black shirt to make it lay straight. A corner popped back up. He hadn't been born to this world of smoothly painted walls and family portraits.

The week with Donald had given him more stories about Eric and opportunities to ride horses through the vineyards. That didn't make him high society.

"How can I act like this if that's what it takes?" When he glanced down the stairway, Eric had disappeared. Sighing, he shifted his gaze out the windows in the front of the house.

Amethyst stood on the porch with the late afternoon sunshine forming a golden shield around her body. Claiming fatigue, she'd slept the day away, and somehow assumed that meant she didn't need to get dressed. Her long, slender legs appeared as pale as mother of pearl. A black, silk camisole clung to her curves.

How erotic to pull the jeweled pins from her bun and let her curls down. He could push her against the railing and slide his fingers over her thighs, lifting the lace hem of her camisole. He could explore what lay beneath while she moaned against his mouth.

Coughing to scatter his thoughts, he hurried down and jumped off the bottom two steps since no one lurked in the foyer. Donald stood on the back porch with Georgette; both turned to face him when he opened the door.

"I was telling Donald how much we'll miss him." Georgette dragged her painted fingernails over his jacket in a teasing fashion.

"You'll have to stay longer, my dears." Donald pecked her cheek. "Actually, there was something I wanted to bring up."

Clark schooled his expression to remain stoic.

"I need to visit my mines to make sure everything is running up to par," Donald continued. "Would it be all right if Clark and Amethyst accompanied me? It would be better on my old bones if I had pleasant companions."

Clark widened his eyes to appear surprised. "Which mines?"

"Don't worry, son." Donald lifted his hand. "It would be nowhere near Tangled Wire. This mine is farther into the desert. The travel might be a bit rough. Of course, this all depends on Georgette's approval."

"Would you like to, Clark?" She frowned, twirling her parasol.

"I haven't experienced too much of the country." Clark hoped the sentences didn't sound too rehearsed. "I'd be honored to accompany you. Learn more about my father." *My real father.*

"It does sound like fun," Amethyst trilled from behind him.

Georgette's hands froze on the parasol's polished handle. "Am, I really don't think—"

"I've never seen a mine before!" She looped her arm through Clark's and leaned her cheek against his shoulder. "It would be so exciting to get to know my new brother more. What an adventure."

He stuffed his hands into his slacks pockets. It would make him look like even more of a scoundrel if he ogled the shadow between her breasts, the whiteness of her chest, the way the hem of her camisole barely covered the curve of her buttocks.

"Your father has plenty of mines," Georgette said. "You also hate adventures. In every letter, you stress how you despise the west."

"I'm doing this for you," Amethyst whined. "You'll love me more if I love your land."

"We love you—"

"Please?" Amethyst flicked her wrist at Donald. "He asked. It would be rude to refuse."

Georgette gave her parasol a hard twist. "Think on it. We can tell Donald our decision in the morning. I'll be leaving. If you want to stay with him, I'll leave you enough money for a new wardrobe."

"I'm sure I won't change my opinion." Amethyst winked at Clark.

He would need to learn how to twist propriety to fit his needs.

"Where to next?" Amethyst stretched her legs across his bed and flexed her bare toes, the nails painted purple. They shimmered in the light of the gas lamps.

Clark leaned over the desk in his bedroom. "You should get back to your room."

"Mother goes to bed so early and Donald sleeps downstairs. Who's going to care? The slaves?"

"They can gossip." He trailed the lead pencil over the route Eric had helped him mark on the map Donald had provided.

She laid back against the brocade coverlet and fanned her curls over his pillow. "Will you do me a favor?"

"Sure." He set the pencil beside the brass candleholder. "Eric said it should only take us a month. I don't want to disregard your father's hospitality."

"I looked through your saddlebags. I'm sorry."

He narrowed his eyes at her. "Back at the ranch? Not much in them."

"I...found stuff." She licked her painted lips.

161

He searched his brain for what he might've stored. A flask, extra bullets… "I didn't steal any of that." She couldn't think that of him.

She rolled onto her stomach and held up a flat package two inches across by two inches. "Why do you carry rising wraps with you?"

Clark covered his mouth with his fist to hide his chuckle. "I'm a man, sweetie. I saw my mother suffer because she raised me alone. I wouldn't do that to a woman."

Amethyst tossed the rubbers across the bed and sat up. "Make love to me before we leave."

Clark blinked. The corners of his eyes burned and his right one felt as if something had lodged against his eyelid. "What?" She couldn't have said that.

She kicked off her slippers; they hit the floor with twin *thumps*. "I want you, Clark." She lifted the hem of her camisole. "You've saved my life. You've taught me to protect myself. I've never been so…I've never been like this before." Cherries blossomed in her cheeks as she slid the silk over her head to drop it atop her slippers.

He averted his gaze to the bedroom door. "I won't take advantage of you." The trauma had disrupted her brain. In the Bromi camps, they would have inauguration rights for the men and women who took another's life. They would mediate in a tent, alone, for a week, while eating mushrooms and drinking cactus juice. When someone took a life, that person needed to come to terms with the deed before it darkened them.

"You should rest," Clark whispered. "You need to think more. Rest. We can wait; Donald will understand."

Her footsteps padded across the hardwood floor until she stood behind him. "Don't you want me?" Her hands slid over his shoulders and hesitated at his throat. "You have a tattoo."

His hair or bandanas covered it most of the time. "It's a Bromi tribe symbol." He traced where he knew the sun and crescent moon shape was beneath his ear. "It means that everything must happen, like how the sun rises and sets, and how everything must share its place. When the sun is up, the moon is down."

She didn't tug at his shirt buttons like a Tarnished Silver would have, and she didn't nip at his ear. Her sigh brushed the back of his neck.

He folded his hands over hers. "Amethyst…."

"Don't give me nonsense about how I'm so much better than you. I don't believe in that."

He chuckled. When he first met her, he would've doubted that. Spoiled girls didn't want to make love with paupers. Amethyst, however, didn't live for propriety. She lived for her. Everything had to do with her.

The murder might have altered her perspective, but if it had scarred her, she would've fixated on it. She really did want him.

He turned as he stood, clamping his hands around her waist and pinning her against his chest. He slanted his mouth over hers and ran his tongue along her lips. Skin, soft and smooth, beneath his callused hands; she could've been porcelain about to break.

He might be a bastard. Wanted by the army. A mining town brat. A fugitive among the savage Bromi tribes.

A con-artist in a wealthy family.

But he could keep her safe.

CHAPTER TWENTY-EIGHT

D onald tipped his hat, the sun making the silver bead on the rim glitter. "Good luck to you both."

Clark nodded. "Your words are well thanked." A Bromi statement. His gaze wandered to the town behind them, the last before this stretch of desert. He'd first fled there, to Barrera, after his mother's death. Past Barrera, desert made farming impossible, and only the Bromi dared navigate the rocks and dunes.

He'd run, knowing the army wouldn't think to look for him there. He'd fallen near nightfall, parched and weak. Darkness had come, death without pain. His body felt nothing. With holes in his knees and elbows, his shirt torn and one suspender hanging loose, he'd lifted his hands and closed his eyes.

A tingle through the numbness had forced him to look again; a little girl floated above him, her body shimmering—a ghost. He'd seen enough of them by then, skirting from town to town while the army pursued.

From her knee-length black hair and fringed skirt, she had to be Bromi. She'd pointed at him, wordless, and might have smiled.

Next time he opened his eyes, at dawn, he'd panted. Already the heat baked off the rocks, Barrera lost behind him. Another Bromi girl knelt at his side. Alive, since she didn't shimmer. Ankle-long black hair, set in two plaits, showed off her tribal neck tattoo. Bare feet with copper rings on her toes. A blue skirt and a deerskin shirt. His mind wouldn't make proper thoughts.

She held a skinsack to his lips to pour water over his mouth. He'd coughed, but it had been his salvation. A man—her brother, he'd later discovered—followed minutes after to carry Clark back to their tribe.

"You're certain we have enough supplies?" Amethyst fanned herself with her hand. Perspiration dotted her flushed cheeks.

"Don't waste it." Donald squeezed her shoulder, but he stared at Clark. "The town is abandoned. You shouldn't find anyone there. Spend the night and move on."

"Move on to Quencher." Clark patted his jacket pocket, which housed the map. "I'll send you a message when we get there."

"You would've gotten along well with Eric, my boy. Nothing slowed him."

Clark turned his attention to the desert to hide the shadow in his eyes. Instead of living in luxury with people who seemed to actually care about him, he chose to ravage the desert to help his deceased father. Yup, life was screwed.

Amethyst tucked her hair into the helmet Donald had given her and fastened the strap. "Ready?" She winked at him.

He could taste her skin on his tongue, a mixture of lavender and her. Maybe not so screwed.

Clark settled his helmet over his head and swung onto the steamcycle Donald had bought for him.

Another stranger had purchased something for him. Clark had promised to pay him back once he had his father's inheritance, but Donald had lifted his hand. "If your father had lived, I would've seen you a few times a year. Eric visited often. I would've spoiled you rotten, son."

Clark revved the engine while Amethyst settled behind him, her bosoms pressed against his back. Her arms slid around his sides to his front. If they had Eric's helmets, they would've been able to talk during the ride.

"Squeeze extra hard if you need to stop," Clark shouted over the engine and through the thickness of the helmet.

"Yes," she yelled back.

The steamcycle shot into the desert.

After three hours, judging by the sun, she squeezed her arms around him beneath his ribs. Clark slowed the cycle and turned it off. They would still need a few more hours until noon to ride. According to Donald, they should reach the abandoned village by evening.

"What is it?" He adjusted the helmet strap where it rubbed on his chin.

"I…." She pulled off her helmet, eyes bright. "Where are the toiletries?"

Did she think she should fix her perfume? "You're beautiful." The dark blue of her suit made her eyes shimmer.

"To…." She licked her lips. "Relieve myself."

Mirth bubbled from his belly to make him laugh. Actual funds, a girl who liked him, a future worth living for, and a new steamcycle. Life hadn't gotten too harsh.

"You're rude!" She slapped his arm.

"Sweetheart," he said, "you go wherever you want."

"I don't see an outhouse." She turned her attention to the stretching plains.

"There aren't any out here." Poor sheltered puppy. "Go wherever you need to."

"I just *what*? I squat?" She flapped her hands. "I can't do that in front of you!"

He stroked her gloved palm. "I've seen your private parts. Don't be embarrassed. I've seen girls pee before."

"That's crass. An ugly word." She swung her leg off the steamcycle so fast she stumbled. Her bladder must have been really full to put up so little a fight. "Don't you dare look."

"As you wish." He scanned the plains for a glimpse of the Bromi, but nothing stirred.

A Bromi wasn't seen until he or she wished it.

Brown dots rose onto the horizon. Amethyst sagged against him too heavily; he pushed with his shoulder to jolt her awake. Her body stiffened and her arms clenched around his waist.

"We're there," he shouted over the rumble and through their helmets.

Wind blew dust across the main street in the town. Skeleton buildings rose over it, nothing beyond the outskirts but an empty wilderness. Broken glass left darkened holes in the windows. A ragged curtain blew through one.

Clark parked in front of the building with a faded sign that read **BN1** in red.

"Bank." He tugged off his helmet. "Looks like some of the letters are missing."

Amethyst staggered off the back of his steamcycle and stretched her legs with a groan. "Donald wasn't kidding about this being *nothing*."

Eric appeared over her head. "This once bloomed. They got as much as they could from the land and left it. The claim wasn't deep."

"The perfect place to hide a weapon." Clark repeated Donald's words. Eric nodded as he pointed at the **BNI** building. "Right, the basement."

"Are you sure we're safe out here?" Amethyst shivered, clutching her helmet against her chest.

Only the Bromi dwelt in the wilderness and they wouldn't harm him. She'd be safe by association. "We're fine. We'll find shelter for the night and finish in the morning." Clark unlatched the steamcycle seat to pull out their canvas sack of food and the two quilts. With Amethyst following, still clinging to her helmet, he kicked open the bank door and stepped inside. The yellow glow of twilight streamed through the broken windows across abandoned shelves and a desk covered in bird droppings. A rat scurried across the floor at the noise the kick made.

Amethyst yelped and ducked back outside. "Clark, that was—"

"A rat," he snapped. "Try living with them constantly." As a child, they would crawl into his bed and nip his toes. His mother would wrap vinegar rags around his feet, but the smell would make his stomach cramp.

He worked his hand lamp from his pocket and pressed the lever to make it light. Clark shone the white beam into the back room. The safe door hung open. A criminal had been there, taken everything and left it for the vultures.

Eric promised no one knew about the secret safe in the cellar.

Clark joined Amethyst at the front door and kissed her lips. They trembled, her eyes wide.

"It's fine," he whispered. "I'll keep the rats away."

"Where will we sleep?"

"Against the wall."

"Sitting *up*?"

She shouldn't have come. Every night she had a bed. Every morning a servant helped her dress. "I'll keep the first watch. You can put your head in my lap."

She licked her lips. "When's the second watch?"

"Daybreak," he lied. She could sleep. He was used to going without slumber for days.

He set one quilt over the floor and sat against the wall, resting one hand over her shoulders to ease her down. She curled into a ball with her head against his lap. He handed her the canteen and after she took a sip, he broke a biscuit in half for them to share.

"Tell me a story." Amethyst tucked the second blanket around her and his legs.

He watched the night consume the street. "You sound like Mabel."

"Little sister?" Amethyst snuggled into his stomach.

He ran his fingers through her curls. "Sort of. I miss her." A rat scurried across the room.

A man floated near the desk, translucent, blackened eyes. He hovered as if staring at Clark before he disappeared through the wall. Harmless.

"When I lived with a Bromi tribe," Clark said, "they taught me how to hunt. The chief wanted me to marry one of the girls. They loved my yellow hair. I couldn't, it didn't feel right."

"Mmm," Amethyst mumbled. Asleep.

Clark stroked her earlobe. "Good night, Ames."

In the morning, he left her curled on the blankets while he located the loose boards in front of the safe. With Eric overseeing, he pried them up using the knife—five down. Numbness encased his brain as he stared at a metal trapdoor. Why did he do any of it? For years, his life had focused on escaping from the army. Finding random objects wouldn't help that.

"You need a real purpose," Eric rambled. "You're doing a good deed. Can't have any of these things being used by them."

"By Horan." Clark twisted the metal lever to the side twice and up once. Gears clicked inside and he lifted it. The beam of his hand lamp revealed a dusty chamber with a single canon. "That's it?"

"Should be two," Eric muttered. The ghost twisted his hands. "Must be two."

Clark leaned forward to shine the hand lamp at the rest of the nooks. "Only one. Are you sure you want it destroyed? I've never heard of a canon that shoots lasers."

"Haven't heard of it because I made the only two," Eric squawked. "No one else dreamed up the idea. They're all in my imagination."

Clark tucked the hand lamp into his pocket and dropped into the safe. Only six feet wide, he could still reach the top if he held up his hands. He crouched behind the canon and worked the back metal plate off the base to reveal a nest of wires.

"Cut them all," Eric urged. "We can't move the canon and I don't want others using it. We don't need laser cannons."

"That we don't." Clark sliced the wires with his knife. A blue wire sizzled, but the others remained still. "What about the other?"

"I don't know," Eric murmured.

The dust didn't seem disturbed, and the safe was small. His father must have forgotten how many canons he'd actually built.

"Sir?"

Senator Horan signed his name to a bank note. "What is it, James?" Birds tweeted outside his office window and farther in the yard, a steamcoach honked. It would be a perfect day for a ride with his wife, if he managed to wrangle her from her bed.

The servant in the doorway coughed. "I was monitoring the recordings."

"Yes." Senator Horan lifted a fresh banknote. As soon as his office duties ended, he'd drag his wife from her room. The people should see them riding together.

"Two people went to the safe in Dust Point."

Horan's hand froze with the stylus pressed between his fingers. "*What?*" Bromi went to Dust Point on occasion, but no one knew about the safe.

"One destroyed the canon and then burned down the town." James gulped. "Sir."

The safe had been a secret. Only a select few knew about it, and none of them would care after so many years to go after it. Senator Horan stabbed the stylus point into his desk and bared his teeth. "Have a sketch made of their likenesses. They're to be found and brought to me." It couldn't be a coincidence. If someone knew about the safe, they might know about the others.

CHAPTER TWENTY-NINE

Heat beat against Amethyst's temple as she leaned against the pole outside the general store in Sweet Dust. Almost every blasted town had a perverted name about the miserable weather. Any place with that much dust shouldn't be inhabited. Grit clawed at her throat and stuck in her nostrils. She pulled her handkerchief from her pocket and blew her nose. A cough scratched up her throat.

"Bah." She'd never blown her nose in public before. How disgusting. Who cared here, in a town that contained only six—she'd counted— streets? The horses at the watering trough didn't look her way. The man walking down the street spit tobacco juice into the packed dirt.

She tucked the silk scarf Clark had insisted she bring over her mouth and ducked her head. Her heels clicked the stones underfoot as she wandered along the buildings. They were squished together like in the city, but they only had one or two stories, with cracks between the wood. Most of the windows had shutters without glass.

Amethyst paused outside the sheriff's office, the building barely bigger than her closet at the ranch. Through the window, she saw the sheriff seated at a desk, his feet propped on the edge while he whittled a hunk of wood. Behind him loomed the bars of a cell.

"I feel so safe now," she muttered. The man's stomach pressed against the buttons of his shirt. Officers of the law needed to be fit and stable...like Clark. He would make an excellent sheriff. Maybe they could found their own town—they had enough money. He could be the sheriff and she could rule over the rest. They would have dance clubs and a fancy hotel. People would come from everywhere. They could call it No More Dust.

Laughing, she turned to head back to the bank where he wheedled with the attendant to give him access to his father's safe. According to Clark, Eric accompanied him to tell him the passwords to get into the metal box.

Her gaze fell on the Wanted posters tacked to the sheriff's front door. The one in the middle made her lick her lips.

A crude sketch of Clark. She wouldn't have recognized him except for his name. *Goes by Clark Treasure, Four-Hundred Dollar Reward, Wanted by the Army*. Should she tear it down? That might seem suspicious. Her father would protect Clark if it came to it, and Donald would too.

The poster beneath it made breath snare in her lungs: two pictures with a thin line drawn between. A man and woman, eerily familiar in looks, as though someone had copied a photograph of them. Them. They weren't labeled, but it had to be her and Clark. They even had the same clothes on.

Wanted by Senator Horan.

How had he figured out what Eric wanted them to do?

He didn't have their names yet. That had to be worth something. Oh, bloody horror. Hopefully he didn't recognize her from all the newspapers. Girls mimicked her looks all the time. She ground her teeth as she ripped the poster down and stuffed it into the front of her jacket.

Clark stared at the money in his hand and licked his lips. Even in the desert, when he'd almost died of thirst, his mouth hadn't been so dry.

That money, the bills in the new leather billfold, belonged to him. He owned over one-thousand dollars.

"I shouldn't have taken so much out," he murmured. The gas lamp made the bills seem to glow.

Eric hovered in front of him with his shimmery arms crossed. "You left another five-hundred in the bank. It will keep gathering interest. That money will help both of you."

Amethyst leaned over the bed to stare out the window, the lace curtain clenched in her fist. She hadn't stopped trembling since she'd found the poster. He doubted she could see anything in the night outside.

Clark set the billfold on the dresser and crossed the room to her.

He slid his arms around her waist and pressed her hips back against his groin. "Relax."

She whipped around with widened eyes. "We're *wanted*, Clark. That's not good."

He chuckled. If only she knew how time took away that fear until it became a dull pain and then only a nagging reminder, an annoyance. An amusement. "They won't find us. Hundreds of people look like us."

"There's only, like, ten people here," she exclaimed. "None of them look like us!"

He rubbed his thumbs into her shoulders to relax her muscles. "We're about fifteen miles from Sweet Dust. We're on the river again, so there will be people everywhere." He'd driven to the river just to find a place more populated, rather than stay in Sweet Dust as he'd planned.

"Senator Horan," Eric said. "He must've used one of my moving photographs. He can survey what's going on wherever he keeps the lenses. He won't hear voices, though."

"Great." Clark narrowed his eyes at his father. "Another awesome invention on your part. Do we need to steal one of those soon too?"

"What?" Amethyst turned her attention back to the window.

"I have the plans...." Eric began.

Clark peeled her hands away from the window and forced her to sit down. "We'll be safe. They may know what we look like, but they don't know who we are. We'll be fine, honey. Your father will protect us. He wouldn't believe we were doing horrible things." Clark grinned to show off his teeth. "Such horrible, nasty things."

She blinked at him, her hair falling across the pillows. "You called me honey."

Clark brushed a curl off her cheek. He'd called Mabel "honey" when they were growing up as a name for a flustered, pretty girl who didn't know when to calm down.

He leaned forward to touch his lips to hers. "I can keep you safe. I've been wanted for years. I know how to stay a step ahead." Even if they were caught, Garth Treasure would protect them. That name could do wonders. No one would expect his bastard son to be wanted by the army, either. They'd used Amethyst's name to rent the room to be safe, but he'd paid.

Clark unfastened the top button at Amethyst's throat. "The door is locked. No one will bother us." Laughter meandered from below in the eatery. "We can be as loud as we want."

Her eyes still wide, her body still trembling, her lips parted...she didn't shy away. He kissed her as he started on the next button. "Trust me. We'll be safe."

"Clark?" She tipped her face up and his lips landed on her neck. Despite the scent of sweat and dirt, she still held the lavender odor of her soap.

"Hmm?" He nibbled the flesh where shoulder met neck.

"Can we go to Hedlund City?"

He nuzzled the underside of her chin. "The capital of Hedlund?"

"I have a house there," Eric said from behind the bed. Clark shifted to glare at his father. He'd assumed the ghost would disappear once he started acting amorous. Did Eric want to watch? Clark bared his teeth at the ghost and Eric lifted his hands in surrender as he vanished.

"Take me there," Amethyst whispered. "I really want to see the city. I miss the clubs and...everything."

They could break from the mission. "We'll go there next...honey." The inventions were hidden away, unused. Senator Horan wouldn't attack with them, or whatever he plotted, if they took a short detour.

CHAPTER THIRTY

Clark clutched the metal gate of the brass fence surrounding the mansion. Adam Street in Hedlund City, where houses had upwards of five stories and were surrounded by locked fences. The yards were green, lush, with flower beds and trees. A paradise in a city that bordered the ocean on the left and the desert on the right.

"We'll have to fix the yard up," Amethyst said from beside him.

Clark clenched the bars tighter. This yard, belonging to his father's mansion, had overgrown with weeds.

Not his father's mansion. His.

"We can hire a gardener," she continued. "I know my father has a house here somewhere. I've never been there, but he mentioned it in a letter. He uses a gardener."

"A gardener," Clark murmured. Behind them, steamcoaches rattled by on the cobblestones. Wind rustled Clark's hair and ticked the backs of his ears bared by his ponytail.

"The code is 7925326," Eric said.

Clark stretched his fingers before he entered the code into the touch pad on the gate. Seldom-used gears creaked and Clark held his breath. They might have rusted. The gate might no longer work.

The two doors parted on squealing hinges. Clark clenched Amethyst's hand before he released to grab his cycle, pushing it through the gate.

She followed him, wrinkling her nose at the shaggy bushes. "We'll figure something out with those."

Clark retyped the password to make the doors slide shut, sealing them within…his home. He actually owned a house. Clark whistled.

"I used to love sitting in the garden," Eric said. "I would lounge on one of those benches and jot notes about upcoming inventions. Sometimes I would have luncheons here. My housekeeper loved putting together a party."

Clark stepped off the path of weeds growing over stone slabs to brush vines away from a bench. Gears had been engraved into the stone back. More flowering vines hung off a table beside it.

"We could do luncheons out here," Amethyst gushed, as though she'd heard what the ghost said. "We can get matching outfits, entire new luncheon wardrobes."

He'd never fantasized about new clothes because of how rarely he got them. Now, he could actually afford a wardrobe, not just one item. He could get a suit that matched and fit, tailored to his body.

"We can do a luncheon every Wednesday. No, every Monday." Amethyst spread her arms and twirled, her heels clicking against the stone walkway. "We'll be famous throughout the city. They'll say things about us. We'll be famous in all of Hedlund for having outrageous Monday luncheons. We'll do themed ones, like circus themed or train themed—"

He yanked her around and shoved his mouth over hers. None of it could be real, yet it was. He had the girl, he had the money—he had a bloody mansion!

"Let's go see the inside." She spun away and skipped up the steps to the double front doors decorated with stained glass windows. She could have been a child, swinging her arms and humming.

Clark jogged after her and entered the code into the pad beside the brass doorknob.

"We'll have to get maids in here to clean," she prattled. "Everything is atrocious, but it will all look stunning when it's done. I'll have to take you to New Addison City. Wait until you see what life is like there! We can gather ideas for ways to decorate here."

"We can't stay here." His hand trembled as he turned the knob and pushed the left door open.

"Why not?"

"Your parents would wonder. We're supposed to stay with them. I'm not supposed to know anything about Eric Grisham."

"You deserve all this," Eric said from behind. "It should all go to you, my boy. My son. My heir."

Clark's skin tingled as he stepped into the foyer. Dust had settled over the marble floor and someone, a servant of long ago, had draped white sheets over the furniture. A chandelier hung from the ceiling. The doors on either side were shut, but the wide staircase led upward into a shadowed world of shuttered windows.

"I can invite the gang here to live," he whispered. "Pay them back for all the help they gave me."

"You want…." Amethyst gulped, her eyes wide. She would want to tell him those ragamuffins, or whatever pleasant language she chose, didn't deserve to live in a mansion like the privileged. "We can decorate rooms for them," she finished in a rush.

Clark blinked. "For truth? You wouldn't mind?"

"It's your house," Eric said. "Put whoever you want in here. You should've seen some of my guests. No one was ever turned away."

Amethyst crossed on her toes as though the dirt on the floor would poison her, and kissed Clark's cheek. "It's your home. If it makes you happy to help them, that's fine."

"My house." Clark slung his arm over her shoulder.

"I'll hire servants. We'll get everything cleaned up, and a landscaper can help with the yard. We can paint, too. My room in New Addison City has blue walls with white clouds painted on. Everyone says how gorgeous it is. If you don't mind." She peered up at him from beneath her lashes.

"I wouldn't know where to start," he admitted. "Would it be a waste to fix this up when we can't stay?"

"Nonsense! I've always wanted to fix up my own place. Even if we don't live here all the time, my parents won't mind if we take seasonal trips here. Father and Jeremiah come to their home here for months at a time. Mother wrote to me about it."

"Do what you want with it." Clark yanked off his glove so he could touch the wall. Everything in it belonged to him, and it had all along. All of it, *his*.

"I'll use some of my money, but you'll have to add some." Amethyst opened the right-hand door and peered into the room. "What a gorgeous front parlor. A bit faded, but we can have the settees reupholstered. We'll have to open the windows to air out the must, too." She hurried back to him with her hands outstretched. "It's almost suppertime. Let's buy new clothes and go out to a restaurant. A real restaurant and not that *shack* in the rubble where my parents choose to live."

"We can bring food back here…." Clark's voice trailed off. They didn't need to save their money in hopes of being able to eat the following day, or even the following week. They could purchase new clothes and eat at a restaurant. "I've never eaten at one of those places, just saloons and inns."

"You've got plenty of money," Eric said. "Take the girl out for a grand time. Court her proper."

Clark glanced at the ghost. "I'm not courting her."

"Eric's here? He better be telling you to have fun. We can get the rest of the inventions later, right, Eric?" She looked at the front door, even though he stood near the staircase. "We're Treasures. We deserve to party. I hope they have a nightclub here."

Clark squeezed her in a hug. His shoulders ached from driving the steamcycle all day, but it might help to…relax. The last time he'd relaxed had been with Mabel when they'd gone to what remained of the dried-up stream in Tangled Wire. "No, you're a Treasure. *I'm* a Grisham."

Amethyst leaned against the counter at Pastorella Boutique. "It was positively dreadful! The steamcoach caught fire—I told my Clarky not to buy one from *that* shop—and it ruined our trunks. Positively ruined everything." She pursed her lips. "What can be purchased immediately while we have attire custom made?"

Clark kept his face expressionless as the shopkeeper peered over her gold-framed spectacles at them. Amethyst had felt the need to conjure a story about why they needed to buy clothes and not have them tailored or designed. He would've preferred asking for outfits without explanation, but if it embarrassed her, her story wouldn't hurt.

"We'll find something to fit you both." The shopkeeper pushed back her chair and rose. "If you'll follow me, please. Sir, our men's department will find you a suit while, ma'am, our ladies area will help you try on dresses."

Clark slid his hands into his pockets to keep from cracking his knuckles. Gentlemen didn't mutilate their fingers like that. What if they saw he was a fraud by the way he acted?

The poor sometimes became the wealthy. A ranch could take off, a new invention might make it big, a hunk of gold might be discovered in a stream. He'd never pondered those lucky fellows before, but they had to feel as he did, sweat on his skin and his eyes bugging.

The men's section dwelled on the left side of the establishment. Bolts of fabric in colors he knew well and some he'd only glimpsed on well-to-dos covered shelves along the walls. Velveteen settees adorned the center of the room, with dressing screens across, and tables covered in tape measures and pin cushions.

A tailor in a pinstripe suit bowed low to Clark. "Welcome to Pastorella Boutique. What might you require this afternoon?" His thick brown mustache bobbed over his lips as he spoke.

Clark coughed to keep his voice from squeaking. "I need a suit…to wear now."

"And another to be made specifically for your body?"

Georgette had required his measurements at the seamstress in her town. They'd sent him two suits, with the promise of more on the way in a variety of fabrics and colors. "The one will be fine."

"You have money." Eric shimmered into existence beside the dressing screen painted with fish. "Order what you want. Enjoy it."

Clark didn't need hundreds of suits. A serviceable pair of work pants and— "Do you only have suits?"

The tailor laughed. "I can make you anything you desire. This is the city, my boy. You're not from here, are you?"

"No." Clark wiped his face with his handkerchief. The man would wonder why he was so hot when fans purred around the room to keep the temperature cool.

"What is it you like?" The tailor lifted a tape measure off his neck. "We can set you up with a suit today and anything else for next week."

Next week. How long would they be staying? Eric's inventions could wait a little longer. His father was encouraging him to party. Maybe not *party*, but at least be happy.

"I would love a pair of Hedlund pants. You might not see many in the city, but they're useful for ranches. They're wider at the hips and thighs for movement, and then button from the knee to ankle. Great for boots and not getting caught in equipment, or in a steamcycle."

"I know exactly what you mean. What color?"

"Black."

Eric floated closer. "If I could, I would buy you one in every color. Get a few pairs. There's more than enough funds."

He shouldn't waste it. But... "Could you do three pairs? Black, brown, and blue? I've always wanted blue pants."

"Blue pants require a smart vest to go along with them. Black, with two rows of brass buttons. I can do a shirt as well." The tailor winked. "I grew up on a ranch in the prairies. I know how to make serviceable attire. Lots of pockets in the vest and reinforced elbows on the shirt. Not a blouse, nothing frilly. Buttons from elbow to wrist and some extra on the collar to keep them in place. Sound right?"

Clark wiped his forehead again. "Sounds amazing."

"Would bullet holders be appropriate for the vest?"

Eric laughed. "You'll be happy with your girl's choice of a boutique, eh?"

"That would be great." Clark gulped. He had to have enough money to cover the cost, or Eric wouldn't be so instigating. Hopefully. "How much will this be?"

"We can put it on your tab." The tailor lifted Clark's arms straight across to measure over his shoulders.

"I do have some money with me."

"We'll see. I'll take your measurements and we'll find you a suitable suit for today." He snickered. "Suitable suit. I love myself."

Clark laughed with him. The normal routine for acquiring clothing involved picking off a dead body or scraping enough coins together for a pre-made item in a general store.

The tailor chose a black suit lined in blue silk. "Since you love blue." The white blouse beneath it lacked frills and fit well beneath an indigo vest.

Clark set the box with his clothing folded within tissue paper on the front counter. The tailor had provided a slip detailing the item for the shopkeeper to charge. She glanced at it before opening a leather-bound ledger.

"Name?"

"Clark...Grisham." He glanced at Eric hovering by the entrance.

"Have you got a tab?"

"I'd like to pay with cash for now." No matter how unseemly that was for a gentleman.

She nodded without looking up. "I can start you a tab."

"I already have a tab, although it's old," Eric said. "Let her know she can revive that."

"My father has a tab here." Clark coughed to clear his throat. "Eric Grisham. It hasn't been used in almost twenty-years."

She lifted her eyebrows, waxed into two skinny worm-like lines. Bloody gears, why had he said that? She might recognize Eric Grisham, the inventor. News would spread that his son had returned and the Treasures would know. Senator Horan would know. The army might hear, but at least they couldn't connect scrawny Clark from the mine with an inventor's heir.

"Do you want to start one for yourself?" she asked in her monotone.

She didn't know Eric Grisham, then, or she didn't care. "You can just use my father's. I still want to pay with cash."

"I'll mark that a purchase was made in his name. That'll be fifty-four dollars."

Clark's fingers trembled as he counted the bills from his jacket pocket and slid them across the counter. "Thank you, ma'am."

"Your...*friend* is still with Susie. You may sit by the door to wait."

"Can I see her?" The woman's room had to have dressing screens and settees like his.

"Only husbands are allowed in with their wives, and that's only if no one else is in there." A question hung between them. If he claimed her as his wife, he could go in to see her.

"She's my intended." He shouldn't lie if they hadn't decided on it beforehand. She might make a comment that would prove the falsehood. Clark sat on the loveseat beside the door with the box beside him.

"Cigar?" the shopkeeper asked.

"No, thanks." He watched men and women stroll by out the window. In that section of the city, steamcoaches rattled by and steamcycles zoomed, rather than the familiar clip-clop of horses. The men wore suits and top hats, the women wide skirts and bustles.

"I wish I could've brought you and your mother here." Eric sighed. "You could've attended the best private school. She could've worn jewels."

Clark squeezed his eyes shut. Would he have wanted that life? School had never been for him, but his mother would've been breathtaking in a pearl necklace or diamond tiara.

"Clark!" Amethyst whirled out from the curtain separating the woman's room from the entranceway. A seamstress followed with a dress box and a hat box. "Wait until you see my gown. I was looking at a beautiful green, but your tailor called over that you'd gone with blue. My blue is going to match yours." He rose as she approached, grabbing his hands and tipping her face upwards, eyes bright. "We'll be a stunning couple. I hope the photographers are out tonight."

"Sixty-eight dollars," the shopkeeper read off the slip the seamstress handed her. "Mr. Grisham, will that be on your tab or cash as well?"

"We can put it on my father's tab." Amethyst squeezed Clark's hands. "I do that all the time in the city."

"I'll pay," Clark interjected. "A gentleman always treats his lady." Would it be appropriate to kiss her in front of the two women? He pecked her forehead before stepping to the counter, pulling out his bills. "Where would you like to do dinner?"

Amethyst dipped the sponge into the soapy water and slapped it onto Clark's shoulder, droplets spraying across the porcelain tub. He cringed as a few hit his ear.

"You, madam, are the worst bather I've ever met." He cupped his hand into the warm water and splashed it onto her chest where she stood behind him, once safe and dry on the floorboards. As she yelped, water soaked through her white silk chemise.

"I am certain no one has ever bathed you before." She scrubbed at his shoulder extra hard. "If you like, I can hire a maid to help out next time." She leaned forward so that her nipples, taut from the water, poked against his back through her chemise. "If I'm such a bad helper, that is." Her lower lip stuck out in a pout worked on him—a frown creased his forehead.

"You belong in here with me." His voice emerged from his throat in a growl that sent the fine hairs rising across her arms. She should have laughed, tossed her braid over her shoulder, and made a remark about being too proud for such a suggestion. The old Amethyst would have done that, and had him crawling to her.

This new Amethyst bit her lip, dropped the sponge into his lap, and lifted the undergarment over her head. As it drifted to the floor, he lunged to his knees and grabbed her around the waist.

"Clark!" She laughed, couldn't resist, and closed her eyes as he wrestled her into the tub with him. Candles flickered from around the washroom. They'd seemed more romantic than the gas lamps. Somewhere in the house, a clock chimed the hour. They would need to go out, but as she nestled her head beneath his chin, his arms still around her and the water lapping her shoulders, nothing had ever felt more divine.

The clubs could hang. Dinner could hang as well.

"So." His lips touched her hair. "You were saying no one has ever bathed me before. My mother did when I was a little one, but I'm sure it wasn't half so fine as you with that sponge. I reckon she never got a drop in my ears."

The water would cool, the soap would dissipate, and they would still be sitting against the porcelain, only warm from their body heat. Amethyst sighed, opening her eyes. Since when had she become practical?

"I'm glad you're here to show me how to properly clean," he continued. "I'd hate to have dirt under my fingernails. It isn't as if I never freshened up for your mother."

"I'll make you into the grandest gentleman." Amethyst shifted around to kneel beside him.

"Can I suck on your toes instead?" He wiggled his eyebrows, and her stomach sank again as if to make her into wax.

She gulped. "The grandest gentleman in all of Amston."

He frowned again, with soap bubbles stuck in his wild hair.

"You can't mean to say you don't even know the name of your own country." She smeared the sponge over his chest and lifted his arm to do the curls beneath. "There is more than just the west. Hedlund is just a territory, my dear." She could have been her uncle with that stern voice.

"I know there's more. There's the east, too." He bit her neck, and the sponge slipped from her fingers to splash them both. "The east brought me you."

Her toes curled. "I was bathing you, wasn't I? Yes, I bought the perfect shampoos and oils. You won't even recognize yourself."

Amethyst lifted her hair, turned her head, and pursed her lips to study her reflection in the gilded washroom mirror. She could only do so much with her yellow curls on her own—people really couldn't expect more from her without a handmaiden. The skinny blue ribbon had the perfect amount of innocence as it peaked from within her thin braid. She'd pinned it close to her scalp to let her other curls bounce down her back. It would all have to do.

Amethyst pushed up on her breasts to make the tops appear fuller. She'd worn her hair in that ribbon-braid for the Hallows Eve banquet two, no, three years ago. She'd been an assassin, dressed in a skintight black suit with gold stitching on the corseted bodice, and she'd carried a marbled dagger with her. What fun it had been to hook men through the cravat with the point of her faux blade and drag them close for a kiss!

Clark's reflection appeared near hers in the mirror and her breath stilled when she tried to inhale. Her stomach clenched, and blood drained from her head.

He looked delicious. His roguish self might make her drool, and rip his clothes off, and nibble across the light fur on his chest, but *this* Clark, in a suit, like a gentleman…

She turned, her fingernails dragging across the wall. He shifted his stance while running his hands over the front of his jacket.

"I've never worn anything this nice." He laughed, and the sound sent her legs wobbling. "I swear, this is—"

"A dream?" She slid across the floor to cup his face between her hands. If he stroked her, she wouldn't want to go out. The dressing would have been for naught.

His yellow hair, pulled back in the queue, made his blue eyes seem brighter. The jacket fit his broad shoulders like a hug. She'd never seen a man wear anything that well. Perhaps she'd always longed for someone with muscles, someone who could protect her.

"I was going to say this is a new man, but from how you're looking at me, I hope I am still me." He kissed the tip of her nose. "I'm rambling, huh?"

"You're perfect," she murmured.

"Dinner and dancing. Not a night club. We'll do that tomorrow night." Amethyst straightened his collar and smoothed the lapels on his suit coat. "We need special clothes for that. These are more...." In the light from the street lamps outside the mansion, her cheeks flushed. "I feel regal with you like this. A night club is for booze and flirting."

"If you say so." He couldn't stop smiling. When had he last been this happy? Staying with the Treasures had brought relief and being with Amethyst meant comfort, but the last time he'd been happy had been with Mabel, chasing barrel hoops down the center of the street. Happiness meant forgetting about being tired or hungry or poor; it was living in the moment with a dear friend.

Clark cupped Amethyst's cheeks and lowered his lips to press against hers. "Lead the way, my lady."

She slipped her arm through his and headed down the street. Gas lamps glowed along the street atop poles. Steamcoaches soared by, and another couple strolled on the opposite sidewalk with a little boy skipping ahead.

"It would be best if we aren't Treasures." Her heels clicked against the cement underfoot. "Father will hear we're in town and they'll wonder why we aren't with dear Donald. He'll also wonder where we're staying. You had a good idea not putting the clothes on Father's tab."

"I did it because I wanted to buy you something." He slid one of her curls, coiled atop her head, through his fingers. "I've never courted a girl before." Being with a girl meant camaraderie—a gang member stood up for other gang members—or a quick tumble with a rubber.

"Are we really courting? I can show you how to do it right."

Leave it to Amethyst to come up with a statement like that. "I'll learn along the way."

"But there has to be carriage rides in the park and parties with friends. We have to be seen, so people know we're together."

"Or," he lowered his voice, "I push you against that street lamp, yank up your skirt, and teach you how to muffle a scream."

Amethyst stumbled and he pulled her against his side. "That's...that's not how you court."

"See how much better my method is?"

They turned the corner onto another street of houses. The one after glittered with the lots of shops and restaurants.

"We can be Amethyst and Clark Grisham." Amethyst's voice cracked.

"We'll be from New Addison City. I do hope there are photographers. We can make a show of ourselves."

He stared at the houses with the manicured lawns and glowing windows. Families lived in them. Happy, safe families. "Shouldn't we stay silent? Our faces are on wanted posters."

"Hmm. No one here should be looking at wanted posters. I'd never seen one before I came out west."

"We won't have our pictures taken," Clark said.

"Have you ever had a photograph of yourself? They're grand! You can wear anything you want, and you can pose—"

"No photos," Clark interrupted. "None. It'll be safer." He could surprise her with a quiet photography studio. They could have one of just themselves to hang in their parlor.

She pursed her lips. If he'd hurt her feelings, so be it. They had to stay secure.

The restaurant she'd chosen earlier sparkled with gas lamps at the entranceway. A waiter opened the door for them and bowed.

Inside the door, another waiter stood at a podium. "Name?"

"Reservations for Clark Grisham. Two," Amethyst said. She'd insisted they make reservations. "It's what you do at the grandest places," she'd explained.

"This way." The waiter held up two menus and led them through the linen-covered tables. Groups of men, couples, and families chatted over steaming plates and goblets of wine.

Clark pulled out Amethyst's chair, as she'd shown him back at the mansion, before taking his seat. The waiter handed them each a menu. "Would the lady care for a drink?" He looked at Clark as he spoke.

"My husband and I would love red wine." Amethyst flicked her wrist. "We would also love an appetizer of bread triangles with cucumber yogurt sauce. Thank you." She held out her hand and wiggled her fingers until Clark grasped it. "You're going to love living in the city, Clark. I'm going to show you a magnificent time. I promise I won't get too tipsy."

CHAPTER THIRTY-ONE

Y ou're tipsy." Clark's voice exploded in her ear, too close.
How had he gotten so close?

Amethyst turned. It had to be a good turn, so why did
some of the champagne slosh from her glass onto her hand.
"Darn it, now I'm going to be sticky. Will you lick it off, love? Please?"
She pushed her wrist toward his face, and her stomach flip-flopped when
he cupped her elbow and slid his tongue over her skin.

"Better?" Lights danced over his grin.

"I can't be tipsy yet." She giggled.

Music pounded against the walls, reverberating off the ceiling. The
city's only nightclub couldn't compare on the same scale as the clubs in
New Addison City, but at least it had loud music and alcohol. The music
involved more guitars and fiddles, but it still kept her feet tapping and her
head bobbing. The club also had only one room, rather than multiple
levels each with a different theme. The one room contained barn-red
walls and gas lamps.

"I miss the crystal chandeliers," she shouted over the music. "They
sparkle. It's dizzying."

"I think you're dizzy enough."

She set her empty glass on the shelf that ran along the border of the
room and grabbed his hands. Bodies crushed against them, a sea of
frilly skirts and cowboy hats. She would have to get one of those skirts
that hung long in the back and ended at her knees in the front,
complete with black fishnet stockings and a feather-accented corset.
Most of the females in the room sported that combination, with a
variety of heels and bare feet.

"Trust me." She pressed against his front, lifting their hands overhead, and bumped her hips against his. "Haven't you ever danced?"

"We do lots of dancing on the plains. The Bromis love to get wild." His fingers massaged her knuckles as they swayed in time with the beat.

She pictured the Bromi slaves with their tan skin and eagle feathers woven into their long black hair. "You're joshing. They don't dance, do they? I've never seen one even smile."

He slid his hands down her arms to cup her shoulders. "Why would they do that around their captors? The Bromi love freedom. They want to move their camps to follow the buffalo and the rains. They don't want to be forced into servitude in houses when they're used to open skies and deerskin teepees."

She bounced her bosom against his chest before spinning on her heels to grind her buttocks into his groin. "Do you miss living with them?" She'd never seen a Bromi in New Addison City, but she'd heard of them—wild creatures who were thankful to be taken in by society so they could become civilized. "Will you take me to meet them?"

"You won't remember this in the morning. You're drunk."

"I'm not drunk yet!" She turned to loop her leg around his knee and tip her head back. "I really would like to meet them. How exciting. I can write to my friends. They've never seen a Bromi, I'm sure."

"They aren't meant to be stared at." Clark stroked the back of her neck, exposed by her pinned bun.

"Please? After we finish retrieving the inventions? You must still be one of them if you lived with them for a while."

In the shadows, she couldn't make out his expression. "If you want."

How depressing the evening had become. Clubs were meant for fun, not morbid thoughts of slaves and desert tribes. "Come with me." She tugged him toward the bar near the entrance. "I need another vodka with orange juice."

Clark leaned against the open gate to his mansion, one leg propped up and his arms folded. Amethyst stood near the door with the prospective gardener she'd found at the hiring agency.

"We want beauty." Her voice lifted from across the yard. "I'm thinking flowers and fountains. It's much too dry here, too hot. We need fountains and water."

"You want bushes." The gardener slapped one hand against the other. "Bushes to line the fence and house, bushes to line the walkway. They don't need a lot of water. They'll thrive. You want bushes."

"I hate bushes. I want fountains and flowers."

Clark chuckled. She'd been excited to find a gardener available for work right away. Of course she would irritate him.

"Who do you think will win?" Eric asked from beside him.

"Amethyst. She won't hire someone she can't control."

"Can she control you?"

Clark peered at his father from the corners of his eyes. "No." He might buy her things and protect her, but she couldn't tell him what to do.

"That's why she likes you. You're dangerous and you don't care that she's Amethyst Treasure. How serious are you about her?"

Clark's muscles tensed. "I won't get her pregnant." *Not like what you did with my mother.*

"I didn't expect you would. She thinks this is a game. Is it?"

Clark watched her stomp to one of the benches overgrown with vines and kick it. "You think a *bush* is going to make this look pretty?"

He couldn't do anything more than play with her. He had no future. He might have a house and money, and a little income according to Donald, but he would always be wanted by the army. "At least we both know it's a game." He coughed. "Do you care what happens to the yard?"

"It's been ill-used too long. I can't use it anymore. Do what you want with it."

Footsteps approached from the sidewalk. Clark stepped through the gate to greet the mailman. "Morning."

The elderly man in his green uniform tipped his hat. "Morning, sir. You taking over the place, if you don't mind my asking? Always felt bad to see it so crummy."

"For now." That seemed a safe answer.

The mailman handed Clark a folded paper from the canvas sack slung over his shoulder, tipped his hat again, and continued down the sidewalk. The front of the telegraph paper read **Grisham**. Only Donald knew about the mansion, as far as he knew. Clark ducked back into the yard and broke the wax seal, unfolding the paper.

I write to you at your father's home in hopes you'll stop there on your travels. Garth Treasure has expressed interest in having you and your partner home. Donald

Clark tucked the telegraph into his pocket. "We shouldn't have stayed so long." Three days. How could he have let himself slip? "We should have kept looking for the inventions."

"Garth is a good man," Eric murmured. "Make him happy. We'll plan the next trip. There's a tonic I made with tiny particles that give you energy when you drink it. They flush from your body, but that rush is used to empower soldiers. They don't feel as much pain and can rush at the Bromi faster, harder."

Clark wiped his hand across his mouth. "How many random things have you invented?"

The ghost hovered back a step. "Enough. Inventions were my life."

"This tonic isn't with the army, is it? You know how they feel about me."

"It's at an outpost with one general and a secretary. With careful planning, we'll succeed."

Clark groaned. "At least this gives me something to do." Even though he'd always worked—around the saloon and the mine, and then to survive alone—it had felt soothing to putter with Amethyst, wake up with her head on his shoulder and his arm across her belly. They'd sat on the leaf-strewn back porch, observing the untamed back yard, while eating bakery sweet buns they'd purchased the day before.

"You love this land like I do," Eric said. "We'll make it better."

Amethyst sat beside Zachariah in the steamcoach heading back to the ranch. Clark, across from them, tipped his hat over his face and turned his chin down, hiding his eyes as though he dozed. Zachariah watched out the window.

She picked at her fingernails. "Why did we have to come back? It was *so* relaxing. I know why Father loves this countryside so much." That should make him friendlier.

"I love it too," Zachariah said.

She pursed her lips. "Why are you acting like this? You're usually

189

talking about the army. Constantly."

"They had a Bromi raid," Zachariah snapped, "without me."

Clark stiffened—not asleep after all.

"Is that all you want to do? Attack Bromis and wear your uniform?" She yawned. "How exciting can that be?" The steamcoach turned into the driveway circle at the ranch. "Goody, we're home. I'm so thrilled Father made us come back early." She rolled her eyes.

"There's a guest from New Addison City."

Amethyst's heart skipped a beat and she leaned forward. "Really? Who is it? I didn't think any of my friends would come." She kicked Clark's leg. "I can't wait to introduce you to my friends. They'll love you. A secret brother. How scandalous and delicious."

Clark scowled at Zachariah. Right, the Bromi comment.

It might be Mary. Her father owned a ranch somewhere in Hedlund, too, even though he lived in New Addison City.

The steamcoach halted and the driver opened the door. Zachariah and Clark hopped out; Clark paused to reach back for her before the driver could escort her. She clasped his fingers and lifted her skirt.

When she'd first arrived, her father's ranch had seemed cold despite the heat outdoors. The Grisham mansion, despite the horrendous condition of the yard, had been more welcoming. It didn't involve family that bossed her around. She could drink and control what happened to each aspect.

"You'll love Mary." Amethyst wished Zachariah wasn't looking so she could kiss Clark's cheek. "She has a wonderful laugh. It will make you laugh, too."

"Amethyst, Clark, welcome back." Her mother stood on the porch beside the swing, where a shadowed man sat. "I trust you had a pleasant journey. I'm sorry to cut it short, but I knew you'd want to return for your *friend*."

Amethyst frowned as Clark's fingers slipped away from hers. Did her mother know how Mary had kissed her that once at the club?

The man on the swing rose and stepped toward her, bowing when he reached the stairs. Amethyst's heart clenched and her belly churned. Oh no. He wasn't supposed to be at the ranch. He shouldn't even be in Hedlund.

Her mother smiled at him. "Amethyst, you didn't tell us you'd invited your beau. We've had an excellent spell meeting Joseph."

CHAPTER THIRTY-TWO

Amethyst clasped her hands to her neck as her mind spun. "Joseph. You're here." Joseph, her flirt in the city. Joseph, who she'd imagined marrying. Joseph, who she probably had asked to visit her on the ranch.

Joseph swept off his top hat in a bow, lifting her hand to his lips to kiss. Hadn't they felt warm before? Now they felt oily, as if he'd rubbed too much bees wax on them to keep them soft. Oily, slimy, not warm and firm like Clark's.

"Of course I would come to visit my Amethyst." He stood and straightened his jacket, as if it could never have a wrinkle.

"You should have told us about Joseph." Her mother swept down the stairs, her skirt brushing the dust. "He could have joined you for the entire visit. He can, of course, stay as long as he desires."

"I'm sure I wrote to you." Amethyst clenched her hands behind her back. The letters she wrote home included pages of the people she associated with and the men who fawned over her, tossing around the big names to show how much people loved her. Joseph would've been listed a few times. Her parents must not have paid attention.

"Alas," Joseph said, "I cannot stay for more than a month. My family has a summer camp on the ocean. I would love to take Amethyst with me, though."

Her mother inclined her head. "That would be fine. Amethyst has paid her dues to us." Her mother laughed. "I know the ranch isn't your favorite place, dear."

Maybe not the ranch, but leaving for Joseph's summer camp would take her away from Clark. She almost grabbed his arm before catching herself. "You wanted me to spend the entire summer here. I don't mind. I should be with family more."

Her mother frowned. "Amethyst, by truth, you can go."

"The sailing will be wonderful," Joseph said. "They've forecast charming weather for the east coast. The summer will be memorable."

"But...." Amethyst gulped. The inventions, Eric, the mansion, *Clark*, they couldn't wait. "I'm actually enjoying it here." There, she'd said it. Let her parents preen so long as she remained at Clark's side.

"Your mother told me about your new brother." Joseph stared over her head at Clark. "What an interesting story. I'm sure you weren't expecting to add a new sibling." He stepped around her and held out his hand. "Joseph Velardi. Pleased to meet you." That snippy edge in his voice, the twinge of sarcasm. He thought Clark was beneath him. Joseph placated Clark. Amethyst bit her lower lip to keep from laughing. Clark could punch her "beau" onto the ground within seconds.

"It is a pleasure *beyond belief* to meet Amethyst's esteemed beau." Clark matched snippiness and sarcasm with a wide grin. "Having a sister is more than I could've hoped for when I finally found my father."

"Is this lifestyle different than what you're used to?" Joseph lifted his eyebrows. Her parents must not have told him anything about Clark, other than his presence.

"Much different." Clark gazed at the ranch as though seeing it for the first time. Amethyst held her breath. How much would he tell Joseph?

"I was raised by a Bromi tribe. It's been hard adapting to wearing clothes and not murdering every white man I see."

Amethyst rocked back on her heels, laughing. Her mother giggled, and Zachariah remained glowering at the driveway.

"You...lived with Bromis?" Joseph paled. "Aren't they savages?"

"You haven't the faintest idea until you see them chase down a buffalo and tear it apart with their teeth. It's also been hard getting used to eating cooked food." Clark winked at her.

"They do that?" Joseph took a step back. "Is it safe to live so close to them?"

Clark nodded, his lids lowered. "I protect the family now."

"Clark is our wonder." Her mother stroked his arm before cupping his elbow. "Why don't we retire into the house? I'm sure you both want to refresh. Amethyst, you can show Joseph the town if you like. One of us can chaperone."

"Chaperones won't be necessary, ma'am." Joseph took Amethyst's hand again. "That's an old fashioned rule."

"We still believe in those old fashioned rules." Her mother should scold Joseph and send him away. He ruined things. Amethyst tried to analyze Clark's expression, but he smiled at her mother with genuine admiration.

"Clark can chaperone!" Amethyst reached for him, but he stepped toward the front porch.

"Don't you suppose Zachariah would rather have something to do this afternoon?" Clark clapped her brother on his shoulder. "Get your mind off your troubles."

Bloody gears, he was mad. Scowling, Amethyst stomped toward the house. Her mother led Zachariah and Joseph toward the kitchen—after he kissed her hand again with his disgusting lips—to allow Amethyst and Clark time to change.

She grabbed his bedroom door as he attempted to shut it. "Joseph isn't my beau."

"Be careful, sweetheart, or someone special will overhear." Blast his hooded gaze.

"No one's in the hallway." She slipped under his arm and pushed the door shut, sealing them inside. "I'll slip out through the balcony. Clark, look at me."

He folded his arms and leaned against the door. "I guess I should've asked if you have an intended."

"My beau, not my intended." She winced. "He's not even a beau. I see lots of men." That darkened gaze again. What a bad answer. "Not like that, I promise. Bloody gears, that's what New Addison is like. You flirt and you move on to someone else. They're flings."

"This fling thinks you're serious enough to take a train out here and invite you back to his summer camp."

Amethyst stomped her foot. "That's not how it is at all! I don't love him."

"I must just be a fling too." Clark strode across the room toward his bed, peeling off his jacket. He wore the ensemble he'd ordered at the boutique: wilderness clothes that gave him that roguish air. Her heart skipped faster.

"You're not a fling! You know I don't flirt with everyone when you're around."

He tossed his vest onto a chair. "I'm sure he thinks that too. You'd best go refresh. You and Joseph will have to catch up before your seaside adventure."

"I don't want to go." Her voice rose. "I want to stay with you, here in Hedlund. I want to get the inventions, help Eric. I want to see the Bromi."

"I'm sure your beau won't mind making you happy. Maybe he can take you to the Bromi."

She stormed across the room to seize him by the front of his shirt. "I want Joseph to leave!"

"So I don't know about him? We both understand this is a game. You go back to your home and party with your pretty Joseph. I stay here and hide from the army."

"Bloody gears!" She jumped to clasp her arms around his neck and shove her lips against his. He remained steady, never teetering, and his lips softened. His hands rested on her hips, neither pushing her away nor pulling her closer.

She stumbled backwards. "You don't make me want to keep flirting. Don't you know what that means? I actually went off into the desert with you. Joseph is just whatever. You're *Clark*. I gave you my virginity. I love you."

He tipped his head as he stared at her. "I'm different. That's what you love."

She folded her arms as a chill crept over her skin. "Does it matter why I love you?"

Clark yanked her against his chest by the wrists and kissed her mouth, his tongue shoving between her lips.

She leaned into him, tipping her head up, moaning against his lips. "New Addison doesn't matter. Joseph doesn't matter. *You* do."

"For now." He bit her neck. "You admitted you're a flirt."

"It's all a game we play. Everyone acts like that in the city." She yanked on the front of his shirt to unfasten the buttons.

He caught her hands. "We don't have that much time, sweetheart. Show me tonight how much you care." He kissed her lips, a quick peck. "Let's show your dear beau how much you've changed."

Clark leaned back on the porch swing and crossed his ankles. Amethyst rested her elbows against the railing near him, her head tipped so she could smile at him.

She actually liked him. It wasn't a passing fling, or a one-night hookup. She wasn't a Tarnished Silver or a lost gang member. Amethyst Treasure, a lady of wealth and prosperity, admired him. More than that, she chose him and the dust and the quest over Gentleman Joseph. In the yard, Jeremiah showed him how to toss horseshoes.

"You need to flick your wrist." Jeremiah bent his knees and crouched backwards. "Flick, toss. You need to get it onto the pegs in the grass."

"Doesn't this ruin the lawn?" Joseph still wore his suit, even though Jeremiah had stripped to his shirt and slacks.

"Grass grows back." Jeremiah clapped him on the shoulder. Of course Jeremiah would befriend Joseph, but hate Clark. Clark chuckled. Penniless, wanted Clark had Amethyst.

"Let's go for a ride later." Amethyst twirled her hair around her finger. "Maybe we can explore more of these roads."

"We could see more of the ranch." Clark patted the swing seat beside him and she stepped back to drop beside him.

"Joseph will love that." Georgette sat in a high-backed chair down the porch, her hands folded in her lap. "Were you thinking *horses* or steamcycles?" The emphasis on "horses" allowed no doubt which one she preferred.

"I don't think Joseph would want to get dirty." Amethyst jutted out her lower lip.

Clark scratched his arm as Joseph scowled at them. The man had ridden days to join her, and she outright snubbed him.

"Be nice," Clark whispered. "He thinks he's your beau."

"I am being nice. He hates dirt."

"So do you."

"I'd love to." Joseph's words ground out as though his tongue were mechanical.

"Flick, toss." Jeremiah let a horseshoe sail from his fingers across the lawn to strike the peg farthest away. It spun around thrice before settling into the grass. "That's five points."

Zachariah lifted a horseshoe from the rack near the porch and stepped forward. He'd also peeled off his jacket, but he'd left his army cap over his cropped hair. Poor boy. Did he feel as if he had no place if he didn't participate in the army? Clark scratched the mosquito bite on his elbow. He should do something with him more; help him to feel as if he had a friend who wasn't a mandatory soldier.

The military hadn't helped his physique. His arms and legs stayed scrawny, but his belly strained the front of his trousers from indulgence.

Zachariah's horseshoe hit the second farthest back peg. "Three points." He grinned.

If Clark had been down there, he would've slapped hands with him. "Good job, Zach!"

Zachariah blinked up at the porch before pumping his fist, the grin strengthening.

"Your turn." Jeremiah clapped Joseph's shoulder again.

Joseph stared at the horseshoe in his hands as if he wanted to wrinkle his nose, but feared the act would offend. He drew a deep breath, took two steps forward, and sailed the horseshoe… off to the left, where it landed seven feet in front of the closest peg.

"Good try, my boy." Garth exited from the house, wiping his forehead on a handkerchief. "That was an excellent first try."

Joseph's cheeks and ears burned red. "That was horrible!"

"Better than my first attempt. Don't worry, my boy, this backwards little Out West game gets easier."

Amethyst giggled. "At least it went somewhere and you didn't just drop it on your foot. Remember the time you spilled your strawberry vodka on poor Mary?"

Clark stiffened. He might have won her for a while, but she and Joseph had a past. For all he knew, they might've grown up together.

Joseph grabbed a horseshoe off the rack and held it out to her. "Your turn, Miss Never Spills Her Drink."

Garth coughed, but Amethyst rocked to her heels, snared Clark's sleeve, and yanked him up. "We'll all have a turn. You too, Mother." Her hand slipped down Clark's arm to interlace their fingers and she winked at him over her shoulder. "I'm sure you've played before, haven't you, darling brother Clarky?"

"When I was working on a ranch for a summer."

"Excellent." She pranced down the porch steps with her skirt swirling around her legs. She grabbed a horseshoe, and her eyes widened as she staggered. "Bloody gears, this is heavy! How do you throw this?"

"Language, honey." Garth coughed again.

"With your arm," Jeremiah sneered.

Clark pressed against her back and held her wrist. "Let me show you." He nudged her forward. "We stand at the line drawn in the dirt." Jeremiah had scraped his boot heal to form it. "That's it, now you need to extend your arm and draw it close. You're not chucking it. Think of an easy throw. You want it to spin, not catapult."

"I'll show her." Joseph clenched and unclenched his hands as if he wasn't sure what to do.

Clark smiled at him. "I'm just her brother, chap. I'm sure she'll still look to you for everything else." Which wouldn't include muffling her screams into his pillow late at night.

Amethyst rocked her buttocks into his hips. "Now what?"

"You release." He stepped back, his fingertips trailing over her shoulder. "Remember, easy toss. You only want enough force for it to go, not for it to make a racket."

She bit her lower lip as she tossed it. It sailed straight, but landed feet ahead of the closest peg. She tossed her head and stuck her tongue out at Joseph. "I got closer than you. Nah nah."

"Amethyst," Garth barked. "Joseph is our guest."

Clark pressed his hand to his mouth to stifle a laugh. Zachariah met his gaze and chuckled.

"That was a horrible throw," Jeremiah exclaimed.

"My turn." Clark stepped forward with his horseshoe and released. It hit the farthest peg and spun down to rest on Jeremiah's. "Five points."

Jeremiah scowled. Clark wondered what Garth would say if he followed Amethyst's example by sticking out his tongue. He hadn't done that since he and Mabel were children.

Garth extended his arm to Georgette to escort her down the stairs. "If you all enjoy this, we can have special horseshoes designed with each person's name. We can create quite a go of this."

"It may not be my favorite game, sir," Joseph said.

"Show me again, Clark," Amethyst purred. Holding a new horseshoe, she backed against him. "It isn't my favorite either, but I want to beat Jeremiah."

Clark caught a glimpse of Joseph's lowered lids and his skin prickled. Amethyst was supposed to be his sister—they couldn't allow that act to slip.

CHAPTER THIRTY-THREE

After two weeks, Clark remembered why he loathed ranch life. Each day followed the same pattern, unlike life on the plains. He woke up at dawn and took breakfast with the family, apart from Amethyst and Joseph who slept late—Clark visited her in her bedroom so she wouldn't have to scurry back to hers when he rose. After breakfast, he followed Jeremiah around the ranch helping where he could, but Bromi slaves and hired hands did the routine work. The only jobs he found were odd and few between. Garth taught him parts of the finances so he could help with the bookkeeping, but his handwriting wasn't refined enough. Sick of Garth's hidden grimaces, Clark surrendered that. Target shooting with Zachariah proved entertaining, although Zachariah spoke little and acted as though he knew everything about pistols, despite the fact he missed more than struck the target.

Anytime Clark wanted to be alone with Amethyst, apart from at night, Joseph followed, so he invited Zachariah. The four visited the saloon, went horseback riding, and rode steamcycles—the first for Joseph, and Zachariah had little practice.

The most excitement came from snippets around town: "What happened to them Horan boys? Fellas just took off on their pa." Clark waited for a whisper of murder, but people who knew the young men well must have thought them the type to skedaddle without word. What Rancher Horan thought of the matter never reached Clark's hearing. Sordid gossip might have spiced the town a bit, but he wouldn't have wanted it to bother Amethyst. Then again, she would have rolled right along with it and added some flavors of her own.

"We'll throw a charity ball," Georgette said at supper. "We'll have to plan it for next month to give everyone ample time to prepare. I'm sure you'll enjoy the dancing, Joseph."

"Thank you, ma'am. I do miss the galas in the city. We'd have one almost every night." He tipped his wine glass to Amethyst. She still fumed over being allowed water, milk, or juice, but never alcohol, so she nodded instead of toasting back.

"What charity would you like?" Georgette cut into her steak. "I've always preferred those balls since they assist others. They aren't enjoyed solely by those attending."

Sweet Georgette. No wonder she chose the desert rather than the city. She must've hated the socialites. From what he'd met of other gentlewomen, they preferred silks and caviar to noticing a beggar dying on the street.

"Bromi." Amethyst's head jerked up. "I want the money to benefit the Bromi plight."

"Bromi *plight*," Jeremiah repeated in a monotone.

She pursed her lips in a downturned smile. "Our dear brother Clark had to live with a Bromi tribe *just to survive* before we saved him. They were *so* good to him we should do something to pay them back."

"The Bromi are wild and meant to be slaves." Joseph fidgeted in his seat. He had to hate ranch life more than Clark. At least Clark kept reminding himself that staying there meant he was safe. Joseph had to be thinking about what he missed in the city and at his summer camp.

"Why ever *should* they be slaves?" Amethyst's voice rose in a whine. Did she really want to help or did she want to cause unease?

"Because they need taming," Joseph said. "Without civilization, they don't know how to live. They run around naked."

"They wear leggings and loincloths," Clark corrected. "They have ponchos for at night. The women wear tunics." The clothes weren't called that in the Bromi tongue, but those at the table would understand what he meant. Why did people assume they were naked just because they chose to wear little covering?

"I'm glad the Bromi were able to help you." Georgette leaned over to rub Clark's knuckles where he gripped his fork. "Amethyst, that's a wonderful suggestion. Why don't you start the charity?"

Amethyst paled. "*Start* it?"

"Why yes. There isn't one currently, but the Bromi shouldn't be treated so horrendously."

Clark glanced at the Bromi cook refilling Garth's wine glass. The woman kept her gaze down. What could she think as she overheard the conversation about her people.

"Clark will help me," Amethyst said. "He knows the best way to help them."

He'd wanted to assist them, but until the settlers and ranchers gave them freedom, assistance would be futile. "We can offer them medicine, but they have herbs they use. They don't need clothing, unlike what most people think." Dig toward Joseph. "The best thing would be to help the Bromi keep their land. They're driven farther into the plains each time a new ranch is built. Some Bromi do prefer living in towns, so we could give money to freed Bromi to help them establish themselves." Free Bromi, those who had proven themselves "civilized" enough to live as they chose. Most of the freed returned to their tribes, or whatever was left. Some, who'd been slaves since childhood, didn't know how to survive there, or chose to stay in town amongst familiar settings.

"People won't want to support that kind of charity," Jeremiah said before forking mashed potatoes into his mouth.

"They will if a Treasure starts it." Georgette beamed at Clark and Amethyst.

At the Friday supper, two evenings later, Garth tapped his spoon against the side of his porcelain plate. Clark stopped daydreaming about what it would be like to drive Amethyst into a field, alone, and peel off her clothes to let the sun heat her skin. His lips would tingle when he touched her warmed flesh.

"I wish to congratulate Georgette and Amethyst on their excellent management of the charity ball," Garth said. "Invitations have been sent and the menu is being prepared."

Clark chewed on a boiled carrot, the cinnamon sprinkled on top making his tongue dance. Amethyst had whirled around the house listing off the excitement they would have. Music, dancing, an ice sculpture, an outdoor bar... Joseph had sat glowering from Garth's smoking room with a cigar and glass of bourbon.

Amethyst lifted her chin and flashed Clark a smile. "This will be a wonderful event. You'll never have experienced anything like it. It will put Donald's *party* to shame."

"I'm sure he hasn't," Joseph grumbled. "They don't have many at mining towns or with the Bromi."

Clark swallowed his carrot. "Thank you for suggesting to bring the Bromi to experience the ball."

Amethyst choked on her rice, and Jeremiah stiffened. The Bromi would hate to come—looked at as slaves, forced into an awkward situation, embarrassed at doing the wrong thing when they didn't understand. Joseph didn't have to know Clark would never invite them.

"We can invite the nearest five tribes," Clark continued. "There are only about one-hundred to two-hundred members per tribe."

"Per tribe?" Joseph sputtered. "You can't be serious, man. After all the work Mistress Treasure and Amethyst have put into this event—"

Clark lowered his eyebrows. "I jest."

"It would be a pleasant idea, but I'm not sure it would be the best for them," Georgette said.

Clark met her gaze. "I agree."

"Unfortunately." Garth bowed his head. "I loathe interrupting conversations, but I was hoping to raise an option. Every summer, Jeremiah and I take a camping trip. Zachariah doesn't always attend, and sometimes Georgette chooses to go. This year we could all go."

Clark had seen fathers and sons take trips. They'd come to mining towns to "learn how the miners lived." They'd visited "vacation" ranches and rented cabins for a weekend. Clark had found solace in a few of those, when they'd been unoccupied. The furniture had been elegant, since the cabins catered to those with wealth. They had toilets, although no working water system. He'd thought of them as fancy toilets.

"You mean Clark too?" Zachariah asked.

"All of us, son. Clark, of course. It's time he joined us on family outings." Garth inclined his head toward Clark. "There's no reason Georgette, Amethyst, and Joseph can't come along too."

"Camping," Joseph repeated. Color, which had been a reddish brown from being unfamiliar with the sun, drained from his flesh. "You jest. That's for hunters and trappers."

"We hunt and trap when we need to," Garth said. "Western furs are in high demand in the east. I'm sure you own a few yourself."

"Joseph is right," Amethyst squeaked. "There wouldn't be any…any…stuff."

Clark rolled his gaze at her. "*Dear sister.* Donald took us camping." Relieving herself on the plains and sleeping in an abandoned bank couldn't be any worse than a luxury cabin.

She stuck her tongue out at him. "That doesn't mean I want to do it again."

"Shush, dear." Georgette laid her hand on Amethyst's shoulder. "It really is enjoyable to be that immersed in nature."

Immersed in nature involved looking out a window at a flower garden. In New Addison city, many top floors of the buildings were roofed in glass to prove greenhouses of vegetables and flowers. The building managers charged money for guests to visit for the day, or the hour. It made a lovely retreat for flirting.

That was nature. Stomping through the forest on foot dwelled in a level of torture. Two Bromi slaves had driven steamwagons for them until they reached the thicket. Garth had handed out the packs and away they went.

The packs. Not steamer trunks, like what she'd brought from the east, or valises. Trunks, suitcases, carpetbags. Oh no, the packs were leather sacks with two straps and giant brass buckles that held the flap closed.

Her father couldn't have found something more hideous if he'd hired a Bromi baby to make it. Amethyst winced. Clark wouldn't want her to think like that about the Bromi. All right, if a *regular* baby had made it.

The air became cooler and damper as they trekked deeper into the woods. No one should have to climb over roots and weave around bushes since roads had been invented. Despite the visible dirt path, it was so narrow no one could walk side-by-side with another, and it dipped and rose until her leg muscles ached. Her shoulders throbbed from the weight of the pack. She paused to shift it, seeking a stronger spot on her back.

"You shouldn't have brought so much," her mother said from behind. "I warned you how difficult it would be."

Amethyst narrowed her eyes. Her mother wore denim, like a ranch hand, like a man. Mud had already splattered the denim overalls. Beneath, her mother wore a checkered red shirt that looked like the print off a servant's blanket.

"How can you wear that?" Amethyst demanded, again. "Don't you care how lousy that looks?"

Her mother pursed her lips. "As long as I'm happy and comfortable, what does it matter if the squirrels think ill of me?"

Amethyst had refused the peasant denim offered to her, but she had consented to a pair of thick black pants. Everyone else, save Joseph, wore denim. They could've been a pack of homeless settlers rather than the Treasures. Joseph trudged along at the end of the line, scowling at the path. Good old Joseph. That had been why she liked him so much. She liked Clark better, but she and Joseph were a pair.

She strained her head to spot Clark at the front of the line chatting with her father. Jeremiah stomped—he must've been used to pairing with Garth on the camping trips. After Jeremiah came Zachariah, who watched the trees. They stretched in every direction; she could've believed they were endless if she didn't know the ocean bordered the continent.

"We won't come across any Bromi?" Joseph asked. "Right?"

"They prefer the plains, the desert," Clark called back. "They won't come this deep into the woods."

"Some Bromi tribes once lived in the woods," her mother said. "They've been driven out. We won't see any, Joseph."

"If we do, Clark will protect us." Amethyst waved at him when he glanced back.

A breeze stirred the tops of the trees and a few green leaves drifted toward the ferns. Most of the trees kept the breeze from reaching them, but Amethyst caught the scent of pines and wild flowers. It might have been peaceful, with the gentle creaks of branches and the gurgle of a stream nearby, if it weren't for that blasted pack breaking her shoulders and the burn in her legs. She rubbed her thighs through her pants and scowled.

"Almost there," Jeremiah yelled.

"We've walked a bloody eight hours," Joseph grumbled.

"Forty-five minutes," her mother corrected. Joseph's face turned a deeper shade of red, despite the exertion flush already covering his cheeks. He must not have meant to talk so loud. Amethyst chuckled under her breath. At least she wasn't the only one suffering.

After hiking up a near impossible ridge that everyone else fairly skipped over, they arrived at a clearing with a log cabin and an outbuilding. Amethyst dropped her pack and stretched her arms. It could've been worse. She and Clark had passed by one-room cabins with weathered barns and people wrinkled by the sun and work. This cabin had a front porch, two fireplaces—one for each end of the house, and glass windows.

"How long are we staying?" Joseph asked.

"Usually we spend a month," Jeremiah said. "It looks like it will only be a week."

Garth shook his son's arm. "Only for now. We'll head back up here later on this summer. We'll have our usual good time."

"A week." Joseph dropped his pack beside Amethyst's. "I can see why you didn't want to come out here to Hedlund."

"If I hadn't, I wouldn't have met Clark."

"You would've still heard about him. Your family writes."

"Not the same." She left her pack by the woods to follow the others into the house. Someone else could grab it later.

The furniture happened to be rustic, but not too bad, lots of carved wood and split logs. Stuffed deer heads glared at them from the walls. The kitchen blended in with the sitting room. Her parents master bedroom finished off the downstairs. Three rooms occupied the top floor.

"This can be yours, Amethyst." Her father swept his hand across a small space covered in bookshelves.

"This is closet size," she squeaked. "There's no bed, just all these books."

"What else is there to do at night except read and whittle?" Jeremiah bumped against her. "It's relaxing."

"Reading is for people who don't have social lives!"

"I hear you," Joseph mumbled. When did anyone have a moment to read when balls were being planned and clothing was being fitted? Friends didn't come over to sit around a lamp and read. They wanted games, tea, rainbow-colored lemonade, not a book about an imaginary adventure.

"We have extra bedding," Jeremiah said. "We'll set you up with a bed."

Her stomach clenched. "Where's the bathroom? We looked in all the rooms."

"Behind the shed," her father said. "There's a toilet and a wash basin. It's perfectly sanitary."

"There's no tub?" She smelled already. Her lavender soap had surrendered to sweat.

"There's a tin tub. We get water from the stream." Jeremiah laughed. "You'll love it."

They had to return to civilization. If she were sick, they would. Amethyst pressed her hand to her forehead and collapsed backwards.

Jeremiah kicked his heel against the wall. His sister lay on the floor with her arms bent and her lips parted. Pretending to faint wouldn't help the government install indoor plumbing in the woods.

"Get up," their mother sighed.

Amethyst twitched her leg.

"Boys?" Their father headed down the narrow hallway. "Normally this room is Jeremiah's and this one Zachariah's. You'll have to share with Joseph and Clark. I don't mind how you break it up."

Jeremiah scratched his chin. If Amethyst thought sweat smelled bad, wait until she had to put mosquito cream over her body. That stuff reeked more than rancid chicken.

For the room situation, he would grab Zachariah. Clark and Joseph the Dandy could share the other space. Neither of them belonged there.

"Clark, want to share with me?"

Jeremiah held his jaw shut as he glared at Zachariah. How could his *blood brother* want to share with that illegitimate spoil?

"Thanks." Clark followed Zachariah into the back bedroom.

"Hi, roommate," Joseph sneered. Why couldn't that fop have gone back to the city and taken precious Amethyst with him? Those days she'd spent wandering off with Clark had been bliss, just like before she'd arrived. Amethyst couldn't bother to bestow pleasantries on her real brothers; she had to fawn over brand new Clark.

"Going for a walk. I'll see if the Ottmans are at their camp yet." Jeremiah stormed toward the stairs. At least the Ottmans, if they had arrived, wouldn't complain about wearing denim and not bathing.

Before, Garth would've followed him over. The mile walk wasn't long, the scenery a mixture of relaxation and darkness. Now, he stayed to coddle Amethyst's fainting spell. Zachariah might have trailed behind, raving about how great his latest stint with the army had been, but now he wanted to bond with Clark, off all people.

Jeremiah kicked the stump by the porch on his way to the path. Mr. Ottman lived a few hours from the ranch, so they only saw him at camp. He made his wealth off his ranch, and although it wasn't a huge pile of money, they got by well enough. His son, Myron, was a year younger than Clark, but a stoic man like his father. Even though he didn't say much, his company was pleasant enough. The other boys, all younger, played around the camp. Jeremiah couldn't remember their names.

He spotted one of them when he emerged from the woods beside their rented camp, a miniature version of the Treasure's cabin. All the little boys looked alike with wavy red hair and freckles. The child waved before darting into the cabin. As Jeremiah approached the porch, Mr. Ottman stepped out with a polishing rag in hand.

"Hello, boy. We wondered if you'd all gotten here yet."

"Just got here a bit ago." Jeremiah shook his hand. "I see you're getting your guns ready."

"Of course." A laugh rolled from Mr. Ottman's flat belly. "We got here yesterday. The girls have been hyper for you all to arrive."

"Girls?" Jeremiah tensed. If Amethyst found out the Ottmans had brought hired hands, she'd scream about how the Treasures didn't bring servants.

Mr. Ottman tucked his rag into the back pocket of his denim overalls. "My daughters. Your mother wrote to ask me to bring them along since she and your sister were coming. I'm afraid my wife couldn't make it, she's been feeling weak lately. Whenever the hay comes out, she suffers terrible migraines."

"She didn't mention that." His mouth dried. They would see what a brat his little sister was.

"Come out, girls," Mr. Ottman called.

"My sister isn't feeling well." She might have still been on the floor pretending to twitch. If the Ottmans thought Amethyst was sick, they might not come over, but they'd accompanied the men to the cabin just to see Amethyst and Jeremiah's mother.

A red-haired young woman stepped into the doorway. "What is it, Father?" Denim pants hugged her body from ankles to round hips. She unbuttoned her shirt to reveal cleavage, no camisole.

"Hi," Jeremiah breathed.

CHAPTER THIRTY-FOUR

The wooden dock built into the stream pressed against Clark's legs. To think that he, the wanted miner, would have nothing to do except hold a fishing pole over the stream and wait for a fish to take the worm bait.

"Sometimes, the army fishes," Zachariah rambled from Clark's right, on the edge of the dock. "We all get together. It turns into a big old feast. Usually the food isn't that good for the common soldier, so they get that with hardtack. Have you ever had hard tack?"

"Sometimes." Whatever was available became food.

"What do you expect us to do with the fish?" Amethyst shrieked from the shore. "I'm not cooking it. I'm not cleaning it. Bloody gears, I'm not even *touching* it. You're disgusting."

"Amethyst." Garth held out the fishing pole to her. "You can sit next to Joseph. You won't have to touch the fish. We can do that. Just be sociable."

"Joseph doesn't want to do it either." She whirled away from the shore. "I'm going back to the cabin to *read.* Come on, Joe."

Clark drummed his fingers against his pole. Amethyst had promised him she didn't care about Joseph in that way, but thinking about them alone in the cabin prickled his skin. Joseph didn't know her feelings.

"We'll go for a walk," Clark said. "We can see more of these woods."

"A walk would be great." Jeremiah jumped to his feet and yanked the girl next to him up.

"I thought you wanted to fish and we were getting in your way," Joseph sneered. Clark stifled a laugh. Good for Joseph for pointing out Jeremiah's snipped attitude.

Jeremiah beamed at the Ottman girl. "Ashleigh, wouldn't you love to go for a walk? I can show you the best views. It doesn't get more peaceful than the woods."

Clark scowled before he steeled his expression. If he wanted private time with Amethyst, then Jeremiah wanted the same with his new Ashleigh…who stood there smiling. Just…smiling. She was pretty enough, with her ginger hair pulled back in a bun, but she didn't say more than pleasantries.

"It is nice weather," summed up her conversation at the dock. She'd also rubbed her head a lot, as though it pained her to be outside.

She accepted Jeremiah's hand. "That would be nice." She massaged her forehead again.

Amethyst, however, kicked at a fern and screamed when it caught on her hiking boot. "Argh, look at this. Why don't we have paths? This is atrocious. Outrageous!"

"It's nature," Georgette said. "Nature doesn't have cement paths."

"It should." Amethyst wrinkled her nose.

Clark chuckled as he set his fishing supplies on the dock. If only she knew the type of land he'd trekked through. A dirt deer path would've been heaven compared with roots and hills and weeds. Mosquitos the size of silver dollars would really pinch her nerves. Add in the constant glancing back to make sure he wasn't pursued, and being careful not to leave too much of a trail left a man skittish. More times than not, he'd gone without sleep to avoid being ambushed while he dozed. The only time he'd relaxed had been with the Bromi and the outcast gang.

Jeremiah led the way through the woods with Ashleigh, in her denim overalls, on his arm. He brushed low hanging branches aside and lifted her by the waist over roots.

"Be careful," he said when they reached a particular nest of blueberry bushes, and stomped around the nearest oak to clear her a new trail.

"Thank you, how nice." Ashleigh rubbed her forehead.

"How nice," Amethyst sneered to Clark and Joseph, the three of them maintaining the rear. "If I have to hear 'nice' one more bloody time, I swear I'm mixing food coloring in her hair wash."

Clark snapped a tiny branch at Amethyst so that it swatted her arm. "Be *nice*."

"Ow," Amethyst shrieked. "You tried to kill me."

"Once," Joseph said to Clark, "Amethyst had a particular row with a new girl in the city. Her family had just come into some wealth, but she wasn't nice in the least." He snickered. "Obnoxious little chit she was. Amethyst invited a group of girls for a slumber extravaganza and put green food coloring in her hair wash. How that blonde chit carried on. Well, not blonde anymore. Think grass green. She never went out in society again, and her family moved across the ocean."

Clark pictured Amethyst standing in the back of a room with a tiny smile and a wicked sparkle in her eyes while her so-called enemy ranted about her new hair color. "Don't worry, Am. No one will ever call you nice."

She snapped a branch at him, but it stilled before hitting him. "I've never wanted to be that."

Clark winked at Joseph, who snickered again. Maybe he wasn't that horrible. In another setting—if Joseph didn't want Amethyst and the army didn't want Clark—they might've been friends. Clark sighed. Friendship didn't work that well for him. Friends tended to be left behind.

Sunlight dappled across the underbrush and the breeze made leaves drift around them. A deer gallivanted beyond the next ridge. Ashleigh gasped, but Jeremiah patted her arm.

"I'll protect you," he said.

"From a deer," Clark whispered. "They are very deadly."

Joseph glanced in the animal's direction. "You josh, right?"

Clark clapped his shoulder. "Definitely. They're one of the least dangerous animals out here."

"Does Jeremiah have many paramours?" Joseph asked.

"How should I know?" Amethyst yanked a wet clump of leaves off her shin. "He'd better not marry her. What a wretched sister-in-law she'd make."

"She'd be a *nice* one," Clark offered.

Joseph narrowed his eyes. "You wouldn't need to worry. They'd stay out here and you'd be with me in the east. I doubt you'd see her more than once a year, if that."

Clark stiffened, coughing. Amethyst met his gaze with pursed lips.

"This is my favorite view." Jeremiah's voice drifted to them. "I come here whenever we're at camp. Doesn't it feel as if it goes on forever?"

"I bet I know what she's going to say." Amethyst grabbed Clark's sleeve as she stumbled over a gully in the path where rain had washed out the dirt.

"Let me guess," Joseph said in a monotone.

"What a nice view." Ashleigh nodded.

"I must see this." Amethyst marched ahead until she stood beside her brother and folded her arms. "All right, it is a bit breathtaking."

Joining them, Clark searched his memory for the views that left him with that reaction. Happy memories rose to the surface: playing hide-and-go-seek with Mabel when they couldn't sleep at night, feeling his mother's curls against his cheek when she hugged him, Amethyst curled up at his side. For unhappy memories, he pictured Tangled Wire with its weathered buildings and miners scarred with dirt from being exposed for years without end. The Bromi men who danced with eagle feathers around campfires to call upon the spirits of the land—he'd hated that, because they'd appeared for him, begging him for help or offering guidance he didn't want. The gangs crowding together for protection, a unity that would stand tough despite pain in their pasts. The Treasure ranch might be beautiful, but everything he ran from clouded it.

Clark frowned at Jeremiah's favorite sight. The ravine lay deep below with a wide stream gurgling through it. Weeds and trees grew alongside it, boulders jutting from the water that glistened in the sunlight. Forest stretched on the other side of the stream, thickening until it became a dark wonderland. For a man like Jeremiah, who spent his time on a ranch in the desert, it would be majestic. For Clark, he pictured how cold it would be to dash through that stream with the army after him. The ravine would be hard to scale, but he could hide among the foliage.

"I understand why my brothers and father find camping to be so nice. What tree is that?" Ashleigh pointed at a stout one that blossomed with pink flowers.

"Lilac bush," Amethyst said.

"It isn't," Jeremiah snapped. "That's just a vine growing over a baby oak."

"Let's pick one of those flowers for Mother!" Ashleigh started down the near vertical ravine with her arms outstretched.

"You can't; it's too steep." Jeremiah seized her hand and she screamed, twisting her ankle. Her body crashed forward and she tumbled sideways. Jeremiah's footing slid and he lunged forward, the weeds slashing across both of them as they fell down the ravine.

CHAPTER THIRTY-FIVE

A stone slashed across Jeremiah's face. He yelped, earning a mouthful of dirt that coated his tongue and mouth, suffocating him as it crept down his throat. A weed caught on his leg, jerking his ankle, and pain sizzled up through his back before more exploded along his arm when he hit another stone. Bloody torment. What had happened to Ashleigh? A thump sounded nearby—could it be her? She was lighter than him; she might not fall so far.

Something exploded nearby, then again, that ringing bang that caused a numbness to spread through his body. His head. He'd hit it. A roaring built up in his ears and he tried to speak, to say he felt funny, but the world faded.

"Bloody gears." Clark braced his legs and took a step down the ravine, digging his heels into the dirt to keep his balance. Jeremiah lay still halfway down. He must've struck something and hit his head, since he didn't move. Ashleigh had disappeared into the brush along the stream.

"You'll fall too, man." Joseph grabbed his hand. "We'll run back and get help."

"Yes, go." Clark jerked free. If they were dead, he would have to save them—alone. Clark met Amethyst's widened gaze. "Get help. I've scaled ravines before, I can make it down. I'll do what I can until the others arrive." Garth had camped before, so he should know what supplies to bring.

"Be careful." Amethyst bolted forward to kiss his cheek before catapulting down the path. Joseph paused with a final, pale glance down the ravine before stumbling after her.

Clark worked his way down leaning backwards, dragging his fingers over the rocks and dirt to keep his balance. The pace had to stay even; if he ran, his momentum would build and he might lose his footing. The air had become dry despite the dampness in the forest. His throat tightened, but he steeled his nerves. If they were dead, he could bring them back, but he had to do it before the others returned.

Jeremiah lay with one arm flung over his chest and the other above his head. Blood soaked into the dirt, dripping across the stone he'd struck his head against.

"Don't you know not to fall for a pretty girl? Literally." Clark hopped beside him and knelt to keep his balance. Jeremiah's eyes, the lids lifted, centered on the sky, his lips parted, as though he'd sought a particularly interesting shape in the clouds. He'd tried to be a gentleman, sharing his special place with Ashleigh and he'd tried to help her with dire results.

Clark rolled him onto his side to inspect the gouge. If it was too severe, it might take some work to fix, and it had to be soon, before time ran out to bring him back. Blood had soaked into the collar of his plaid shirt and the cut ran three inches across. More tears covered his clothes, trimmed in blood where his skin had ripped.

He'd seen people fall from heights, and he'd seen them die, witnessed them suffering. His stomach clenched, but he fought down that too. Jeremiah had never been nice to him, but for the Treasures' sakes, he'd fix him up. No one deserved to die.

Except maybe the army, and Horan, and everyone else Clark had ever killed.

He untucked his blue shirt and ripped off the bottom strip. Holding his breath, Clark felt around the cut for a break in the skull—he could do nothing for him then—but the bone felt solid, other than the blood gushing from the wound. Clark tied the rag around the man's forehead to staunch the bleeding. Jeremiah's neck seemed awkward, bent too severely right. Clark snapped it back and closed his eyes to find the dead place.

It came to him, with the sharp colors and desert atmosphere. A shape wavered into view. Darkness enveloped the body, but it was tall, thick, a man's spirit.

"Jeremiah, come." Clark took the spirit's hand and the darkness dwindled away, replaced by Jeremiah's widened eyes.

"Where…?" Jeremiah sputtered.

"Come back to life." Clark yanked them from the dead place. Air rushed back and he coughed, opening his eyes. Jeremiah had hesitated at the last second, but he'd gone. The body in front of Clark jerked as the spirit returned.

Jeremiah blinked his eyes and gasped, his muscles caught in a spasm. "What happened?"

"You knocked yourself out." Clark stood and wiped his bloodied fingers on his slacks. "Stay here and don't move. You're bleeding. I'll get Ashleigh, and then we'll climb up. Amethyst and Joseph went to get help."

"I need to find her!" Jeremiah flailed his arms as he attempted to stand, tumbling back down and wincing.

Clark scowled. The man should know when to stay down. It wouldn't make him weak to recover. He'd kill himself again if he didn't relax. "Stay still. You'll open the wound. You don't want to die." Again.

"Ashleigh!" Jeremiah remained on his back, but he dug his fingers into the ground and panted. At least the blood loss would keep him still.

Clark maneuvered back down the ravine toward the stream. Lucky him, saving the careless few. Ashleigh should've known better than to try to scale an incline. Jeremiah, the gentleman rancher, couldn't be blamed, but her—definitely.

Trees and thicker weeds grew along the stream bank, feeding off the water. Clark ducked beneath an apple tree and scanned the greenery for a glimpse of her red hair or clothes.

He saw a flash of white by a bush. She'd worn a white blouse with a denim collar. Clark fought through the weeds to reach her. She'd landed half in the stream, her head covered by water. Ginger curls floated in the current, freed from their confines, and one arm lay twisted behind her back. He would have to snap that one back, and pump the water from her lungs. He could do that after she awoke, though.

Clark lifted her by the waist to pull her from the water and laid her on a fern. Her lips parted, her skin a pallid gray, eyes open and glossy: quite dead. He gritted his teeth and snapped her shoulder back into place. It would be less painful for her if he did that before she revived. He'd learned that by helping a ranch worker once after he plummeted from a hayloft.

Her ankle had broken as well, jutting to the left instead of the right. He twisted it back. She wouldn't be able to walk, but it would be better than getting it back into joint awake.

"What are you doing to her?" Jeremiah yelped.

Clark jerked his head up. Jeremiah staggered toward them and dropped beside Ashleigh. Curses on him, he should've stayed away. Clark held up his hand. "You're not well, you shouldn't move."

"I need her." Jeremiah reached for Ashleigh and pulled her against him. Her head flopped against his shoulder. Blood trickled down the back of his neck.

She needed Clark. He couldn't save her in front of Jeremiah without exposing himself.

He couldn't let Ashleigh die, though.

"I know what to do for her." Clark reached for Ashleigh, but Jeremiah twisted to the side, grimacing. His head had to be dizzy from the bump and blood loss.

"You're not a doctor," Jeremiah rasped.

"That doesn't matter. Doctors don't help the poor. You learn to mend yourselves or you don't get mended. Let me help."

"She'll be fine." Jeremiah trembled. Garth and the others needed to arrive soon. Their son needed them, and Ashleigh needed Clark.

"She's dying," Clark hissed through clenched teeth.

"She'll wake up. She'll be fine." Glossiness spread over his eyes.

"Just let me—"

"I said *no.*" Jeremiah jerked the pistol free from his waist holster. His hand wavered and the barrel pointed to the sky, off to the left of Clark. Saliva dribbled down Jeremiah's chin.

"Do you really trust me that little?" Clark stood. "You're self-righteous and stubborn, but I can't fault you for that. It's your personality. Living with gangs taught me that much about people."

"Let me…help…Ashleigh." Jeremiah rocked with her in his lap and the gun plinked against the stones.

"Do you feel bad about me leading Amethyst's rescue? I don't want to be the hero."

"Ash…." Jeremiah moaned, sagging forward.

Clark stepped toward them, and Jeremiah moaned again. He crouched to press his fingers against Ashleigh's neck, cold and clammy from the stream. He could pull her back...

"No!" Jeremiah snarled. His lips didn't close, more saliva dripping from his mouth.

"Hello?" Garth's voice carried over the ravine. "We're here. Where are you?"

Clark closed his eyes, his fingers still on Ashleigh, and leapt to the dead place. She'd gone.

Amethyst huddled beside Clark on the sofa. Zachariah had built up the fire in the hearth, wood crackling and sparks sizzling. The night closed in as if someone had sealed them in a wool blanket.

"How can Joseph sleep?" She rubbed her arms to still the goose bumps on her skin.

Zachariah stabbed at a log with the iron poker. "Some people do that to help them deal."

"Ashleigh *died.*"

"Lots of people die," Clark said.

"I can't believe Jeremiah wouldn't let you save her. He's so...that's awful of him!" Zachariah wouldn't know what she meant by "saving" and Clark had explained to everyone how he'd attempted to help her. Because of her brother, a girl was dead, and she'd only been camping to be company for Amethyst. She pressed her wet eyes against Clark's shoulder.

"You know Jeremiah." Zachariah stabbed the log with more force, splitting it in half. "He's always right."

The others had gone to the Ottman camp, including Jeremiah with his bandaged head. He'd refused to stay in bed, insisting Ashleigh would be fine, even though her father had wrapped her in a bed sheet to take home.

"You should tell him you saved his life," Amethyst whispered.

Clark shook his head.

"Do you suppose Mother will still have the party?" Zachariah asked.

Amethyst picked at the white polish on her fingernails. In the city, a party went on even if someone passed away. They'd actually been near when it happened, though. "Nothing stops a party." New Addison City kept that as an infamous motto.

"Mother will probably use it as a diversion, or a way to keep us together. Remember the party she threw for me when I joined the army?"

Zachariah had joined when he turned fourteen, the legal age, and he'd been a part of it ever since. After three years of schooling, he'd been granted leave to flit back and forth between home and the barracks.

She'd faked an illness so she wouldn't have to travel to his farewell party.

"I'm sorry I wasn't here for that." They might not be best friends, but Zachariah hadn't deserved that. It wouldn't have hurt her to visit if only for a week.

Her brother shrugged. "Most of it was Mother and her friends. You're lucky you grew up in the city." He set the poker in its rack beside the hearth. "I had a tutor. I never got to make friends. The only guy I had was Jeremiah. That's what I love about the army. There are actually friends."

Amethyst pictured the brick private school she'd attended since she was five. The other mothers had cooed over her, since she didn't have hers available toward the end, and she'd gone to lunch at the park with her friends. She'd never had to feel lonely. How alone he must have been without companions or a club. The town certainly didn't offer extravagance.

"I'm sorry."

Zachariah shrugged again.

Clark turned his head as though to kiss hers, but he whispered into her hair, "Ashleigh is here."

Amethyst stiffened. The air hadn't shifted, keeping the same damp feel she'd sensed since fleeing from the ravine for assistance.

"She wants Jeremiah to know it's not his fault." Clark's lips stirred her curls. "The doctors told her there was a lump in her skull. The headaches would worsen until the lump expanded enough to kill her. She didn't want to survive."

CHAPTER THIRTY-SIX

onald's party should have prepared Clark for the excess of tonight—ribbons hanging from the ceiling and wrapped around anything available, and heaps of food that could have fed the gang for years. No one should starve when one family filled a room with tables overflowing with bowls and plates. Donald had been extravagant, but Georgette Treasure's menu surpassed that.

Clark leaned against the railing overlooking the main hallway where a Bromi man accepted the coats and wraps of entering guests. He pictured the younger members of the gang, not yet ashamed to show weakness, crying because their stomachs were so hungry they ached. Georgette could've invited three-hundred people and they would still have food left over. As it happened, she'd invited one-hundred.

"That's all?" Amethyst had asked. "In the city—"

"I'm afraid there aren't as many people here close enough to make it," Georgette had interrupted. Clark wondered if that had been a dig, since Amethyst had avoided family gatherings to stay in New Addison City.

Georgette hovered by the door greeting her guests by name, kissing the females on the cheek and curtsying to the men. "Mr. Roberts, hello! Mrs. Roberts, you look stunning. Might those be new diamonds?"

Clark had lined up in the hallway with the rest of the family. Georgette's true purpose for the party shown through when she said, "I'd like to introduce you to Clark, who I wrote to you about, and Joseph, my daughter's beau."

Most guests stared at Clark with pressed lips and raised brows, fidgeting with whatever they held, as if unsure how to react to a bastard.

He didn't belong with the Treasures. His life involved mining and fleeing, taking whatever job he could get, shooting off pistols and riding his steamcycle until the wind numbed his neck.

"Jealous of Joseph?" Eric appeared behind him.

Clark scowled, pushing off from the railing. "They're ignoring him. They don't know Amethyst, so he doesn't mean much."

"Jeremiah's glowering in the study."

"Let him. He deserves his misery. I never got to mourn Mum. You don't have time to be sad if you're running."

"Georgette wants you to become part of her family."

"For your sake." Clark lifted his gaze to the chandelier. The gaslamps along the walls reflected off the hanging crystals. "I'm thankful. I can't tell you how much. This just doesn't feel right. I don't deserve any of this."

"Clark!" Amethyst stood below, waving and rocking on her heels. Peacock feathers hung from her pinned curls and a gold chain dangled across her forehead with a sapphire in the center.

He lifted his hand in a wave. She should've been glorying in the attention she received for finally appearing in Hedlund, not seeking him out.

"What's really bothering you?" his father asked.

Clark glanced over his shoulder at the ghost. "What's my purpose in life now? Save your inventions and pretend to be a Treasure? I can never marry Amethyst. The world thinks she's my sister."

Her heels clicked against the stairs as she hurried up. "What are you doing up here? Who are you talking to? Oh, is Eric here? What's he saying? I bet he wants you to stop being a hideaway." Amethyst seized his hand, lifted it, and twirled until her back pressed against his front, his arm pinned across his chest. "I miss you. Come to the ballroom with me. Mother will have the dancing start soon. Have you eaten? The cook made these delicious apple fritters. Have you ever had apple fritters before?" She yanked him toward the staircase. "You won't be a hideaway when I'm around, not when people want to know more about the Bromi."

Jeremiah scowled into his glass of bourbon. It should burn, but even when he gulped it, that numbness lingered. Ranch hands died. A ranch could be a dangerous place. He'd seen a bull ram his horns through a man's chest. He'd held that workers hand while the life left him, and they'd buried him in the ranch graveyard out in the back field.

Children died from illness or carelessness. Lawless men roved through town and killed a few before roving out.

Ashleigh shouldn't have perished. He'd stood next to her. He should've been faster, could've saved her if he'd reacted better.

"Bullocks." He scowled into his shot glass. His father expected him to move on. Double bullocks. A young woman had perished in front of him. He'd held her dead body in his arms.

Jeremiah knocked back that glass and turned in his chair to the table beside him to pour another. Laughter sounded from outside the study door. Maybe he should've locked it, but his father had the key in the billfold he always carried. If Jeremiah asked for it, his father would tell him to socialize.

The only light drifted in through the windows from the yard. If anyone walked by, and they probably would since his mother had transformed the gardens into a wonderland, no one would see him within the darkness.

Clark had told him not to feel bad, that Ashleigh hadn't been healthy. *You don't suffer from physical pain in death.*

Clark's words danced through Jeremiah's mind. People didn't suffer from anything in death. It brought blissful peace. Not that it helped him feel better for Ashleigh, but what did Clark mean? His mother had died, but something about the way Clark spoke sent ice over Jeremiah.

He frowned into the bourbon. What else could a person suffer from in death?

Amethyst linked her fingers with Clark's to lift their hands overhead, her hips swaying to the music. Although the band her mother had hired played what had to be a western tune—it involved banjoes and guitars—the beat did make her feet want to tap along.

"You have to admit dancing is fun," she shouted over the music.

He laughed, jerking her closer. "It's not bad."

"I can't wait to take you to a real club in New Addison City. You'll love it too."

"I doubt it." He winked. "I'll go anyway."

The song faded and the dancers paused to clap. A man in a cowboy hat and fringed leggings stepped forward on the stage in the ballroom. He waved his cap. "Hope y'all are having fun. I've had a request by yours truly, Zach Treasure, to do a line dance. Now, I know it's not what most of you are familiar with, but let's give it a go."

Amethyst sought her brother near the stage. He clapped hands with the man. "What's a line dance?" she asked, turning to Clark. Of course the west would have to ruin a perfect party.

"Never done it before?" Clark's heated breath tickled her cheek. "You follow what the man says. We'll stay in the back so you won't be noticed if you make a mistake."

"It's a new step? They never mentioned line dancing at school, and I took dance lessons since grade one." Amethyst Treasure knew every dance, and the way she moved made everyone gawk. Stumbling through a new dance would shatter that image. "I'll just watch this one—"

"No, you won't." Clark steered her toward the back.

"I'll demand they do a different song!"

"Don't do that to Zachariah."

"How does he even know that man?" she sputtered as he pushed her against the back wall. "A hostess doesn't fraternize with the band."

"Zachariah knows him from the army. Did you hear him request that band?"

Amethyst blinked. "When did he say that? I don't ignore him that much."

"Ready?" the cowboy hat man asked. The crowd of men and women in suits and ball gowns cheered. No, they should be demure, polite. They should clap and smile, not cheer and whistle. Those manners belonged in a club, not a charity ball.

In unison, her family's guests formed straight lines. Clark pulled her into the rear queue.

"What are we doing?" she snapped. "This looks ridiculous." They would think her a fool. At least ten people had commented on seeing her in papers or hearing her name mentioned when they were last in the east. "I have a reputation!"

"Swing your partner round and round," the band leader chanted. The lines split into partners, men grabbing a woman's waist, and they spun.

Clark did the same for her, but he tucked her head under his chin and spun slower than the others twirled. The band struck up another loud, fast beat.

"Right leg in, right leg out!"

One arm still around her waist, Clark shook his right leg forward and then back. The others did the same, almost in unison. How dare they do such a disgusting move? Legs stayed under a person's torso, not waving about. That belonged in the bedroom, not a ballroom.

"Do-Si-Do, Do-Si-Do!"

Clark and all the other bumpkins placed their fists on their hips and stomped forward, sideways, backwards…a blur of skirts and suits. The man on Amethyst's other side bumped against her. She stumbled, her slipper heel twisting. Gasping, she grabbed Clark's shoulder to right herself. People laughed. Could it be at her?

Face hot, Amethyst whirled away and stormed toward the door. More people stood in the doorway clapping with the music. She shoved past them into the hallway, her chest heaving beneath her beaded corset.

"Am, what are you doing?" Clark jogged to her side. "It's fun."

"It's embarrassing." Hot tears pricked her eyes. "I'm a perfect dancer. This song isn't fair."

His smile slipped away. "You can't be perfect at everything."

Maybe she should've played along. He actually enjoyed it. Amethyst folded her arms, stomping toward the dining room. "I'm hungry."

"Do you want me to teach you?" he asked as he followed her.

"Go back and enjoy the dance."

"Not without you."

She rubbed the corners of her eyes to banish the tears. "I'll be fine." Fewer people mingled amongst the food than in the ballroom. They paused to smile at the newcomers. How polite. Too bad her cosmetics were probably running all over her face. Leave it to Zachariah to ruin the party for her.

Clark brushed his hand over her back. "Remember when we danced outside at Donald's party?"

"Yes?"

He took her hand, kissed her knuckles, and steered her out the glass doors in the back of the dining room. Night air bathed her flushed cheeks and she closed her eyes, allowing him to lead her down the stone pathway.

"Tonight was supposed to be wonderful," she muttered. "I was going to take Hedlund."

"You don't have to take everything."

"That's what I do. They call me the princess of New Addison City."

"You're my princess."

She lifted her eyelids to blink at him. "That's such a courtship saying."

They'd come to the gazebo behind the ballroom. Music vibrated through the walls. Clark rested his hands on her hips to draw her closer.

"Let me teach you out here," he whispered.

She looped her arms behind his head. "That's another courtship saying."

"Maybe I'm trying to court you, then." He lowered his lips until they touched hers, his tongue brushing her mouth with a sweetness that made her legs tingle.

"I thought you were already." She lifted to her toes to press their lips tighter.

"Too bad I don't have a loose sister," Joseph said. "We could've been having so much fun."

CHAPTER THIRTY-SEVEN

Clark's stomach clenched and his breathing rasped as his throat tightened. He shouldn't have allowed Amethyst to get in the way of his survival. He didn't have time for a lover. He didn't even have time to find his father's blasted inventions. Staying with the Treasures had been a mistake. If he'd gone onward, he would've been safe. He could've had time with the gang, with the Bromi, found other quick jobs at ranches.

Joseph stepped from the shadows with a smoking cigar between two fingers while he clapped, his expression cast in darkness.

"I was teaching Amethyst how to line dance," Clark said. His last hope would be to lie smoothly enough.

"I'm sure that's how all siblings learn to dance." Joseph leaned against the gazebo. "Continue. I'm curious to see where this lesson leads."

Amethyst clung to his sleeves. That made the situation so much better. She distracted him too much; he forgot to watch for people. Keeping her to himself had poisoned his mind.

"It's dark out," Clark said. "I'm not sure what you saw, but if you want to join the lesson, we won't mind."

"I'm thankful Mistress Treasure thought to light the pathways. It provides a clear view, and even if it were dark, my ears don't lie."

"Joseph." Amethyst tipped her head to the side, her earrings jingling. "No one will believe you over me."

Of course she had to ruin their chances of lying to freedom.

"It will certainly cause a scandal, won't it?" Joseph blew a puff of smoke at them. "I'm not surprised, Amethyst. I knew you were flirty. You've had so many courtships. I thought I was a bit different, though.

Then I see you here with your brother." He cleared his throat. "Bastard half-brother."

Amethyst bit her lower lip. "That's what we do. We court and we move on."

"Amethyst," he growled, "we court so we can marry. My parents are in love with you. You're Amethyst Treasure. Do you know how amazing they think it is that we might wed?"

"It's just courting."

Clark winced. Was that how she viewed him? The world she grew up in saw flirting as a natural way of life. She'd never grown out of that mindset, but Joseph had, and he wanted to settle down to raise children in that same environment.

"You wanted to propose," Clark whispered.

"My parents were excited about the summer camp for good reason," Joseph said.

Amethyst shifted her stance. Some corner of her had probably wanted a catch like Joseph.

Joseph blew another puff. "I could understand if you had a fling with a ranch hand. You're right, I know how you are, but your brother, Amethyst? Really?"

"Don't do this to me." Amethyst stepped toward him. "Don't, Joseph."

Even if the family didn't believe him, the rest of the world would gobble up gossip about Amethyst Treasure making out with her brother. Clark wanted to peel off his skin to cover her, to protect her. He hadn't felt that way about someone after his mother and Mabel had vanished. She'd wrapped herself in her own misery by playing the social game, but she didn't deserve ridicule. She shouldn't have led Joseph on, either; Clark should've insisted she end that as soon as he'd arrived.

"I'm not her brother." Clark met Joseph's eyes in the flickering light. "Her parents are using it as a ruse to protect me."

Amethyst sucked in a breath and Joseph lowered the cigar from his mouth.

"My real name is Clark Grisham. My father, Eric Grisham, was friends with Garth Treasure."

Joseph crossed him arms. "Everyone thinks you're Garth's bastard."

"They want everyone to think that. The man who killed my father wants something he invented. They're protecting me." Clark steeled his emotions. The excuse sounded ridiculous.

Joseph dropped his cigar and squashed the smoldering tip with the heel of his boot. "Let me guess. If I ask anyone, they'll deny it."

And be shocked that Clark knew about his true past. "Yes."

"It's the truth. Look up Eric Grisham if you don't believe us." Amethyst's voice wavered. What had become of the strong, selfish girl who assumed everything she did was perfect? He wished he could pull her against his chest and hold her, but that would add fuel to Joseph's intimations.

"This charity ball is a front to make everyone further believe Clark is a Treasure," Joseph said in a monotone.

That had to have been part of it. "Yes."

"I'm heading back to New Addison City in the morning." Joseph stared at Amethyst, his lips in a line. "If you want to come with me, have your bags packed. We'll go together. If you want to stay here with whoever this Clark man is, then do so. You won't hear from me."

Clark cupped Amethyst's shoulder and turned her to face him. "What do you want? If you want to return to the city, I'll understand."

Amethyst shook her head, her lips parted. "I want to stay here. You know that."

Clark glanced up at Joseph, but he'd slipped along the path where the light didn't reach. "Bloody gears, I hate relying on others." If he had to, he could run again, and Amethyst might even go with him.

If she wanted.

An owl hooted from the tree in the yard. It would fly off soon, once dawn took a firmer hold. The Bromi slave loaded Joseph's trunks into the steamcoach. Amethyst folded her arms as she stood on the front porch. The breeze sent goose bumps across her skin beneath her velvet robe and silk camisole. Clark would wonder where she was, but she'd chosen to go to bed alone, and then kept herself awake to watch for Joseph's departure.

Standing beside the coach, he tugged his leather gloves over his fingers and glanced up at her. "I left Master Treasure a letter with my thanks and apologies for leaving so abruptly."

She would have to find the letter to make sure he hadn't written anything incriminating. "You don't have to leave."

"Don't." Joseph shook his head. She could hear her words in his. *Don't, Joseph.*

"I'm sorry." At least she, Joseph, and the Bromi slave were the only ones available to overhear.

"At first I thought when you showed up here this morning you were coming with me." Joseph opened the door to the coach. "Goodbye, Amethyst Treasure."

The old Amethyst might have screamed at him to come back. She deserved worship, not to be tossed aside. Joseph should try to win her back. He could woo her with chocolates and hair ribbons.

She didn't care about Joseph. How he acted towards her didn't matter in the least. She had Clark.

The steamcoach sailed down the driveway, morning mist parting for its passage. It would burn off fast in the desert heat. At least the house stayed cool. If she hurried, they could snuggle before the day grew too hot.

"Amethyst," her mother said from the doorway.

She froze, her hands clenching into fists. Everyone should be sleeping off the party that had ended only an hour before.

"Why did Joseph leave?"

"I thought you were asleep." That would be a safe comment.

Her mother wore a brocade bathrobe tied around her waist, the lace of a nightgown peeking from the hem. "I can never sleep after a soiree. Much too excited."

"Same here." A lie. She'd learned to fall asleep as soon as she retired so she could be ready for the next night's entertainment.

"Joseph left." Georgette didn't make it a question.

"He thought it would be best." Another safe comment.

"You're no longer courting?"

Not him. "What's it matter? He left. He saw Ashleigh die. What else do you expect him to do? Stay here forever?" She pushed past her mother and ran for the stairs, her slippers slapping the floor.

"I'm sorry." Her mother's voice drifted after her. Let her mother think Amethyst mourned Joseph's departure.

She locked her bedroom door and hurried across the balcony to Clark's room, tapping thrice against his door. He might be asleep. She bounced on the balls of her feet. She needed to see him, talk to him, remind herself he was real even if Joseph wasn't anymore.

The curtain parted to his face. Without smiling, he opened the door and she grabbed him around the waist, her face against his chest, breathing in the scent of sandalwood her mother used on his clothes.

"I love you," she whispered. "Marry me, Clark."

CHAPTER THIRTY-EIGHT

Captain Greenwood paced his office. The world map glared at him from the wall, as if taunting him to find that Clark Treasure. The world might be large, but it didn't stretch forever. That bastard dwelled somewhere. All Captain Greenwood had to do was locate him on the blasted map.

The army captain shoved his leather-bound ledgers off his desk. They struck the floor and papers slid. A glass stylus rolled under the filing cabinet.

Captain Greenwood slapped the telegraph sheet onto the cleared off space of his desk and dropped into his chair so hard the carved feet scraped the hardwood floor. His secretary should've sent him that paper sooner. It was too important to be left in the stack awaiting his return. The wretch could've shipped it to him. That was what he got for vacationing on the east coast. Boating, stretching his toes in the sand while his children frolicked in the waves, eating lobsters with his childhood buddies…none of that mattered when Clark Treasure had been spotted back in Tangled Wire almost *a month before*.

He adjusted his gold-framed spectacles as he squinted at the paper. No, it had been more than a month ago. "Blood and balls."

A knock sounded on his office door. "Captain Greenwood?" Why had he hired such a timid mouse for a secretary? Who cared if she was his best friend's daughter? The girl didn't have enough common sense to boil water.

"Come in!"

The pause let him know his growl had made her bite her lower lip. Again. The brass knob turned, the door creaked open, and the little chit took a step in. She clutched a tome to her chest, her arms trembling as if she were a leaf about to be ripped off a branch by a windstorm.

"Sir?" She gulped. Stray brown hairs escaped from her chignon to cling to her face and neck. Others stuck straight up. Could she never look neat? "I found w-what you w-were looking for."

"Bring it here," he snarled.

She ran, stumbling over her shoes, to drop the tome on his desk. It covered the telegraph.

"Not there, you imbecile!" He shoved it off the paper. "Did you find which coat of arms matched the description in the message?" The man who'd spotted Clark Treasure back in Tangled Wire had described the brand on the steamcoach he'd driven off in. Captain Greenwood might have to send one of his soldiers to retrieve the spy if they needed more information.

"I-I did, sir." The top button of her white blouse had popped open and he caught a glimpse of her lace chemise. How unladylike. Couldn't she find a way to keep her clothes from coming undone? "Sounds like the Treasure brand, sir."

Captain Greenwood clenched his hands into fists. "Impossible. The Treasures wouldn't help a criminal. They're upstanding citizens. By the gears that run our country, they own more than half the state of Hedlund."

"His last name is Treasure. Perhaps he's related?" She tugged down her brown under bust corset as it rode up. Why did she wear such things when she didn't have enough bosom to support them?

"He's not blooming related," Captain Greenwood scowled. "His mother was a Tarnished Silver. He worked in a mine, for crying aloud. You think Captain Treasure would let a family member grovel like that. No, they take care of their own. Lots of folk adopt the names of the well-to-do, make them feel like they mean something in the world." He smiled to make his secretary cringe. "I killed his mother myself. That's the kind of bloody lot they are."

Her eyes widened. "Did she deserve it?"

"Every Tarnished Silver deserves what she gets." Captain Greenwood chuckled. "That woman begged me to look after her son, not to hurt him. Oh, we won't hurt him. We need him more than that."

"How did you kill her?" his secretary whispered. Her skin had paled more than usual, the rouge on her cheeks looking like two apples shoved into an unbaked pie crust.

"The general who'd finished pricking her held her down while I slit her throat." Captain Greenwood flipped through the tome until he came to the Treasure crest: an eagle flying over a mountain. It fit the spy's description. Could Clark Treasure have gone to Captain Treasure seeking protection?

If he did, Captain Treasure would turn him over as soon as Greenwood asked. Clark belonged to the army. He still had the serum working in him, blast it all.

If Captain Treasure didn't know much about Clark—the boy might not have told him the last name he claimed—then he might become suspicious if Greenwood started asking about another Treasure. The army needed Clark as soon as possible.

Captain Treasure's son, Zachariah, had enlisted in the army. Greenwood could pay a visit to the ranch to contact Zachariah. He could imagine some sort of mission for the lad. Zachariah was always easy to manipulate; he'd fall for whatever excuse Greenwood told. Once there, he could explain about how dangerous Clark was, or even see him. He could bring a wanted poster.

"Make train reservations. I'm going to the Treasure ranch tomorrow."

Amethyst breathed through her nose to calm her racing heartbeat. Clark had taught her that trick. According to him, it helped the body more than hyperventilating through the mouth.

"Mother, Father." She glanced at both of them, careful to stay a minute on each face. Clark had promised her a professional attitude would help her plea more than whining. "Clark helped me to learn to speak more rationally." That would give him some points, prove he was a good influence on their princess. "Joseph thinks I'm materialistic and childish." She drew another deep breath through her nose. "I don't want to be like that anymore."

"Am, honey." Her mother stood beside her father's desk, where he sat rubbing his chin. She held out her hands to Amethyst, but she leaned back. "I apologize for not taking a firmer hand in your upbringing. I shouldn't have allowed your…tendencies."

"I can write to Joseph," her father began.

Definitely not. "Please don't." Amethyst met his gaze. Clark promised that would help her case more. "Joseph is right about me. I want to change, and having my father tell him I'm a good person won't help me to seem mature. I really like Joseph." He was entertaining, as a friend.

"How can we help you?" her mother asked.

Perfect. Amethyst offered a weak smile. Looking too eager might ruin the act. "I would like to spend the rest of the summer finding myself and getting to know Clark better. He's really opened my eyes to what matters in life. Survival. Being a strong person. He hasn't been able to travel as we do."

Her father frowned. "Are you considering travelling overseas?"

She shook her head. "Around Hedlund would be nice. I would like to get to know this state more."

"We could all take summer trips," her mother began, but Amethyst shook her head, sighing.

"If I do this with one of you, I may fall into my normal tendencies, and those are the things I want to change. I'm sorry if this hurts you." Clark had insisted she add that sentence. "Clark is new. I can be someone different. Does that make sense?"

Her father squeezed her mother's hand. "They have traveled already, and it didn't hurt either of them."

Her mother patted his arm. "I think it would help Clark as well. He seems uncomfortable around all of us."

"Clark and I will plot out a route to show you." Amethyst curtsied. "Thank you, Father. Thank you, Mother. Your permission is incredibly kind."

If they let her parents know exactly where they would be at all times, it could further show how mature she'd become. She wouldn't be blocking them out any longer.

As Jeremiah headed upstairs from the kitchen, he swirled the water around his cup. The heat didn't usually affect him, but since Ashleigh's death, he'd lain awake at night watching the stars outside his window.

A knock sounded on the front door.

He paused, his hand on the banister. No one visited at night, and it had to be almost midnight. The servants and slaves slept. If a ranch hand needed his father, they would go through the back door and ring the bedroom from the kitchen.

Jeremiah wiped his wet mouth on the back of his hand and opened the door. The light outside, coming only from the moon and stars, revealed the shape of a young woman. A cloak covered her body, but a round belly protruded from her front.

"Are you here for one of the ranch hands?" Jeremiah stifled a yawn. It wouldn't be the first time one of them had impregnated a village girl. Garth would insist they married.

"A ranch hand? No." Her gentle voice slid from beneath the hood. She had to be dying of heat in that wrap.

"You're one of Amethyst's friends." A city girl. Maybe she'd gotten in trouble with a boy and come to Amethyst for help, or she was another friend who'd decided to visit unannounced. "I'm sorry, but she's traveling with...our brother." Same excuse as when that boy, Joseph, showed up on the doorstep. At least he'd arrived in the morning.

"I'm Ashleigh's sister," the figure said. "Alyssa Ottman."

Jeremiah clenched his fist around his glass. Maybe he had fallen asleep after all and he dreamt. "You're her sister?"

"Yes. You met me at the camp. You might not remember. I know things became terrible."

"Why...are you on my front porch?"

"I had to find you."

He shook his head, stepping back. "Come in, Alyssa."

"Yes." She sashayed in and pushed back her hood. Curls frizzed around her face.

He shut the door. "Follow me." He led her into the parlor where he lit one of the gas lamps. In the light, he saw she wore a green traveling gown. The lump he'd supposed was a swollen belly happened to be a leather reticule.

She set it on the floor and knelt beside it, rifling through the contents before she lifted out a small book. "This is Ashleigh's diary."

"Does your family know you're here?" Of course the sister of the girl who'd died would show up at midnight with her diary.

"They do. It was important for me to come find you." She rose, holding out the diary. "I would have come sooner, but I couldn't find a ride from town, so I walked."

"You walked from the train station?"

"Yes. I apologize for the intrusion, but my heart broke when I saw how upset you were. I don't want you to blame yourself for my sister's death."

Jeremiah sank onto the settee and set his glass of water on the floor. "I was next to her. I could've grabbed her." Pressure built behind his brow and he rubbed his hand over his face. "I shouldn't have taken her to the ravine."

Alyssa set the diary in his lap. "Please, Mr. Treasure. I found her diary and I read it. I know it was naughty of me, but I needed to connect with her again, at least one more time. My sister was ill. Ashleigh knew she didn't have long to live. She wrote about how she hoped to have an accident while on the camping trip."

Jeremiah studied the sincerity in her eyes as they reflected the gas lamp. "You're serious?" Clark had hinted at the same thing.

"I'm positive. I wanted to show you the diary so that you could move on. Please, don't harm yourself over this. We can both be sad, but Ashleigh is happy now."

"Was the diary at the camp?" How had Clark known? He might've seen the book if Ashleigh had it there.

"She kept it in her desk at home. She didn't take it to the camp."

Ashleigh might have told him.

"Ashleigh must've suffered with such a secret," Alyssa said, as if she knew his thoughts.

Somehow, Clark had known. How?

Clark's heart pounded and his head whirled. His mind spun in a circle as if it couldn't grasp a tangible point. Let it all rot! He'd lived in fear of the army, but they couldn't touch a Treasure. They couldn't harm a Grisham.

Amethyst stood in front of him, her hands resting in his. She'd purchased a white dress from a shop. It didn't fit as well as her other clothes, the corset with gold embellishments squeezing her breasts up too high, a silk chemise peeking over the top. Her lips, painted scarlet, curved into a smile.

"You're certain?" Clark whispered as the sheriff of Little Rock Detail meandered across the court house.

"Of course." She blinked her painted lashes.

"We can't tell your parents yet." They'd find a way somehow. "We'll do this one step at a time. Inventions first."

"Is your father here?"

"By the door." The ghost beamed, hovering near the secretary who organized a stack of wanted posters. There wouldn't be one of Clark Grisham in there. Clark Treasure, yes, but not the newly discovered Clark Grisham.

The sheriff cleared his throat. "I bind you both in holy matrimony. You'll be together until the ends of your days. Clark Grisham will be husband of Amethyst Treasure. You'll protect her with your life and offer her your name. That agreeable?"

Clark smiled into Amethyst's blue eyes. "That's more than agreeable."

"Amethyst Treasure, you agree to do all this Clark Grisham tells you to do. Keep his house and bear his children?"

Her cheeks flushed, but she didn't break his gaze. "I do."

The sheriff set a paper on the desk in front of them. "You'll both sign here and it'll be legal." He held out a glass stylus.

"Thanks." Clark signed his name on the first line. It was time he did something for himself. His mother would've liked Amethyst, and his father approved. His real father liked what he did.

Amethyst accepted the pen. "Thank you." She signed her name with a flourish across the second line.

"You're married." The sheriff stamped the paper. "I'll make you both a formal copy of this and you'll be set. Congratulations, Clark and Amethyst Grisham."

Clark lowered his lips to his wife's, the softness of her mouth parting without resistance. He could ignore his floating father so long as the woman who loved him leaned against his chest and dug her nails into his shoulders.

His father cleared his nonexistent throat. "Behave, boy. You're in public."

That was a little harder to ignore.

ACKNOWLEDGEMENTS

My mother decided to introduce me to her childhood so I wouldn't miss out on anything. This endeavor might have been partially due to our satellite television offering a channel of old time shows. During dinner, we watched the Big Valley, the Lone Ranger, and countless others. I'd never been that into Westerns – not like my mother, who grew up wearing moccasins, holsters, toy guns, and riding a rocking horse – but something about the shows caught my attention. The setting was dangerous and the characters, although tame by today's standards, had rough hero qualities. I began to wonder what those stories would be like with steampunk aspects.

Along came Clark Treasure, a noble bad boy. He had to have a love interest, so hello feisty Amethyst. They needed a Wild West setting, a prosperous ranch, angry neighbors, and a corrupt villain. You might feel that Hedlund reminds you of America's "Wild West." The story needed something else... so why not add a few ghosts?

I wrote *Treasure, Darkly* in only a few months. The Utica Writers Club deserves gratitude for listening to the rough drafts of my first chapters and for helping me develop the Bromi.

My critique partners not only offered writing advice and caught my typos, but their support has helped me along this winding trail.

Gratifying words from my editor, Jessa Russo, allowed me to walk around the house for days with gigantic smiles. I'm so glad you love these characters as much as I do.

The staff at Curiosity Quills has aided me on this journey. For my agent, Sharon Belcastro, thanks for having my back. My family and friends will forever be my cheering squad. As for the readers, I hope you guys love the feel of the setting sun against your back and the smell of a dusty road at twilight.

I should also acknowledge that without penning this steampunk-western series, I wouldn't have been inspired to purchase a pair of moccasins…or fringed boots…or cowboy boots, for that matter. I also own a plaid shirt and plain blue jeans now. They look wicked awesome with my steampunk corset.

A TASTE OF...

GEARS OF BRASS

A STEAMPUNK ANTHOLOGY

TREASURE'S KISS

JORDAN ELIZABETH

Amethyst exhaled as loudly as she could. The painter displaying his artwork could've had the decency to create exciting works. The paintings in the elaborate frames that covered the walls of the exhibition house couldn't have been less exciting if they were straight gray.

The one in front of her consisted of a cat's paw on green, which might have been grass. How did that count as art?

"How morbid. A paw. What happened to the poor kitty?"

The girl beside her, Mary, covered her ears with her hands. "I swear I'm not listening to you. You're going to make me laugh."

Amethyst sighed again. "I hope the painter at least gave the cat a proper funeral. With all the money he's making off this exhibition, he can afford a gravestone."

"Am, it's art," her friend hissed. "He didn't really chop up a pet."

"I never claimed it was anyone's pet." Amethyst sashayed to the next painting. Society's best milled around her, a plethora of giggles and gasps. Did they truly find art that entertaining?

She leaned against the velvet rope keeping her far enough from the wall to avoid touching any paintings, as if she would. Only one of them contained a likeness of her.

"What do you think of this one, Mary? *I* think someone ate too many gears."

Mary grabbed her arm. "For shame. This one is beautiful."

Brass circles covered a black backdrop. The circles almost made the image of a man's face. Almost, but not quite. The artist probably thought that meant more to the world.

"What are you looking at?" Amethyst rolled her eyes.

"Amethyst Treasure," a male said. She turned to face the caller, smoothing her gloved hands over her gown. A photographer set up his tripod behind her, a grin splitting his youthful face.

"Yes." She drawled out the affirmation.

"A picture, please?" He ducked behind his camera before she could answer.

Amethyst laughed. "Why of course." She slid her arm through Mary's, pulling her friend against her side, and parted her rouged lips to give him a glimpse of her perfect teeth. Mary, wearing a simple dress suit, would complement her gown well; let everyone know Amethyst spared no worry for too much extravagance.

"That's *the* Amethyst Treasure," an elderly woman whispered to her companion. "Did you hear about her sixteenth birthday party last month? They say she rented an elephant from the circus to give her guests rides."

The flash bulb went off and she blinked to clear the white stars from her eyes. That had been her best birthday yet.

"Miss Treasure?" A hand brushed her elbow.

"Yes?" She turned to smile at whatever adoring fan wanted her autograph next, and her breath caught in her throat. A young man stood behind her, his top hat in his hands. Black hair curled around his forehead and neck, silver spectacles propped on his nose. His suit remained crisp against him. A red velvet cravat decorated the collar of his white shirt.

"Miss Treasure." He bowed. "I'm pleased to make your acquaintance."

"Likewise," she breathed. His skin had a perfect tan, his teeth were even like hers, and he had to be a foot taller. Lifting her chest, she tipped her head to the side. "I'm afraid I don't know who I'm addressing."

"Kenneth Marshall." His words rolled off his tongue with a slight accent. It reminded her of how her brothers spoke.

"Are you from the west?"

He blinked his clear, emerald eyes. "Yes, I am. How did you know?"

"I'm a language expert." At least in regards to people who moved west. They developed that rolling drawl. This Kenneth didn't need to know she was limited, though.

Kenneth shone that fabulous smile at her again. "I might sound a bit like... Well, I've traveled overseas for the past few years."

"Oh my." She removed her sandalwood fan from her sash to flip it open. "I've been longing to travel overseas. My uncle offered to take me, but it wouldn't be wise for his health." Plus, overseas they might not realize how important she was.

"Perhaps someday, I might be able to show you around there." Kenneth extended his arm. "Would it be too forward of me to ask you to lunch?"

Amethyst glanced back at Mary, who ogled a painting of an enlarged pocket watch. "I'd be delighted."

"Welcome to Charles Belle." The hostess curtsied to Amethyst and Kenneth at the entrance to the café. "Will it be two this afternoon?"

"My favorite table please." Amethyst flashed Kenneth a smile. He should know she knew her way around New Addison City. "I come here quite often with my uncle and my friends." He should also know how important family was to her, and how popular she was. Men loved popular girls.

The hostess led them through the room to the stairs, leading them up to the second floor balcony where they could overlook the ocean. A steamship glided into port and smaller fishing vessels mingled along the docks.

Kenneth pulled out the chair facing inward. "For you, Miss Treasure."

That seat wouldn't do. She needed to be in full light to make her yellow hair glow, and her golden silk dress needed to shimmer. "I'd prefer next to the railing."

He ducked his head. "At once."

Good boy. He pulled out the high-backed chair and Amethyst slid onto it, smoothing out her two skirts. Her white lace petticoat showed when she crossed her legs.

A waitress appeared and handed them their menus. She wore the uniform required of all servers: a dark brown dress with a white shawl buttoned over the shoulders. The uniform fit her slender form exceptionally well. She had blonde hair that hung in ringlets.

Amethyst clenched her jaw, but Kenneth never glanced at the waitress, his gaze on Amethyst. Excellent.

"Two champagnes." Amethyst waved the girl away. "Won't you tell me about yourself, Ken?" A nickname always helped her get closer to a man's heart.

He cleared his throat. "I was born in Hedlund."

"Which business does your family run? My father owns a ranch in the west there, but he also dabbles in railroads and mining."

"Banking." Kenneth rested his hand over hers where she'd left it on the table. "I've heard your father's made himself quite a name."

Amethyst straightened her shoulders. "Indeed he has. He's been said to have a king's worth of money. He's probably the richest man in the world, even wealthier than our leaders."

According to her uncle, it was hard to judge wealth since it came and went so fast in investments, but she liked repeating what she'd read in newspapers.

"Is he here now, in the city? I would enjoy meeting him."

"Oh no." She tossed her head to make her hair shimmer. "My parents live out on the ranch. I prefer staying here with my uncle. There's just so much to do in the city."

"Speaking of things to do…" He rubbed his thumb over her knuckles, making her stomach clench and her nerves twitter. "I've been meaning to rent one of the small airships for a turn over the countryside. Would you be interested?"

She'd never gotten to do that before. How jealous her friends would be that she'd taken an airship ride with Kenneth! "I would love to! It's so very kind of you to ask me."

"Tomorrow morning? We can set out by ten?"

She wrinkled her nose. They needed to spend the evening together, perhaps see a show. She wouldn't rise until at least eleven. "That's terribly early. Shall we agree upon noon? You can call on me then."

He narrowed his eyes and shifted in his seat, pulling his hand away.

"I'd rather meet you at the airship rental."

Amethyst stiffened. Gentlemen always called on her at her uncle's apartment. Ah, Kenneth had to be shy about meeting her paternal figure. After the ride, he would feel more comfortable. "Fine, I'll meet you there."

"Your champagne." The waitress materialized from the shadows of the café, piano music drifting after her.

"We're going on an airship ride tomorrow." Amethyst beamed. Hopefully, it would make it into the newspapers.

The driver opened the door to the steamcab and lifted his hand to Amethyst. "Miss Treasure?"

She slid her gloved fingers into his and descended with slow steps. Once on the pavement, she lifted her head and smiled to the awaiting photographers… only, the media didn't wait outside the airship rental. The brick building had shutters fastened over its windows and a wooden cutout of an airship hanging over the closed door.

"Will that be all, Miss Treasure?" The driver held out his hand.

She pulled a wad of bills from her purse and yanked the drawstring. That should cover the fare and his tip. "Fine." She must not have told enough people she would be there. At least Kenneth would appreciate her attire. She'd chosen a white silk corset high enough to be worn on its own, with detachable sheer puffed sleeves and a full hoop skirt. The top hat and choker matched the pristine, virginal white. Kenneth needed to know how sweet she was, even while she took charge.

Amethyst marched into the rental shop with her chin up, a single curl dangling down her neck from her chignon beneath the hat. Paintings of airships adorned the cream-painted walls. A man sat behind a desk in the corner, and across from him, Kenneth lounged in a sitting area of settees. He rose and removed his hat, bowing at the waist.

"Miss Treasure." He took her hand to kiss it. "Greetings, my dear. I'm glad you could make it. I was worried."

Worried? She almost flared her nostrils. She was only a half hour late. It was better to keep men wondering. "Of course I'm here."

"The photographers were waiting. I don't know how word got out. I called the police to send them away."

"*What?*" Amethyst froze. "You sent them away?" How would her face be pasted across the newspapers the next day?

"Today will be just for us." Kenneth slung her hand through his arm and turned to the man at the desk. "We're ready."

"Right this way." He inclined his head to them before heading toward the back of the shop. "I have the one you requested outside, but if there's another one you'd prefer, I can get a different one."

"It will be fine," Kenneth said. How could he know if he hadn't seen it? It might have advertising on it, and then Amethyst wouldn't be able to ride in it, unless it advertised something of her father's.

The back of the rental contained a mile-long strip of gravel and grass. An individual airship rested in the center, tethered by ropes and metal hooks to the ground. She'd seen airships floating past in the sky, some large enough for groups of as many as three-hundred passengers. An individual would only house up to five.

"Did you tell your uncle where you were going?" Kenneth opened the door in the basket for her and Amethyst glided inside.

"Of course not." She giggled. "He doesn't trust these newfangled inventions, as he calls them." With the giant balloon up top and the basket hanging underneath, he thought of them as floating deathtraps.

"Wise man." Kenneth stepped in and latched the door.

"You know how to fly this?" Amethyst leaned over the basket to stare at the metal propeller, then up at the red and white striped balloon.

"We went over the directions before you arrived," the rental owner said. "You have this for five hours. Any longer and I'll have to charge extra."

"Understood." Kenneth fiddled with levers and buttons on a panel near the door. The machine beeped, sending a chill over Amethyst's arms. Even if photographers couldn't mark her passage, excitement still bubbled in her belly.

He pulled a cord hanging from the balloon overhead and the propeller whirled. The airship lifted, swayed, and lifted higher.

Amethyst waved to the rental owner as she called her goodbye. "Toodles!" How thrilling to be above everyone, watching people who couldn't see her. The airship lifted over the brick buildings, higher toward the clouds. The people became doll sized, then ant sized, and the skyscrapers shrank. The ocean transformed into a blue blanket and a land of stone.

"This is very relaxing." Amethyst held out her hand and spread her fingers, the air rushing over her skin. "Have you driven one before?"

"I have my airship license."

"Really?" What a pity the individual airship didn't have a bench to sit on, but leaning against the basket wasn't too strenuous.

"I've flown a lot."

"Is that your profession?" Plenty of her city companions studied to become lawyers or doctors, or businessmen like their fathers.

"No. I don't have one anymore."

She turned to face him, her bottom against the black wicker. "So, darling, shall we stop to luncheon somewhere? We should've brought along a picnic."

"We'll stop." He gazed out at the world with his jaw set, the happiness gone from his straight demeanor.

"Before we have to land back at the rental?"

"Miss Treasure, did you mention my name to anyone?"

Amethyst licked her wind-chapped lips. She should've brought a gloss. "Um, yes. Lots of people. Why?" She'd told her uncle about charming Kenneth. She'd sent a note to Mary letting her know about the lovely evening they'd spent together.

"My full name?"

What *was* his last name? "Yes." It hadn't meant anything to her. She didn't know of anyone else with that surname, so she'd forgotten it as soon as he'd told her.

Kenneth chuckled. "Good. When the police didn't show up to arrest me, I'd hoped you'd forgotten."

Amethyst curled her fingers into fists. "What does that mean?" Why did he have to ruin the romantic outing by spouting off nonsense? They didn't even have an audience.

"Three years ago, your father ruined my life. He terminated my family's reputation."

"Um…" Amethyst wished she could back up further. Wind pushed at her top hat, so she shoved it up higher to straighten it. "I don't understand."

"Now, I'll ruin his life."

"Kenneth…"

"My family worked at his mine. My father was his mine master. My mother kept it shipshape and I worked the books."

"Yes? I'm sure there's a lot of that out west." The airship swayed in a strong gust.

"Do you know how much we made?" Kenneth rounded on her, his nostrils flared. "*Pennies*. He paid us in pennies!"

Amethyst scurried away from him around the basket. "So? Isn't that what people make out there?" She'd never had to work. Pennies might be special.

"Your father has millions of dollars, but he couldn't spare that for his mine master? My father took what he had to. We all took it."

"You stole?" She forced a giggle. "This is a funny story, but its ruining the mood, Ken."

"It's not a story." He scowled, pushing a few buttons on the control panel. "You rich folk all think alike. You're perfect. You don't have to share. I couldn't believe how lucky I was when I found you."

"You didn't find me…" Her voice trailed off. "You meant to bump into me at the art show?"

"My parents are in prison. Your father wouldn't give them bail. I barely escaped. I found a way to hide on airships to get overseas. I drove these things for rich people. You won't be so rich anymore."

"Ken…" How stupid she'd been to get in an airship with a stranger. "Take me back. Now."

"Never." He chuckled. "Your father made my family pay, so now he's going to be the one paying. If he wants you, it's going to cost him his fortune."

Her uncle had always warned this would happen if she insisted on staying in the light. "You're holding me for ransom?"

"And more, pretty girl. My father deserves that mine."

"You're crazy." She bit her lower lip. Calling him names might make him angrier. "Look, if you set me down—"

"You're mine, Miss Treasure. All of you."

They'd left the city behind and soared over farmland of fields and trees. Something on the control pad had to lower them. If wishes worked, it would pop out at her.

She could call for help. Farms had to have workers.

Amethyst lunged toward the control panel and slapped it with her purse. A lever caught in her drawstring; buttons flashed and beeped.

"*Bitch.*" Kenneth seized her around the waist to yank her backward. The wind tore off her top hat to send it spinning into the air. The airship teetered and swayed, the balloon groaning. As Amethyst tumbled back, she seized the hanging cord and clung to it.

"Let go!" Kenneth grabbed her wrist and she bit into his forearm where his sleeve exposed his skin. Amethyst kicked off him as the airship teetered harder, and the basket disappeared from beneath her feet. She gasped, clutching the cord tighter as she hung. The balloon groaned and vinyl tore. It bounced down so fast her stomach seemed to jump into her throat.

"Stop, it'll blow up. The fire and the gasses—"

Something hit her foot and she released the cord. Weeds slashed across her arms and face, tangling in her skirt. The ground slapped her back.

Amethyst rolled to her knees before scrambling upright, turning in a circle, everything around her cornstalks and weeds. She'd seen those stalks decorating doors in the autumn, a bit of the country to spruce up the city.

To the right, something exploded and heat washed over her. Amethyst yanked up her skirts and ran, weeds slashing her ankles. When she reached a dirt road, she paused, leaning over to clutch her sides. Her lungs strained against the confines of her corset and her eyesight blurred.

Flames leapt in the distance where the airship had crashed.

No one would have to know how he had threatened her. Even if his family had committed crimes, they wouldn't have to know Kenneth had tried to ransom her.

She could pretend the airship had malfunctioned. That wouldn't make her look stupid or careless. Bad. Amethyst Treasure was never *bad*.

Lifting her skirts again, Amethyst stumbled toward the red barn.

Read more of *Treasure's Kiss*

And other Steampunk Stories in…

Gears of Brass

A Steampunk Anthology

Available Wherever Books are Sold

ABOUT THE AUTHOR

Jordan Elizabeth, more formally known as Jordan Elizabeth Mierek, can be found wearing billowing skirts and brocade boots in the summertime. She wears them in the wintertime, too.

Although Central New York is her home, Jordan travels frequently, in particular to historical forts and fairs. She fell in love with steampunk while working at a Victorian Fair when she realized the genre contained her favorite things.

You can contact Jordan via her website, JordanElizabethMierek.com, or on her blog, Kissed by Literature.

She's the president of the Utica Writers Club, which would make a great full-time job, if the organization wasn't not-for-profit.

Fans of the Treasure clan should toss their cowboy hats into the air and check their pocket watches, for more adventures of Clark and Amethyst await in Hedlund.

THANK YOU FOR READING

Please visit http://curiosityquills.com/reader-survey to
share your reading experience with the author of this book!

Escape from Witchwood Hollow, by Jordan Elizabeth

Everyone in Arnn—a small farming town with more legends than residents—knows the story of Witchwood Hollow: if you venture into the whispering forest, the witch will trap your soul among the trees. After losing her parents in a horrific terrorist attack on the Twin Towers, fifteen-year-old Honoria and her younger brother escape New York City to Arnn.

In the lure of that perpetual darkness, Honoria finds hope, when she should be afraid. Perhaps the witch can reunite her with her lost parents. Awakening the witch, however, brings more than salvation from mourning…

Gears of Brass, a Steampunk Anthology

A world like ours, but filled with gears of brass, where the beating heart is fueled by steam and the simplest creation is a complex clockwork device.

Within this tome, you'll find steampunk fairy tale re-tellings, as well as original stories that will send your gears turning.

Welcome to the steampunk realm, with eleven authors guiding your path.

CPSIA information can be obtained at www.ICGtesting.com
Printed in the USA
BVOW07s1241030315

390013BV00004B/53/P

9 781620 076958